**See what everyone is saying
about Mariah Fredericks's books!**

Crunch Time

"The dialogue and thought patterns of the main
protagonists are right on the money." —teenreads.com

"[A] page-turner . . . immediately absorbing."
—*Kirkus Reviews*

"Fredericks writes about high school academics and social
rules with sharp insight and spot-on humor." —*Booklist*

An Edgar Award Nominee

Head Games

"[Mariah Fredericks] again perceptively explores
the psyche of teenagers." —*SLJ*

"The humor is welcome and the
intelligence penetrating." —*BCCB*

"[Will leave] readers with the same wistful
feeling as 'Game Over'." —*Kirkus Reviews*

The True Meaning of Cleavage

"Laugh-out-loud funny and way twisted!
A VERY realistic (and painfully familiar!) story."
—Meg Cabot, author of *The Princess Diaries*

"No one in this great novel is an annoying stereotype—
it's full of characters you might find in your own
school cafeteria." —*YM*

★ "A modern-day *Forever* . . ."
—*VOYA*, starred review

Also by Mariah Fredericks

The True Meaning of Cleavage

Head Games

In the Cards: *Love*

CRUNCH TIME

A Novel

MARIAH FREDERICKS

Simon Pulse
New York London Toronto Sydney

This book is a work of fiction. Any references to historical events, real people,
or real locales are used fictitiously. Other names, characters, places, and incidents
are the product of the author's imagination, and any resemblance to actual events
or locales or persons, living or dead, is entirely coincidental.

SIMON PULSE
An imprint of Simon & Schuster Children's Publishing Division
1230 Avenue of the Americas, New York, NY 10020
Copyright © 2006 by Mariah Fredericks
All rights reserved, including the right of reproduction in whole
or in part in any form.
SIMON PULSE and colophon are registered trademarks
of Simon & Schuster, Inc.
Also available in an Atheneum Books for Young Readers hardcover edition.
Designed by Ann Zeak
The text of this book was set in New Baskerville.
Manufactured in the United States of America
First Simon Pulse edition June 2007
2 4 6 8 10 9 7 5 3 1
The Library of Congress has cataloged the hardcover edition as follows:
Fredericks, Mariah.
Crunch time / Mariah Fredericks.—1st ed.
p. cm.
"A Richard Jackson Book."
Summary: Four students, who have formed a study group to prepare for the SAT exam,
sustain one another through the emotional highs and lows of their junior year in high school.
ISBN-13: 978-0-689-86938-9 (hc)
ISBN-10: 0-698-86938-X (hc)
[1. Friendship—Fiction. 2. Interpersonal relations—Fiction. 3. Scholastic Aptitude Test—
Fiction. 4. High schools—Fiction. 5. Schools—Fiction.]
I. Title.
Pz7.F872295Cr 2005
[Fic]—dc22   2004020008
ISBN-13: 978-1-4169-3973-3 (pbk)
ISBN-10: 1-4169-3973-3 (pbk)

For Pearl,
who took me to the opera

Acknowledgments

The author would like to thank the following people for their help and support in writing this book:

Dick Jackson, for his staunch resistance to anything boring, cowardly, or untrue;

Ginee Seo, for her passion and generosity, and for her invaluable insight into the parents' point of view;

The Deep Throats, who revealed the mysteries of SAT prep and testing theory;

Maureen McMahon and Helena Santini, who kindly vetted the book for errors. If there are any left, it is solely the fault of the author;

Jeannie Ng, who tempers ferocious professionalism with patience and a sense of humor;

Hilary Goodman, for a hilarious train ride back from Philadelphia;

Kristy Raffensberger, who stepped in heroically and saved me from looking stupid more than once;

My nephew Gabe, for giving me the first line of this book;

Kristen Sard, who is one of those amazing people for whom no proper test can ever be devised;

Allyn Hartstein, who is another;

Josh Weiss, for bringing basset hounds and a few other things into my life;

And in memory of my mother, who throughout her life faced tests way more challenging than the SATs and passed them all with brilliance, grace, and courage.

MAX

They never list the names. Just the numbers.

Every year the school posts the SAT scores in the lobby, where anyone can see them. But they don't put the names—like Jeff Stein got 2340, Susie Chen got 1160. They just put the numbers and let you guess who got what.

Which, of course, is what everybody does.

It's easier than you think. Like some kids, the math geniuses and future physicists, you can pretty much figure out they're the 2300s. If someone gets 2400, it always comes out who it is. "Oh, don't tell anyone, but I got 2400." Yeah, right. Next day everyone's like, "*He* got 2400. *He's* going to Yale."

And it's not too hard to figure out who's at the bottom of the list. Who got in the 1200s—when they give you 600 points just for writing your name. You think of the stoners, the jocks, kids who just say, "Screw it." Because some kids do. They say they don't care what they get, and they mean it.

Then there's everybody else, all clumped together in the middle. The pretty goods, the fines . . . also known as the not good enoughs, the not quite acceptables.

Last year when I took the PSATs for the first time, I told myself I wouldn't look at the list.

But I did. And there it was: my score. *This is where you are, Max. This is how much you count for.*

Sometimes I think, *What's worse? Doing just okay, or*

totally bottoming out? There's a weird honor in completely screwing up, in scoring so low that no college'll take you except the ones that take everyone, including mental cases and paint eaters. The kid at the top has that spot all to himself. But so does the kid at the bottom.

When you're trying to figure out who got what, you remember—who looked happy the day after you got the scores? Who looked bummed out, who was crying?

Mr. Crowley, our college adviser, always says, "The top colleges can only take so many kids from Dewey." Only a few of you, maybe even only one of you, are going to get to go to Yale or Harvard."

In other words, like it or not, you're all in competition with one another.

Part

I II III IV

Pick Up Your No. 2 Pencil. Begin.

LEO

In New York everybody knows everybody else. Well, there are all these people you totally don't know—like cabdrivers and the freaks in the park—but they don't count. The people who count, the kids who go to your school or schools like your school, we all know one another. It's like a club. "Dalton, check. Prada, check. Summers in Europe or the Hamptons, check." We all want the same things and we all do the same stuff to get them.

Like college. You can pretend you don't want to go to Yale or Harvard or Brown—but you do. Unless you're a nose picker. In life there are those who count and there are nose pickers. Very few people actually count for anything—even though everybody likes to think they do.

Anyway, I'm not surprised when I walk into the SAT prep class in the last week of summer vacation and there's at least three other kids from Dewey.

Without even thinking, I size them up.

Daisy Stubbs. Plays b-ball, dates b-ball. Heavily into saving things, from the planet to the guy at the party who thinks it's a cool idea to mix tequila and schnapps. I've been to a lot of parties where Daisy's holding somebody's head while they puke. She's a lot of guys' dream, but I never saw the big deal.

Strictly state school. No threat.

Of course, next to Daisy is her best bud, Max. Max

is a little guy. Those who can't play, write for the school paper. He'd probably tell you it's all about the game, but it's like, dude, girls in shorts? Who are you kidding?

Max is smart. He could be thinking Ivies. Maybe Columbia.

Then there's Jane Cotterell. When she came to our school last year, we were like, "Sweet, Julia Cotterell's daughter *and* she passes for a babe." But Jane speaks to no one. Shy or stuck-up? Can't tell. Guess when your mom's a movie star, you don't mix with the little people.

Possible threat. But only because of Mom.

I take a seat, look around. No sign of the teacher, and it's almost time to start. While we wait, I open my notebook and start a list, "Five People I Don't Know Who Count."

1. Bill Gates
2. Quentin Tarantino (or Steven Soderbergh)
3. Bono

And maybe, just maybe, Jane Cotterell.

Jane

I really, really hope they don't make us go around and say our names. I hate that. Somebody always asks, "Hey, is your mom Julia Cotterell?"

I have two standard answers: "Um, yeah" or "No, but I get that all the time."

I hardly ever do "Um, yeah," because then you get, "Oh, I loved her in *Persuasion*," or "She totally deserved the Oscar that year." And then what do you say? "Thanks"?

My mom would be so on me right now. There are three kids from Dewey here, and she'd be like, "Why don't you say hi? Why don't you talk to them? They don't have fangs, for God's sake."

Mom, believe me, Daisy and Max would find me utterly boring, and Leo Thayer is a BP who talks only to other BPs.

Where is the SAT guy, anyway?

MAX

Just when I'm thinking *Is this class ever going to start?* this bald guy sticks his head in the door and gasps, "Can't find the booklets. Stay put, I'll be right back. . . ."

I feel Daisy's notebook nudge my hand. I look at what she's written.

"It's a sign. Let's split."

I write, *"Can't. Must learn secrets of a, b, c, d, or e."*

Daisy scribbles some more.

"a. This is lame.
b. This is boring.
c. This sucks.
d. All of the above.
e. LET'S SPLIT!!"

Last year Daisy and I both said prep was elitist and sick, and we swore we wouldn't do it. Then we got our PSAT scores, and well, I guess things change.

I tell myself everyone does prep. Even Tory McEwan, who got the one perfect score in the school last year, did prep. There's no shame in it.

I just feel . . . disgusting, that's all.

The SAT guy is back. He pants, "Just a few more minutes, I'm arranging for backup."

Then he disappears. Leo Thayer makes a big show of looking at his watch. "That's ten minutes gone. This one class costs a hundred dollars, this guy owes us each ten bucks."

A girl with pink fingernails who obviously thinks Leo is hot says, "Totally."

I tell myself I don't hate Leo Thayer because he's one of the Beautiful People and so many women think he's hot. I tell myself I hate Leo Thayer because he's an egotistical schmuck.

And I almost believe myself.

Then Daisy says loudly, "Screw the ten bucks. Let's just walk out."

Daisy

Well, someone had to say something.

I mean, God, we were all just sitting there like, *Oh, please, Mr. Brilliant SAT Man, share your wisdom with us. We have paid you hundreds of dollars for the wonderful privilege.*

And those who don't have hundreds of dollars, well, screw them.

And those who don't go to private school, screw them, too.

I said to my parents, "Doesn't it bother you, just a *little*, how unfair this is? How the whole system is completely and disgustingly rigged?"

And they were like, "Yeah, but you're going anyway."

Yay, principles.

Last year Coach said she would bench me if I didn't quit arguing with the refs all the time. So I've been trying not to lose it so much. But this whole scene is just too obnoxious. I say it again: "Let's walk out."

If this were a movie, this would be the part where the crowd rises up with a huge roar and burns something down.

But all that happens is Leo Thayer rolls his eyes and says . . .

LEO

"What, because the guy didn't show?"

Because yeah, I'm annoyed the guy is late, but that doesn't mean Daisy gets to piss on the whole thing. I know *exactly* what she's thinking. And I'm sorry, I know some kids go to lousy schools and never learn to read—but how is me screwing up my SATs going to help?

I tell her, "You think there shouldn't be any test at all.

Colleges should just take us because we're nice and kind to animals. Not 'cause we're . . . smart or anything."

Daisy cocks her head like she's thinking about it. "Well, if we're so smart, how come we have to pay some jerk to teach us how to take a freaking test?"

She looks me right in the eye, and I have a weird flash. Some party where this girl was following me around, all boo-hoo, because . . . I don't know, she had ideas. She got herself totally trashed, and Daisy took her home. When they were leaving, Daisy looked back at me, and I was like, *Not my problem*. Daisy gave me this look: *Whose problem is it?*

I said then and I say now: not mine.

Although it's seriously pissing me off that this guy is so late. . . .

MAX

Probably most of the kids here think Daisy's kidding. *Yeah, she says "Let's walk out," but she doesn't really mean it.*

Except she does. She totally means it.

I look around the classroom. Here's what I see: a bunch of kids who know the whole college game is stacked against kids without money and connections.

And . . . a bunch of kids with money and connections.

All of a sudden Daisy gets up, goes to the front of the class, and says, "Everyone who thinks the SATs are bogus, the time for pizza is now."

Okay, Max. Here's where you stand up. . . .

I think of my dad: "Hey, how was SAT prep?" "Uh, well . . ."

Then all of a sudden I hear this little, tiny voice: "I'll come." I look toward the voice, see . . . Jane? Jane Cotterell?

Daisy sees her too, smiles at me like, *Insanity time . . .*

And that's that. If Jane Cotterell's walking out, I certainly have to. I stand, say, "I'm up for pizza."

The rest of the kids stare down at their notebooks. I go stand with Daisy and Jane at the door. Daisy looks back at the class. "Last chance."

Then Leo says, "Screw it," and gets up.

And before anyone has a chance to do anything, Daisy yells, "Sayonara," and we run out the door.

Jane

This is wild.

I've never done anything like this. Just leave and slam the door, good-bye!

I've seen people do it. My mom used to do it all the time when she was fighting with my dad. I wanted to tell her, "Hi, Mom, this is not a movie, we're not your audience. . . ."

Except this time we're the ones everyone's looking at. I guess they think we're crazy. I should feel embarrassed, but I don't. It's like, *You're the fools.*

When we get out to the hallway, and we see the SAT guy—still looking for his stupid books—and Daisy says, "Run for it," we get nuts running down the hall, charging down the stairs, and someone, I think Max, starts laughing because it's so nuts, and then we're all cracking up, even me, and I'm worried because I'm running so fast I'm going to fall down and break my neck, and we jump down the last few stairs, and Leo shoves open the door and waves us all through, and suddenly we're out on the street and we're free and . . .

And I think, *Maybe we are crazy.* But crazy's really good.

Then Leo says, "Okay, now what?"

Max and Daisy look at each other. If no one says anything, we'll all just walk away. . . .

I say, "You could come to my house."

LEO

One of my basic rules in life: Never ever turn down a chance to meet a famous person. So when Jane asks us over, I immediately say, "Sure."

Daisy says, "Yeah, cool." She's so psyched she got us all to walk out she'll agree to anything: "Take a swim in the reservoir? Yeah, cool. . . ."

Only Max looks doubtful. Probably thinking he's too dorky to meet Julia Cotterell. He's right—but I'm not going to let that stand in my way.

MAX

Frankly, I thought once we were out of there, Daisy and I would go and hang on our own. We don't know these guys. And when it comes to Leo, I seriously don't want to know him.

But somehow we're all going to Jane Cotterell's house. Not that Jane is so terrible. But I don't know her, and I have no idea what to say to her. I know she used to hang with Lily Previn, but they don't seem to be buds this year.

And of course, Jane's insanely gorgeous, and I can't speak to insanely gorgeous females. The most I can manage is, "Uh, duh . . ."

She really looks like her mom, with this cloud of black hair, huge gray eyes. Thin, perfect skin—she's like from another planet where they build everyone perfect. Whereas I'm from a planet where they build everyone short and weird looking.

You don't want to be supremely uncool and say, "Hey, I saw your mom in the newspaper." But I don't know what else to talk to her about.

The only other thing I know about Jane is what everyone knows about her. And that you really can't talk about.

What people say about Jane is that her stepfather watches her naked. They also say she lets him.

I have to admit, sometimes I look at Jane and the thought of her naked and being watched is not the worst thing to think about.

Then I look at her face, the way she never really looks anyone in the eye, and I feel like if that's true, it's really ugly, and someone should do something.

Jane

I can't believe they're actually coming. I wish I had the first clue what to say to them. Everything I've thought of so far has either been somewhat stupid . . . or really stupid.

Like, I know Max writes for the school newspaper, but I don't read it. I know he's into sports, but if I talk about that, I'll sound like a complete idiot. "Uh, baseball, that's the one with the bat, right?"

Daisy is way cool. Everybody likes Daisy. You can't not. But I know she's into politics and stuff. She'll probably think my house is totally gross and richy rich. "Oh, my God, I went to Jane Cotterell's house? You could feed a family of twelve with what they spend on toilet paper."

Leo, I know, just wants to meet my mom. Too bad for him she's not home.

I've never had this many people to my house before.

I wish I knew how to do these things.

Daisy

We are definitely a weird little group.

Me. Max. Jane Cotterell. And Leo Thayer.

We hardly say anything on the walk to Jane's house. In the elevator we look at one another, thinking, *How did this happen?* Actually, I don't care how it happened. I am so damned psyched we stuck our finger right in their face: "You thought you had us? Think again. . . ."

Mariah Fredericks

Jane's place is really nice. This is how you live when you have serious money. I look around for an Oscar or something, but no dice.

I say, "Cool apartment."

Jane looks embarrassed. "It's way too big."

She takes us into the living room, then runs into the kitchen. When she comes back, she's got her arms full of glasses and bottles of soda. Leo leaps up to help her. I glance at Max, *Check out Mr. Sua-vay,* and he rolls his eyes like, *Is he for real?*

Then Jane says to me, "We can order pizza. I mean, if you still want to."

I had totally forgotten about the pizza, but I say, "Yeah, sure." So we do. When it comes, Leo, of course, has to "help" Jane by going to the door to get it with her. Max rolls his eyes again, but I punch him because he's going to make me laugh if he keeps it up.

There are three couches in an open square. I sit down next to Max on one. Jane's hovering, like she's not sure where to sit—in her own house. I pat the center couch, and she sits down.

Leo sits on his own couch, spreads himself out. "So, when's everyone taking the test?"

Max says, "March," which is news to me.

Jane says, "I guess March."

Leo looks at me, but I'm like, "I don't *know.*"

I look at Max like, *How did you know?* He never told me he was taking the test that early.

"You should do March," Leo tells me. "You should take it as many times as possible."

"I heard that colleges don't like it when you do that," says Jane. "Like, they hold it against you."

"How would they know?" asks Leo.

Max says, "I heard every few years some colleges only take the kids with the best scores. They don't look at anything else—just to see what kind of student they get." He leans in and takes a chip. "Can you imagine if you wanted to go to that school in the wrong year?"

Jane swallows. "I heard they score the tests wrong sometimes, but no one ever finds out."

"Sometimes people fill the dots in wrong," says Max. "Supposedly one kid used the wrong pencil, and the test didn't count."

Leo laughs. "Did you hear about these two guys who knew they'd be sitting next to each other, so they swapped sections? They did their own essays, but the kid who was good at math did the math, the kid who was good at verbal did that. I think they got into Brown."

Max shakes his head. "That sucks. That's evil."

LEO

Which you would totally expect from a guy like Max. "Oh, it's evil." Dude, it's a system. You work it however you can.

Then Jane says, "Does anybody else have nightmares? I have this dream that I do horribly, and *People* puts on the front cover 'Julia Cotterell's Daughter Flunks SATs!'"

Max says, "The other night I had the dream where you're like, 'Wait, the SATs are *today*?' and you're running, thinking, *Man, they better let me in. . . .*"

Daisy laughs. "I have this nightmare that I do horribly and . . ." She shakes her head, embarrassed.

I say, "What?"

"Well, money's kind of a scarce thing in our house, so I'm going to need some serious financial aid." Daisy pulls at a ring on her finger. "So I'm worried if I blow this thing, it'll be like, 'Forget it, you can't afford to go to college.'"

Jane

I feel awful. I should never ever have said anything about *People* or my mom. Not when people have, like, real problems.

To get past it, I say, "Is it me or is everyone at this school really competitive about this stuff?"

Leo snorts, "No."

While Max says, "Only insanely."

Daisy says to Leo, "Come on, remember the Twenty-four Hundred Club?"

I look at Max, and he says, "Last year some seniors formed a club. You could only be in it if you got a perfect score, and you were *only* allowed to hang with other Twenty-four Hundreds."

Daisy adds, "It was the height of obnoxiousness."

Leo grins. "What's so evil about having a club?" You can tell: He had friends in that club. Nobody minds clubs when they think they can be in them. Like girls who say they don't have cliques, they just don't want to be friends with *you*.

I say, "Where you can't even talk to people unless they get the same score?"

Max grins. "We should have numbers on our butts." He turns to Daisy. "Hi, I'm a two thousand. Nice to meet you."

In a haughty accent she says, "Sorry, I only date twenty-one hundreds and above. . . ."

We all laugh—even Leo. He can probably be nice sometimes. But you can tell Max and Daisy think Leo's just a BP and they're above BPs, and Leo probably thinks, *Well, they're* not *BPs, so who cares about them?*

I don't get it. Why we have to rank ourselves all the time.

Then Daisy asks me, "Is your mom psycho about the college thing?"

Grateful that she doesn't think I'm a jerk, I say, "Not so much college, but she's always telling me how I've had everything, and if I screw up, it proves I'm this big spoiled brat."

Max nods. "My dad's pretty intense about it too." Daisy nods, like, *Is he ever.*

Then Leo says, "That's funny. My dad's the total

opposite." He breaks a pretzel. "He thinks I take it way too seriously."

It's weird. A few minutes ago someone would've said, "Yeah, you do, and it's annoying." But somehow the fact that Leo admitted it means we can't. Like he's one of us now.

Like . . . there's an us.

Daisy

I'm about to ask if anyone else is sick of hearing, "They're going to be judging you this year. They're going to be looking at your scores and your grades and your extracurriculars and the size and smell of your farts . . . ," when all of a sudden Jane sits up and says, "Wait."

We all look at her.

"Maybe we could do, like, a different club? A study group or something. We could meet here if you want to."

Jane is practically bouncing on the couch, she's so eager to do this. I can't help thinking, *This girl has bucks, a famous mom, and absolutely* no *friends. What's up with that?*

On the other hand, it does occur to me that hanging at Jane's house would be a lot better than prep— although I don't see what we'd learn.

Max must be thinking the same thing, because he says, "How would we do it?"

Jane shakes her head. You can tell she hadn't

thought that far. But Leo says, "Like, everybody does one practice test a week. Bring it in, and if somebody gets something that you screwed up on, they explain it to you."

"Right," says Jane, like that's exactly what she was thinking. "So?" She looks around uncertainly.

If you could read minds, Leo'd be thinking, *No way, except maybe I get to meet the mom.* Max'd be thinking, *I don't really have the time.* And I'm thinking, *No way do I want to waste a second more than I have to thinking about this test.*

But none of us says what we're thinking. You can't. Jane is just way too psyched about this. So we all end up going, "Yeah, okay. That'd be cool."

And in my case, wondering, *What are we getting into here?*

LEO

I'm pretty sure I'll be busy whenever Jane decides the next meeting is. But there's no point in saying that now.

Instead I ask, "So, does anyone know when their Crowley meeting is?" Daisy and Max groan, fall around on the couch.

Jane says, "What's the Crowley meeting?"

I say, "Crowley's the school college adviser—"

"He's evil," says Daisy.

I ignore her. "In your junior year you have a meeting with him and he gives you a list of schools where he thinks you should apply. He breaks it down: reaches, possibles, and safeties."

Jane frowns. "What if you want to go somewhere that's not on his list?"

"It means Crowley thinks you can't get in."

"Or that you're not worth his time. What he does," Max tells Jane, "is decide how many kids from Dewey can get into the top schools and limits the number of applications so the top kids have the best chance. Like if I want to go to Yale, and Crowley's thinking, *Okay, Leo and Jane have a better chance of getting in there than Max does,* he won't put Yale on my list."

Jane frowns. You can tell it's hitting her for the first time. Like, yeah, maybe we're going to hang out, go over some SAT crap together, be all supportive. But when you get right down to it, it's every man for himself.

MAX

On the way home Daisy says, "Are we really going to do this?"

"It's better than prep," I say.

Daisy nods. "I am *not* going back to that heinousness."

We keep walking. I don't say, "I am." Don't say, "I have to." Don't say, "Otherwise my dad'll kill me."

The great thing about Daisy, she always says what she thinks. But she doesn't make you do the same. Mostly because she already knows. She knows most things about me.

Like she knows that when I got my PSAT scores, I took them to my dad and said, "Hey, not too bad, huh?"

He just looked at them for the longest time. I waited for him to say, "Not bad at all!" or something like that.

Instead he said, "Well, you could do better." He looked at me. "Don't you think?"

"Well, yeah, but . . ." I didn't know what to say. Because I thought the scores were not bad for the first time around. "I bet a lot of kids didn't get this high."

"I don't care about a lot of kids, Max. Forget them. Do *you* think *you* can do better?"

And I was like, *Wait, I have to remember everybody else when I'm not doing as good as they are, but when I do better, I* still *have to worry about everybody else? When do I get not to worry?*

For a second I wished my mom were there, so she could say what she thought. Which was entirely stupid because dead people don't think about SATs. Or anything else, for that matter.

My dad said, "Do you know how many kids are going to take the SATs next year?"

"A lot."

"That's right. Do you know how hard it is for colleges to choose? How many outstanding candidates there are?"

I wanted to ask him, "Do you think I'm an outstanding candidate?" But instead I said, "They look at a lot of stuff, not just SATs."

"Sure. But grades, an interview, your recommendations, your essay—all that's subjective. The SAT is the only hard, solid number they have to go by. And you can't let them use it against you. If it's a choice between you and someone just like you but with better scores . . ."

I kept thinking, *But these scores are okay.*

Then I saw my dad's face, and I knew if I thought these scores were acceptable, then I was a loser, a guy who was just okay in a world where you have to be frigging amazing.

Just okay is not okay.

So I said, "I think you're right. I can definitely do better."

My dad smiled. "I know you can."

That night I get out a piece of paper, draw a line down the middle. At the top I write, "My Life." Then on one side of the line I put "If I Do Well on the SATs," and on the other, "If I Don't Do Well on the SATs."

If I Do Well on the SATs

- I will make my dad happy.
- Go to a decent school with people who have half

If I Do Not Do Well on the SATs

- I will make my dad seriously pissed off.
- Get into some dumb-jock

a brain and who don't necessarily care that you're not a sex god.
- Meet someone.
- Fall in love, or close approximation thereof.
- Be happy.

school where girls sleep only with dumb jocks.
- Be stunted by lack of sexual experience in college; never get anyone to sleep with me. Ever.
- Die a miserable virgin.

Then I close the notebook.

Daisy had her hair in a braid today.

LEO

I paid for the pizza. I don't think anybody noticed that, but I did. Which really annoys me. Like, "Oh, he's got money, let him pay." Gee, you're welcome.

Since the day is shot, I head home and zone. I'm sitting in the living room, flipping channels, when my little brother, Alonzo, brings his monster truck screaming up to my sneakers. Yelling, "Road block, road block," he crunches the car over my feet, and I say, "Man, you are lucky these are my old shoes."

He looks up grinning. Kid's only seven. Monster trucks are kind of his life.

If you want to get technical about it, Zo is my half brother. He became a fixture in the house when he was two. That's when my dad decided maybe his girlfriend and his kid should live in the same house with him.

Jenna's okay. She's young, which might sound weird for me to say, but she is young; she's only twenty-seven, and I don't get the sense that she's got the biggest clue. Although she figured out how to get my dad to pay her rent, so there you go. Not so dumb after all.

Once, we all went out to dinner, and the waiter thought she and I were the couple, that we were together. She and my dad found that most hilarious. I was like, *Right, moving on . . .*

Zo's okay, though. Look at him, ramming his monster truck into the table leg.

Zo's cool.

That night I try to do the practice test as quickly as possible. I want to get fast on this thing so I can forget about the time pressure.

I'm about two-thirds through when there's a knock on my door. Great, there goes my time. I yell, "Yeah?"

The door opens. *Oh, hi, Dad.* I say, "What's up?"

He says, "Homework already? Man, they work you hard."

He smiles like he's all sympathetic, but what he really means is, *I can't believe you're working. Get a life already.*

My dad used to be all about work. He used to get it: You want something, take it, nobody gives it to you. Then he flipped out, decided he wasn't "living"—whatever that means. Bye Mom, bye job, hello Jenna and acting like . . .

Whatever. I say it again, "What's up?"

He points back to the living room. "We rented some movies, wanted to know if you were up for it."

I hold up the SAT book. "Kind of busy."

After he's closed the door, I feel a little bad.

But then I'm like, *What do you want from me?*

Do you have any idea how competitive it is out there?

No, you don't, because you decided you didn't give a crap.

Well, I don't have that choice. So don't make me feel bad that I can't watch some stupid movie with you.

I go back to the test.

Daisy

I'm not a mega-talented basketball player. But I read the court well. Like, I can tell which way players will go—and I can usually fake them out.

That night at dinner, with my folks, I'm in for a major fake-out session.

First my mom. "How was prep?"

Fake left. "It was cool having Max there."

Then my dad: "Did you find it helpful?"

Fake right. "The guy couldn't find the test books."

Mom and Dad glance at each other. I can tell I'm about to be doubled-teamed.

A lot of kids will tell you how much their parents suck. They think it makes them cool to say they're barely surviving the torments of their evil mom and dad. And I always have to say, "You know, my parents are okay. They're pretty cool, all in all."

Which is why I can't lie to them. Unfortunately.

I expect screaming. But when I tell my parents I skipped prep—and that I'm not going back—they just get really, really quiet. Which is, frankly, worse.

My dad turns his fork over. "The basketball's not going to do it, honey."

"I know."

"And your grades are good, but . . ."

"Not amazing, I know. I'll make them better. I promise."

My mom says, "It's a lot of money, Daisy."

Which makes me feel wild and desperate, and I start saying, "I know. I know . . . ," anything to get them to stop talking about money. I feel like it's the only thing we talk about anymore: "Your dad's out of work. I'm working full-time and going to school. Things are really tough right now."

When the PSAT scores came in the mail, we all knew they weren't the kind of PSAT scores that get you scholarships. That's when my mom and dad said, "Maybe we need to think about prep."

I say, "I will make this work, I totally promise, okay?" I look at both of them. "Okay?"

My mom smiles, puts her hand on mine. "We know you'll try, it's just . . ."

The money. "I know." Then: "You know, a bunch of us are going to get together and study. Sort of a group. Do practice tests."

My mom smiles. "That," says my dad, "is an excellent idea."

After dinner I try one of the practice tests. I think of what Leo said: "Bring it in, and if somebody gets something that you screwed up on, they explain it to you."

Yeah well, Leo, I'm going to need a whole lot of explaining. I mean, look at this:

> The lapdog is an excellent companion animal for those dwelling in cities. Its small size is well suited to apartment life. Its pleasant temperament makes it an ideal pet for people who have less time to walk an animal, as it will not become aggressive or restless due to lack of exercise. Which of the following is the best way to combine sentences 1, 2, and 3?
>
> *a.* The lapdog is a good house pet because it is small and unaggressive.
> *b.* The lapdog is an excellent pet because of its size and temperament.
> *c.* Many people who prefer lapdogs require small, good-natured animals.
> *d.* WHO CARES??????

I throw the stupid book across the room.

Jane

My mom is always on me about friends. Why I don't have them. Why I should have them. I've told her a million times, not everybody can be universally *adored*. But since she is, she doesn't get that. Like because I'm her daughter, everyone should be dying to be my friend.

So I figure she'll like hearing about everyone coming over. That'll make her happy.

At dinner I keep waiting for my mom to ask how it went. The prep thing, so I can tell her how I met these guys and they're kind of cool and maybe I'll see them again.

But she doesn't ask. Instead she talks to James the Pain about his gallery and how she thinks he's getting screwed.

I should explain: James the Pain is her husband. Not my dad. My dad lives in Connecticut. With his wife, Pam.

James the Pain is a sculptor. James the Pain thinks he's brilliant. My mother agrees.

I do not agree.

Like this dinner. It's typical. James the Pain going on and on and on, and my mother going, "Oh, I know, honey, I know," and Jane . . . Jane who?

I don't think they'd notice if I got up and walked out the door. Maybe I should try it. Maybe I should get up, walk out the door, into the hallway . . .

Get into the elevator, go down to the lobby . . .

Walk straight out into the street . . .

And just keep going.

I'm actually inching over in my chair when I remember Daisy standing in front of the class, how she just stood there by herself, with everyone looking at her.

I say loudly, "Me and a bunch of kids bailed on SAT prep." Immediately my mom and James stop talking.

My mom looks at me. "Excuse me?"

"We bailed. Because the teacher didn't show up, so we . . ." I shrug.

My mom says, "He didn't *show*? I can't believe it. If that happens next time . . ."

"I don't know if I want to go back." I start poking at my rice. "I think I might think the whole thing is bogus."

James groans. I want to stick him with the fork, I swear to God.

"Bogus?" My mom smiles.

"Yeah. Unfair." I try to think how Daisy would put it. Unfair is not anything my mother will understand. My mother has gotten everything she has ever wanted and much more than she deserves because she's . . . *Julia Cotterell.* "This girl in the class was saying how the whole testing and scores thing is out of control. Like that has anything to do with how smart you are . . . it's an unfair judgment."

My mom laughs again. "Honey, as you go through life you will learn that life is full of judgment—and most of it is a lot more unfair than any standardized test."

She picks up her fork, waves it at me. "Wait till your friend turns forty, she'll find out how unfair life can be."

I want to say, "My friend—who is not my friend, by the way, not yet—will not care when she's forty, because my friend is smart and a good person and doesn't need to be beautiful and *adored* to feel like a human being."

I don't say any of this. But thinking about it gives me an idea. "I asked them over. I was thinking maybe we could study together. Like a club."

"That'd be great," my mom says, smiling. "But you're going back to the class, too."

I say, "Sure." Because I can invite them over here. That's all that matters.

At the end of last year when I found out that Lily, who I thought was my one friend, was not my friend at all, I thought this year was going to suck. Nobody knows me. Nobody wants to know me. . . .

But now I think maybe I was wrong.

Maybe this year could be okay.

What: The first meeting of the SAT Survival Club
Where: Jane's house (153 East 73rd Street)
When: Thursday, September 12, 4:00 p.m.
Why: Because the SATs suck

MAX

There's a saying in our school: The road to Harvard starts in Mr. Crowley's office. Still, it's not a place you want to be. There's a rumor that some kid, the first time he saw Mr. Crowley, his hair turned white and he lost his mind.

That's *probably* not true. But looking at the pamphlets outside Crowley's office, you can see how it might be.

> *The SATs and YOU! Beat the Stress and Win!*
> *Finding the Perfect Fit: What You Need to Know*
>   *About Getting into College*
> *Interview Skills 101*
> *Complete the Circle: Strategies That Really Work*

I tell myself you cannot get heart attacks from looking at flyers in the college admissions office. However, I could be the first.

I can see it now: SIXTEEN-YEAR-OLD BOY DROPS DEAD FROM SAT STRESS! HIGH SCHOOL PRINCIPAL SAYS, "HE WASN'T HARVARD MATERIAL, SO WHO CARES?"

I pick up an *SATs and YOU!* and open it.

> *Are YOU ready for the SATs???*

Gah! No. I crumple it up, then pull it open.

> *Are YOU freaking out???*

Er, yes sir, I am.

Do YOU need help???

Frigging duh.

Is it my imagination, or are they trying to make you as freaked out and insane as possible?

Our first SAT meeting is today.

LEO

You hear it all over school. When people talk about their summer vacation, it's not about Maui or the Hamptons anymore. It's "I interned at my dad's law firm," "I volunteered for Amnesty International," "I was a gofer at Sotheby's."

In other words, people are getting serious about the college thing.

But I can play this game. A little smile, a shrug. Nobody has to know the Thayer family hasn't done Maui or the Hamptons in quite a while. I have a voice I use with people I don't care about but have to be nice to. I think of it as Leo Basic. Usually I use it with my mom or teachers. It's friendly, laid back, but not too out there. If you listened closely, you might hear, *I am so freaking bored by you.* Most people don't listen that closely. But I get a kick out of knowing it's there, that note.

At lunch I run into Kyra Fleming. She's sitting at one of the tables, writing in her notebook. Kyra doesn't have to get serious. She's been serious all along.

She wants Yale. I want Yale. It's something we joke about—most of the time. She's definitely Little Miss Entitled, but someone I like—most of the time.

I sneak up on her, whisper, "Dear Diary: That Leo Thayer is so hot, I would do anything to have him. . . ."

She turns, whacks me with the back of her hand. "Leo, you are sick!"

I sit down, and she shows me the notebook. "Check it out. This summer I made a family tree and I put down all the schools everyone went to. Legacies are *muy importante*. My dad's been giving money to Williams since he left." She smiles. "Mom and Yale the same."

I smile back. "Sweet." Then, so she doesn't totally get the upper hand, I say, "I just started prep. Have to brush up on the test skills."

Kyra wrinkles her nose. "I'm not doing prep. My parents hired a tutor. It's, like, two hundred dollars an hour or something and totally worth it—if you can afford it. My mom says classes are useless because you just get treated like everybody else."

I smile. "I'm tough. I can handle it."

"Really?" Kyra cocks her head at me. "Because sometimes I worry about you, Leo. You can't just be a grade grubber or test monkey. You have to be a well-rounded individual. Show school spirit. You're not real big on school spirit, are you? I mean, your extracurricular's a little"—she smiles—"puny."

Some girls think they're being hot when they kick your ass. Right now, among other things, I'd like to tell Kyra, "Wrong. And by the way, some of us don't have mommies who went to Yale and daddies who went to Williams. So some of us have to do the work and get the grades, and that doesn't leave a whole lot of time for bogus shows of school spirit. . . ."

I shouldn't let Kyra and her crap about school spirit bug me. It's part of the game: She teases, I act like I don't care. Because I don't.

Just sometimes the game can get a little tiresome.

Oh, man. Almost forgot. That thing at Jane's is today.

Daisy

Tryouts
for Women's Basketball Team
September 12, 3:00, the gym

I don't have to do tryouts anymore. Once you've been on the team for three years, you get a free pass. But I always like to go. Just to say, *I don't take my spot for granted.* I figure if Luisa Martine, who's our best player, can go, I can.

It's funny, watching these kids try out. Some of them look fierce—*Give me the ball, I'll show you what I can do.* Most of them look like, *Uh, why did I think this was a good idea?* I remember the first year I tried out, I thought,

Just let me disappear. Now I'm smiling at them, letting them know it's okay, we won't torture them.

While Barbara, our coach, explains to them how try-outs work, Luisa Martine comes over, says, "Hey, Daisy," and holds up her fist. I give it a light tap.

When I was a freshman and Lu was a sophomore, she was my god. Every once in a while I still can't get over the idea that we're friends. It's like, *Wait, you're Luisa Martine.*

"Check it out," Luisa says, and shows me her sweat-shirt. It says PROPERTY OF U. PENN. "I went over the sum-mer. *Loved. It.* Already started putting together my freshman wardrobe." She grins.

I nod. "Excellent."

"Yeah, it's kind of a reach for me. Crowley doesn't think I have the SATs. But I figure I'll show the love by applying early."

Barbara blows the whistle, and we start practicing for real. Like they say in the ads, I love this game.

A lot of people are like, "Ew, sports, that's for dum-mies." And yeah, maybe you don't win the Nobel for basketball, but when I see people play music, it's the same thing. They're just into it, riding the wave. And when they're good, they take you along; you'd never have found that wave on your own, they had to create it. It's not "A is to B as C is to D, and the answer is pi squared." It's not a logic thing. You know it because you feel it.

Barbara switches over to running exercises, which are boring and exhausting. She does them to weed out the kids who won't want to work. Lu and I decide to take a pass.

I'm getting salt-'n'-sugar water from the machine when I hear Luisa say, "Mighty Max!" and see Max heading toward us. He says, "Ready to go?"

I look back at the freshmen. In the worst way I want to be one of them and not going to this meeting. I say, "Yeah, give me a sec."

Luisa says, "Where are we off to?"

"Jane Cotterell's," says Max. "SAT study group."

Luisa groans. "Don't remind me. I have nightmares about that freaking thing. Have fun," she says, and runs off to join the layup line. I wish I could too. I'd even do the stupid running exercises—anything but the SATs.

Part

I **II** III IV

Put Your Pencil Down. Turn Your Test Booklet Over.

Your Checklist for SAT Success!

1. *Good study habits.*
2. *Strong concentration skills.*
3. *Fun. We know it's hard, but if you can relax, your chances for success will SOAR!*
4. *Friends. A strong support system is a must!*

—from *The SATs and YOU!*

Jane

One thing I read in this book on entertaining: Good food is essential to a successful gathering. So here's what I've got:

Coke, Diet Coke, Sprite, water.

Popcorn and pretzels.

Chocolate chip cookies and peanut butter cookies in case anyone's allergic to chocolate. (Although what if they're allergic to peanuts?)

Anyway, I think, I *think*, it's enough.

Now all I have to do is get rid of my mom.

I don't want her around when the guys come over. I haven't even told her they're coming, because the second I do, she'll be all, "Oh, I want to meet them." She wants to pretend she's just any other mom, but what it's really about is that she loves it when people get all goofy around her. I remember when she met Lily. That was the day I found out Lily wanted to be an actress. News to me.

Now she's reading a book in the living room, where we have to be.

As I bring in the bowls of popcorn and pretzels she looks up, and I say, "Some friends are coming over. We're doing SAT stuff."

She brightens. "This is that group?"

"Yeah, sort of." I set the bowls down.

"Well, I'll get right out of your way." She starts gathering up her book and teacup. "When are they coming?"

Which means "When do I get to meet them?"

"Well, the thing is, this is the first time we see each other's scores, so it could be a little weird if people were around." My mom glances at me. She doesn't hear no a whole lot and always makes a bigger deal of it than it is. "Maybe you can say hi next time?"

She hesitates, but then I get the smile. "Well, don't let things get too crazy, or I'll have to come in here and break it up." She heads down the hallway, then turns. "Is Lily coming?"

"No."

"What ever happened to Lily?"

You did. "Lost touch."

Then the bell rings, and I go to answer it.

LEO

So, yeah, it's not supposed to be a competition. But I'm pretty sure I'll have gotten the highest score. Frankly, I should get the highest score. I'm the only one who takes this thing seriously.

I'm the first to arrive. I'm about to ask Jane how she did on the practice test when Daisy and Max buzz. While Jane goes to let them in, I take my test book out of my bag. Then I put it back. I don't want people getting pissed because they think I'm showing off.

Max and Daisy come in, sit on "their" couch. Max takes his book out and places it carefully next to the cookies. Then Daisy takes hers out and shoves it alongside, almost totaling a bowl of pretzels. When we started this thing, I told everyone we had to have the same book: *Score! The Insider's Guide to SAT.* That way we could all do the same tests.

Then Jane finally sits. Her book is on the floor.

"Okay," I say, "so how'd everybody do?"

Crunch time.

I don't want to start this off. But nobody is saying anything, so finally I go, "I got nineteen ninety. Not bad, but I want better. Verbal I killed, math I screwed up a few places."

I look at Jane, who's staring off down the hall for some reason. I say her name and she jumps. "I got, uh . . . sixteen ten."

"Is that what you wanted?"

She shrugs. "It's what I got. I mean . . . I don't know what you mean." She looks at Max and Daisy.

Max says, "You can get into decent places with that score. But if you got it higher, you'd have more choices."

I say, "Definitely. Okay, Max. Hit me."

Max meets my eye for a moment. The guy doesn't like me. He opens his book, looks at his test sheet. "I ended up doing okay. But I froze up a lot. If I'd been doing the real test, I wouldn't have finished." He looks up. "My score was twenty-one fifty."

As Daisy whoops and high-fives him all I can think is, *Twenty-one fifty. And he calls that okay.*

Twenty-one fifty, could go higher. Bet he writes a kick-ass essay. Writes for the school paper, teachers like him . . .

Is Max thinking Yale?

I say, "Great, man." Max smiles. He knows he just kicked my butt, and he knows I know it. We have a thing here, ladies and gentlemen. A definite, bona fide thing.

I say, "Daisy?"

Daisy

When Leo says my name, I want to say, "Let somebody else go." But there isn't anybody else.

Now batting, Daisy Stubbs . . .

There's only one way to do this, and that's fast. With a big-ass smile on my face, so nobody gets all, "Poor you!"

Really quick I say, "Twelve twenty."

Then when nobody says anything, I raise a fist. "Whoo-hoo! Lowest score to Daisy!"

It is real hard to keep smiling when nobody's smiling back.

LEO

Daisy's score is so lousy, at first you're like, "You're kidding." But as we go through the questions we screwed up you can tell: She wasn't kidding.

But at the end of the meeting, when I say we should write down our scores so we have a record, I'm honestly not thinking about Daisy. But when Max gives me a dirty look, I think, *Oh, duh . . .* , and say, "Forget it."

But Daisy says, "No. Absolutely. Write it down." She takes out her notebook, and we all give our scores again. Then she holds up the book so we can all see:

> Record for the First Meeting
> Max: 2150
> Leo: 1990
> Jane: 1610
> Daisy: 1220

All I can see are those first two lines. Max, then me.

When I get home, I feel like I'm going to explode. One person asks me one wrong thing and it could get seriously ugly.

Luckily no one's at home. There's a note saying they've taken Zo to a movie and they're eating out. I should order whatever I want.

But I don't need to order what I want. What I want is right here.

Normally I don't do this during the week. It's just not a good idea with the 'rents around. And unlike some people I know, I don't believe in going to school wasted. It's not worth the potential hassle.

Tonight, however, I need something. A reward of some kind for all the crap I just went through. It's like a performance. You gotta come down somehow.

I go to the liquor cabinet and examine the possibilities. My dad is a Scotch man; Jenna, strictly wine. So those I leave alone. Those they would notice. Fortunately my preferred beverage is rum. I'm partial to Cuban, but Bacardi, which is what my dad buys, will do. Cola helps cover up the cheap aftertaste.

I have had old Captain Jack, but I admit, he kicked me on my ass. I told my dad I had a wicked stomach flu and stayed in bed all day. I like the idea of martinis. You know—Bond, James Bond. Shaken, stirred, whatever.

But when you're on a stealth quaffing mission, there's no time to shake or stir. You pour in a glass and chug it down.

I let the first one settle. Then pour another. Then I can let it into my head.

No matter what you do, it's never enough. They put it out there, "Ooh, maybe, maybe you can get this. Maybe, just maybe, you can have that. . . ."

Then at the last minute they say, "But only if you do this, this, this, this, and this. . . ."

Mariah Fredericks

If Max wants Yale, man . . . he's exactly the kind of nerdy jerk college types love.

Then for some reason I think of Kyra. How easy this is for her.

I put the glass down before I throw it against the wall.

MAX

On the bus ride home Daisy says, "Did you see Thayer's face when you said what you got? A-mazing."

I know she wants to talk about my score because she doesn't want to talk about hers, so I say, "I think he was a little surprised."

"Yeah, just a little." She grins. Then she says, "So, what's the verdict on Jane? Hot or not?"

I think Jane's got the whole waifish thing going on, but she doesn't seem to know she has a body. Also, people give signals. How they feel about the whole physical thing. Like, *Yeah, I am definitely into it.* Or, *Don't touch!* Jane's definitely a Don't Touch. (Which kind of makes you wonder if the whole thing with the stepfather is true.)

I say, "She looks like her mom."

"Knew it! You're hot for the mom."

"Uh, no."

"Into older women . . ."

I put on a Cockney accent. "Like 'em young and fresh, I do."

"Perve."

"Look who's talking." I look at Daisy, then all of a sudden can't. "Nah, Jane doesn't do it for me."

"So, who does?"

Lately Daisy's been teasing me a lot about women. I'd kind of like to know why.

"I can think of some people."

That night I make a list.

Daisy asked me who I thought was hot . . .

   a. Just to say something.
   b. Because she really wanted to know.

Let's say *b.* She really wanted to know.

So, Daisy wants to know who I think is hot because . . .

   a. She's curious.
   b. She wants me to have a girlfriend.
   c. She wants to *be* my girlfriend and is wildly jealous that I might find another woman attractive—even though she doesn't know that yet, because I think if she did know it, she would come out and say, "Hey, Max, I think you're hot." Which she has not said.

I close my notebook. Look over at my SAT prep book. I should not feel good that I got a better score than Leo Thayer. I should not think, *I beat Leo Thayer's ass.* This is not, after all, a competition.

But as Leo says, it is. So I do.

Daisy

Figuring Out Financial Aid
Managing the Perils of Student Debt
Why Does It Cost So Much??
Make Their Money Work for You!

The numbers freak me out: $50,000, 13 percent interest, tuition up 27 percent, grants down 42 percent. After a while it doesn't make any sense. It's all just a bunch of numbers and symbols that add up to one thing: You're screwed.

Certain things, most things, cost money. I get that. Like cars and restaurants and movies and designer clothes. But none of that stuff is stuff people need. Things people need should not cost huge amounts of money. Things like food and somewhere to live and medicine and . . . school. Those things should be affordable. And yet somehow they're, like, the most expensive things in the world. Like, "Oh, you need this? Well, you'll have to pay a million dollars for it. Can't afford a million dollars? Well, you can just drop dead, then."

Sometimes I think they've decided only rich kids should be educated. Everyone else can be stupid. I know that isn't actually true, that education costs a lot, and blah, blah, but there's something about these pamphlets that makes me want to shriek.

You look at the scholarships, the grants, the loans. They ask a million questions: What do your parents make? How much can they afford? What can *you* pay? What do you want us to pay . . . and why the hell should we?

I want to say, "Nothing. Forget it."

Yeah, then what, Daisy? You told your parents you'd check this stuff out. So . . . check it out.

Even though I'm pretty sure that every single one of these things on the tables outside Crowley's office is designed to make you crazy, I open one of the brochures.

A Major Expense

In the last decade the average cost of tuition plus room and board has skyrocketed. A college education can be a crippling expense for many families these days.

Sometimes I wonder, *Is it really worth it? What can I learn in four years that's worth hundreds of thousands of dollars?* Like, I need to spend all that money to study poetry?

Only if you don't, you could be flipping burgers at Mickey D's your entire life. And why is that? Can someone tell me why that is?

Okay, shut up, Daisy. Chill out.

The door to Crowley's office opens. Kelly Thurston comes out with a big smile on her face. Kelly's an Ivy, one of Crowley's little pets, someone who'll make him look good by getting into one of the top schools.

Crowley and I haven't liked each other since ninth grade. At our first meeting he said he heard I liked to sing, so I should take chorus. It'd look good, he said, on the résumé.

I didn't take chorus. And Crowley never pressured me to do anything ever again.

Still, when he sees me, he puts on a fresh smile. "Daisy . . ."

I jump away from the financial aid pamphlets, start looking at the SAT stuff. But that doesn't fool Crowley. He pulls one—*Managing the Perils of Student Debt*—out and offers it to me. "This one is very helpful."

For a second I think about smacking it out of his hand. But I can just hear my mom on that one. So I take it.

If I didn't dislike Crowley so much, I'd ask him, "What score do I need to get money? How high do I have to shoot?" But I can't. There's something about him that feels like teeth: Never show that you need something from him.

As I decide not to ask for Crowley's help his eyes narrow like he knows exactly what I was thinking. I feel like I've failed some test. Or escaped, I'm not sure.

He says, "By any chance, are you thinking of a career in teaching?"

"I haven't really thought about it."

"You might. There are loan forgiveness programs for people who go into teaching. That could alleviate some of the burden."

The burden. Am I the burden or do I get the burden? I guess that's the question.

I totally admit: The first practice test we took, I didn't try. Just got through it as fast as possible and said, "Hey, I get what I get." And when what I got wasn't very good, I acted like, *What's the big deal?*

But the next week I tried. I shut my door, turned off the stereo, and tried.

The SATs are a really weird head to be in. It's like aliens came down to Earth and translated normal human thought into some bizarre language. It looks familiar, but when you try to think in it, you go nuts. Even the essay. It's, like, discuss this incredibly complicated issue people write whole books about—in twenty-five minutes.

I just don't get it. That one question, I thought, *Okay, obviously* c. And it was *d*. I didn't even understand their explanation of why it was *d*.

For a second I thought of calling Max. Primarily to

find out, did the whole world know the answer was *d* except me? Like, am I the only one who doesn't get this test?

But then I thought, *Of course Max put d. Max totally gets this. Everybody gets it, Daisy, except you and a bunch of rock heads.*

So I didn't call Max.

And I got my worst score yet.

So at today's meeting everyone gets to hear about my lousy score. Everyone gets to go, "Oh, poor Daisy, how can we help? Let us explain it to you. . . ."

I can't stand being helped. It's like when someone puts her hand on your shoulder, and you're like, *Get off.*

I hate losing. I hate not being good at something. And I know even if I get a little better at this test, it won't be good enough. Not good enough for money.

They used to call Michael Jordan "Money." Because he was that good. If the Bulls were down, he'd just turn it up and say, "Okay, time to win the game." And he would. He was that stupidly, ridiculously good. You could count on him. The way you count on money.

I always felt bad for Patrick Ewing. He was a friend of Jordan's who played for the Knicks. He was good—really, really good. He deserved a ring. But he never got one because he had the rotten luck to be playing at the same time as the greatest player who ever lived. At least, that's what they said.

Then Jordan left the game for a while, and Patrick had his shot. No Money to beat him.

He still got beat.

I remember watching it, the game where they lost to the Rockets. Patrick put it all out there. He knew what was at stake. Big, galumphing guy. No grace, but tons of heart. In the last seconds of the game he went for one of the most elegant shots you can do, the finger role. And he missed. And he lost.

The next day it was all over the papers, the picture of Patrick's hand stretched to the breaking point, ball teetering on the very tip of his finger. So close, so close . . . not enough.

Everybody had something to say. All those fat-ass sportswriters wanted to know, why did Patrick go for the finger role? And I kept thinking, *The guy tried. Can't you see how hard he tried?*

They saw. They killed him anyway.

Jane

I haven't even put out the soda and pretzels when Daisy arrives. She immediately sees she's the first and says, "Oh, man, am I early? Major social boo-boo."

It takes me a second to speak. "No, definitely. Come in."

Daisy says, "Max got hung up with the newspaper, but I can wait outside if . . ."

"No, really. Come in." I gesture to the kitchen.

Daisy follows me in. She helps me carry all the stuff out. Lily never carried stuff. She just sat there while I waited on her. Once she even asked why I'd gotten cheese popcorn when I knew she liked butter.

Daisy sits, takes a handful of pretzels. "It's really nice of you to do this."

"I like it," I say. "Sometimes I think I'll open a restaurant someday."

"Way cool." Daisy outlines an imaginary sign. "'Jane's.' Would it be seriously fancy?"

"Oh, no. Nice, but for everyone. Like, you could take kids."

"Well, you'll have to let us know when you open, dahling, so we can all come."

"I'll have a special gahla, dahling. Only the elite." Daisy laughs. Suddenly I am a funny person. I can make people laugh. I can feed people. I can open restaurants.

Honestly, when Leo and Max get here, I'm bummed we have to start talking about SATs.

LEO

I say it right up front: "Max—what's the score?" So everybody knows I have no problem with this.

He looks in his book. "I didn't do so good this time. Nineteen seventy."

He's 1970. I am 2020.

I . . . won.

Why does this not feel better?

Because Max is looking at me like, *I know you wanted to beat me. You think I care? How pathetic are you, getting competitive over a test?*

Max makes it look like he doesn't work at all. Like he's that good.

I feel a twinge: *You are not that good. You've never been that good, Leo.*

You can't just be a grade grubber or test monkey.

"Okay," I say, "Jane?"

Just as Jane is about to say her score someone passes by the living room on their way to the kitchen. For a second the woman hesitates, just enough time for me to think, *Oh, gosh, that's . . . Julia Cotterell.*

She half waves, like she's embarrassed, then hurries on. Jane acts like she never saw her. But only when her mom's gone does she say, "Nineteen hundred."

I say, "You went up, that's cool."

She smiles, shrugs. It's weird. Jane started this club. But out of all of us she's the one who seems to care least about the SATs.

MAX

When Jane's done, I feel Daisy tense up, and I know immediately she didn't do well. I almost say, "Why don't we get to the problems?" so she won't have to go through the whole "What'd you get?" thing. Then Leo says her name, and she just says it, straight out.

Worse than last time.

I reach for her book. "Can I see?"

Daisy shrugs. She's all folded up, her arms crossed, her legs tucked under her chin. While I look at her test, she pulls at a loose thread on her jeans.

Leo says, "What screws you up? Is it math or verbal?"

"Math," says Daisy. "And verbal. The whole thing, basically."

> Record for the Second Meeting
> Leo: 2020
> Max: 1970
> Jane: 1900
> Daisy: 1190

Jane

I feel horrible.

Poor Daisy. I mean, as we went over stuff with her she just got more and more frustrated. I felt like we were torturing her. I wanted to say, "You know what, it doesn't matter." Then I remembered what she said about scholarships, and I felt awful all over again. Because for Daisy it does matter.

At dinner, before I can say anything, my mom says, "I'm sorry. I forgot."

I just look at her. James says, "What'd you forget?"

My mom waves her hand. "Nothing. I . . . interrupted Jane's meeting."

James says, "You live here too, as I remember."

I glare at him. *So do you, only no one wants you to.*

But that's not true. My mother wants him to.

That night I put on my favorite nightgown. My mom calls it my *Little Women* nightgown because it's old-fashioned looking with long sleeves and flowers. I really love it. You put it on and you feel completely safe, like a cocoon. And maybe it's lame, but *Little Women* is one of my favorite books. I would love to have a lot of sisters, all living with me, even if we fought sometimes.

One thing I really wish is that I had my own bathroom. Now I have to use the one in the hallway, which is tiny. Since I'm only brushing my teeth, I leave the door open so I don't feel like I'm suffocating.

I'm almost finished when I see him. In the mirror.

James.

He's standing in the hallway. Just standing there.

Not just standing. Looking.

Our eyes meet in the mirror. *I see you.*

LEO

When I get home, I have an e-mail from Kyra Fleming. Probably wants to tell me about a new relative she's discovered who went to some great school.

There's always a question with Kyra. Are we kind of into each other, or do we just do the act? Sometimes I think about pushing it, just for a laugh. Forget the act, do the deed.

Somehow, doing the deed with Kyra seems like one of those life experiences best avoided.

I open her e-mail. It says: *"Hey! I hear you've got a little club. Can I join?"*

I type back. *"Sorry. Quite the elite group."*

I pause, can't resist. *"Someone would have to nominate you."*

"I don't do auditions. You either want me or you don't."

I think, then type, *"Why don't you do auditions? Scared you'll blow it?"*

I know and Kyra knows: There is no answer to that one. I win.

I've got a ton of homework I need to get to. As I stack the books on my desk—calculus, physics, *As I Lay Dying*—I think, *All this work. And the SATs.* I think of Mr. Bennett, who does English. For him, reading Faulkner is some sort of transcendent, wah-wah thing. I don't have time for transcendent, man. Just give me the Spark Notes.

I'm trying to figure out why someone's mother is a fish, when Daisy pops into my head. It's weird. When she was struggling to figure out a sentence-completion question, part of me thought, *Yeah, Daisy, this SAT stuff isn't so easy, is it? Maybe it does take a few brains.*

But I thought, *This is a really smart girl. She's got a brain. Why can't she get it that the missing word is* proficient, *and not* optimistic, gregarious, *or* effect?

Then I thought, *Why should she?*

The test is still the test. You can't sit around

going, "Oh, it's not fair. It's too hard." Nothing's fair. Everything's hard—that's the way it is.

But still.

MAX

"Whatever I am, I owe to strength of will,
character, application, and daring."

—Napoléon

Madame Deschalles has written this on the blackboard. She has a serious jones for Napoléon.

There are some things I have in common with Napoléon. We're both short. Then there are things I don't have in common with him. Namely, everything else.

For example, I am not a daring person. My strength of will is not massive. This probably accounts for a lot of things. Including my almost complete lack of sexual experience.

"Oh, uh, hi, I was wondering if, uh . . . oh, well, you know. Uh, actually never mind, it was stupid. Sorry I bothered you."

Whereas Napoléon probably said, "Be mine, wench." Or whatever the French for *wench* is. *Waunch? Femme?*

I'm sure Leo says something like that as well. He may not have a French accent or be conqueror of Europe, but he is, in fact, not short.

It's been more than a month since Daisy asked me who I thought was hot. Since then two things have happened:

Mariah Fredericks

1. I haven't been able to stop thinking about her.
2. I haven't done diddly about it.

This isn't new. Me liking Daisy. When I first saw her in eighth grade, I thought, *This is the greatest-looking girl I've ever seen—and not in a mill-yun years will she go out with me.* When she started dating some head case named Peter, I thought, *Well, you weren't going to ask her out, were you? She'd only say no, and then it'd be all weird and you wouldn't even get to hang out with her.*

For most of the time I don't even think about it. But it is there, I can feel it. Mostly we're friends. But there is this little part that's something different, and I feel like I'll go nuts if we don't deal with that other part.

Because I think it could be really good.

It can't all be about hotness. It has to be about other things too. And it's when I think about the other things that I think, *Maybe I have a shot.*

Daisy dates jerks, it's something her friends know about her. This guy Kyle was the worst. He was heavily into drinking and heavily into hitting things. At last year's senior party he got mad at Daisy and put his fist through a wall, right near her head. That was it for Kyle.

Daisy hasn't had a boyfriend since then. Maybe she's waiting for me to say something. Maybe she's feeling the same way, but embarrassed.

She did say I was cute. Over the summer she did say that. And she did say that she would never go for someone like Brad Pitt, which, since I am the biological opposite of Brad Pitt, gave me a certain amount of hope.

Sometimes I don't think about it at all. We hang, and it's just cool being with her. Like, *Zap, oh, alive now.*

And then . . . then there's this other thing, and I think, *You are so stupid. Kiss her.*

Napoléon would kiss her.

Le wimp, *c'est moi.*

But maybe it's time that stopped being true.

Jane

I have to admit, I was kind of hoping Max would get hung up at the paper again and Daisy might come early. So when they arrive together like always, I have to not show that I'm disappointed.

I point out to Daisy that I switched to white chocolate macadamia cookies instead of boring old chocolate chip. She says, "Cool," but nothing about restaurants.

It's obvious she's in a bad mood. But I don't know why. I glance over at Max once when she's not looking, and he just shrugs.

Then Leo comes, and we all sit down and say our scores. And that's when Daisy says it.

"I'm quitting."

Daisy

I decided to quit last night. I was four questions into the practice test, and I thought, *Screw this. Why am I torturing myself?*

Because I'm not getting any better. I know I have to take the test in March, and yeah, it'll suck when I get the same lousy score, but why go through this again and again and again? It's like banging my head against a wall: *You're dumb, you're dumb, you're dumb.*

Now everyone's staring at me. Any second now they'll start with the "You can'ts."

I say, "I'm holding you guys back. You spend all this time explaining stuff to me that you already know. It's a total waste of your time."

Max says, "I like wasting my time."

Jane says, "Yeah. Definitely."

For a second I don't know what to say. I only know I can't go on coming to this stupid group and feeling pathetic. I reach down to get my book bag off the floor.

Max says, "Daisy, come on."

I feel a flash of rage. It's totally unfair, but I want to scream, "I don't ask you to do stuff where you feel like a loser. Don't ask me to."

And when I see that Max sees what I'm thinking, I feel like the world's biggest cow.

I so need to be out of here.

But then Leo says, "You can't quit. It's not allowed."

LEO

Daisy says, "Excuse me?"

And for a second I think, *Are you nuts? Let her go.*

But the fact is, there's only one of us who really needs to up her score, one person who'll really be screwed if she doesn't. And if you don't help that person . . . I don't know. What's the point otherwise?

"It's lame if you quit. If you were having a lousy game, would you say, 'Forget it, I'm quitting'?"

"If I was *this* lousy, they'd throw me off the team."

"Can I ask you one thing?"

"One thing." She's still got her backpack on, she's still ready to go. It hits me how much it sucks when you work and you try and it doesn't go the way you wanted at all. . . .

I say, "Can you be okay with the fact that this is a game like any other game, and you learn the stupid rules, and you get by the best you can?"

Daisy's jaw is hard. She's looking at that door.

She says, "I hate this game."

"Right. Then, don't play."

She shouts, "I have to!"

I shout back, "Then, don't quit!"

A lot of girls, you yell at them, they think they have the right to go all boo-hoo on you. Daisy looks half amused, half pissed off. Her tongue works its way all around her mouth while she thinks.

Then she sits down.

"Okay," I say, "let's look at the first question you got wrong."

Daisy picks up her test book. Then she laughs.

"That would be question number one."

MAX

Wait . . .

There's something weird here.

We're going through Daisy's test. And all of a sudden it's like me and Jane aren't even in the room.

Record for the Sixth Meeting
Leo: 2010
Max: 1950
Jane: 1890
Daisy: 1100*
*Unofficial score

Jane

I made Leo put that, about the unofficial score. Daisy didn't want me to, but I really think things will be different for her now.

I feel so good. Like somehow the four of us are going to be separate from the competitive nastiness that goes on at school. "She said this about her, and it was true, and he did this to him. . . ." It's all so petty.

At the end of the meeting I wanted one of two

things: to invite them to stay to dinner, or to go home with one of them. I just didn't want it to end.

I also have this stupid fantasy that somehow we'll all end up at the same college. Or maybe colleges in the same area, so we can visit one another on the weekends. For a while I think about driving to meet Daisy at her school and calling her from the car and talking about our stupid professors.

I kind of hope she and Max figure it out and get married. It'd be so cool to go to their wedding. Maybe I'll have it together by then and I can cater it. And then on Sundays they'll come over for brunch.

Leo will come too. And he'll always have some new girlfriend, and we'll always be like, "Okay, when are you going to settle down?"

I know it's a dumb fantasy. I just want to stay friends with these people for forever.

I pass by my mom's room. She and James are lying on the bed, watching one of the shows they like. My mom's curled up around him, like she's a teenager. The TV makes some joke, and she laughs. Then she looks up at James to see if he's laughing, if she was right to think it was funny.

She sees me, says, "Come. Watch with us."

I say, "No, thanks. Homework."

I do have homework. I have to start *Hamlet*, which we're reading for English. I can't believe how evil Gertrude is. Her son's upset because his father's dead, and she's like, "Shut up, be happy for me." She doesn't care about Hamlet at all. All she cares about is she's got this new husband and everyone's paying attention to her, but she's got no clue about what's really going on. And when her son tries to say, "Hello, maybe Dad was murdered?" she's like, "We're all very happy, and if you can't go along with that, we're going to single you out in front of everyone and say you're crazy."

Daisy

After the meeting I call my mom and tell her I'm going to eat out with Max. She says, "How'd the meeting go?" I say, "Okay."

We go to our favorite place, the Athens Diner, where the waitress says, "Cheeseburger and Coke for the gentleman, veggie burger and coffee for the lady."

When she brings it, Max tells her, "One day I'm going to have chicken parmigiana, just to throw you off." Then he says to me, "So, if you still want to quit, that's cool with me. I'll quit too."

I take a moment, smearing barbecue sauce on my burger. "Nah, I'll give it another shot."

"Seriously. I can help you. We don't need to do this whole thing with Leo and Jane. . . ."

"I like Jane. She's okay." I bite into my veggie burger. "Even Leo's turning out to be semihuman."

I know it's wrong the minute I say it. I don't know why, but "Leo is human" was not the right thing to say to Max.

"I mean, he's still a jerk." *Great, Daisy, bash the guy after he helps you.* "Just . . . not twenty-four hours a day."

Max stares at his cheeseburger. "Yeah, maybe just twenty-three and a half."

Okay. Did not know Max hated Leo that much. We eat for a while, then I think of something much better to talk about. "So, is Jane still not hot?"

Max is glad to be off the subject of Leo. "Definitely not hot. Pretty, but . . . too weird." He pauses. "And for me, interest in sports would definitely be a must. Otherwise she's going to think I'm really boring."

This is so Max—"I'm boring, I'm a loser." I say, "I bet Jane doesn't think you're boring."

Max gives me a weird look. "I'm pretty sure she does."

"Ask her out and see."

"I don't want to ask her out."

I nibble a french fry. "Hm. Embarrassment—a definite sign of attraction."

"Uh, *no,* actually. Cut it out."

Max hates it when I tease him about girls. But he needs to be teased because he's way uptight about the whole thing. I know he's not gay. At least, I think he's not gay. But he has this thing that because he's short and shrimpy, no one's going to be into him.

Now he's looking at me like he really wants to say something, but he's not sure he should. Probably: "Drop dead, you're pissing me off."

I say, "Sorry, I didn't mean to be a jerk."

"No, it's cool." But he says it to the cheeseburger.

"Peace?" I wave my fingers in the air.

Max smiles, waves his fingers back. He reaches across the table, and they touch mine, like that stupid thing you do when you're a kid, prick yourself and swear blood brothers.

Thinking of that, I say, "Friends."

I don't get it, why Max laughs.

Graffiti in the second-floor men's bathroom:

biggest bastards in history

1. hitler
2. osama bin laden
3. j. martin crowley

LEO

A lot of kids think Crowley is evil. They won't even go near his office. They act like it's radioactive. Like the guy's going to pop out his door and scream, "You're never going to college, young man!"

It's because he has power over them. Crowley has your file. He knows where you can get in easily and where you have to get lucky. He makes the list, checks it twice, decides if you're naughty or nice, going to Brown or Hampshire.

I'm pretty sure Yale will be on my list. But you can never be really sure with Crowley. He might decide at the last minute, "Nah," and put Vassar instead.

I'll be seriously pissed off if he does that to me. The first time I met him in freshman year, I said, "Just so you know, I want to go to Yale."

Crowley is tall, but he's thin, balding, and sort of weak looking. Until he looks at you. His eyes are pale, almost without color. But you feel like he sees the ugliness, the stuff you hide from people and only admit to yourself in the late hours of the night, when everyone else is in bed.

That's the look he gave me when I said I wanted Yale. "We'll see."

Now I look at his door, which is always closed. No open-office policy for Crowley. He deals in secrets.

There's a rumor. I don't believe it, but there is this rumor that Crowley meets with the best kids first. Any kid who might get into the Ivies, Crowley meets with them early so they have the most time to prepare their applications. Like Tory McEwan, Little Miss Perfect Score, she's been hanging out in Crowley's office since school started. It doesn't bug me the way it does some people. I figure, hey, best kids are the most motivated. They deserve the most attention.

It's still early, only November. So it's not that I want Crowley to tell me when my meeting is. Or say, "Yes, Leo, I put Yale on your list, don't worry." I just want to make contact, say, "Hey, how are you?"

I figure, the guy knows I want Yale. And if he's not going to give it to me, he's not going to be all open and friendly.

But just as I'm about to knock on the door it opens. I step way back fast as Kyra comes out of Crowley's office. He's still half inside, and she's got her back to me, so neither of them sees me.

She says something, and he laughs. It's like they're colleagues, talking about how they've totally got it over on the rest of us schmucks.

Once Crowley shuts the door, I say, "Hey, Kyra."

She turns. "Oh, hey, Leo. What's up?"

Big smile, Leo Basic voice. "Not much. You?"

"God, I am totally stressing." I don't pay much attention to that. Kyra is always "stressing."

Then she says, "I have my Crowley meeting in a few weeks. But I'm so *nervous*, I had to meet with him and just say, 'Tell me you're not sending me to, like, some junior college in Des Moines.'"

Wait a minute. Crowley's meeting with Kyra first? Meeting with Kyra before I even have my meeting scheduled? What the hell is that?

"You'll do fine," I say to cover up. "You know you will."

Kyra wrings her hands. "That's what he said, but God, I don't know, I don't know. . . ." She seems genuinely freaked, and for a moment I feel like she's a friend. Just another person under pressure and trying not to flip out.

"Seriously," I say. "I know Yale's going to be on your list. Has to be."

She smiles a little at that. Then looks up at me. "When's your meeting?"

And right away I know. Kyra is not a friend.

I say, "Coming up, I forget the exact date."

She gives me a playful push. "Yeah, I figured you'd be in the early group. Can you imagine some of these kids? How Crowley has to tell their parents, 'Hi, he'll be lucky to get in anywhere. . . .' But I'm glad you're in the early group, Leo. Would suck otherwise."

Her smile says it all: *Suck for* you.

MAX

I admit, I'm totally surprised when Daisy announces that she broke 1500 on her practice test. And also disappointed. Which sucks. What kind of friend is disappointed when his friend has a little success?

But when I see her looking at Leo like, *So?* I realize it's not Daisy I'm worried about having success—and if I didn't like Leo before . . .

I could actually kind of hate him now.

Jane

Before the meeting I decided no matter what Daisy's score, I would say it was amazing. Of course I end up saying, "That's amazing!" before Daisy even says anything. Like, I think she gets the "One" out, and I'm yelling, "That's amazing! That's amazing!"

"It's a lot better," says Max.

There's a pause. Without meaning to, we all look at Leo. Who shrugs. "It's okay."

Daisy says, "Gee, thanks." But you can tell, she thinks he's kidding.

But he says, "Sorry. Jump another three hundred points, and you might have a respectable score."

"Well, what if I don't jump three hundred points?" says Daisy sarcastically. "What if I only make it to, like, two sixty-two?"

"Then, I guess," says Leo, "it depends on whether the other kid who wants a scholarship gets two sixty-three."

For the longest time nobody says anything. I know the silence can last only a certain amount of time before somebody says, "Okay, this is over." So why can't I say anything?

Daisy

What an ass. That is all I have to say about Leo Thayer. What a major, colossal, stupendous—and any other pretentious SAT word you want to throw in—ass.

I hope he bombs on the SATs. I hope he gets rejected from every snotty Ivy school in the country.

I hope he ends up working at Mickey D's, flipping

burgers and saying "Yes, sir" to some guy who went to community college and who's a million times smarter than he is. . . .

"Screw you," I say. "Screw this."

MAX

When Daisy gets up to leave, I look over at Jane. She looks like she's going to cry. I want to tell her, "Daisy freaks out sometimes. It doesn't mean anything."

But I'm not giving Leo the satisfaction.

After a second I follow Daisy out. As I say to Jane, "I don't want her to punch anybody out," I look at Leo. "You know, like someone who didn't deserve it."

Jane

I hate Leo. Why couldn't he just say "That's great" like everybody else? Why did he have to make such a big thing of it? Like it's any of his business how Daisy does. He always has to be Mr. I Know, Mr. I Tell It Like It Is. Well, who is he to say how it is? People like that, in my opinion, are the most ultimately clueless.

Like my mom. She's so clueless she can't get it even when you tell her. Over the summer I said to her: "James watches me. It creeps me out."

And she sort of laughed and said, "Watches you?"

I said, "Yes." Wanted to say, "Don't treat me like I'm crazy. He is always there. Whenever I look. Always. He's not supposed to be there, so why is he?"

"Watches you how? When?"

"All the time."

My mother looked at my face, like she was deciding if she liked my performance. She said, "Honey, I don't see it. All the time?"

"What, so it doesn't happen?"

"No . . ." Then my mom realized that she was almost agreeing with me. "I mean, when I see him looking at you, I don't see him *watching*. I don't see anything wrong with it, I guess is what I'm saying. Is there—"

"I don't like it," I said. Because to me, that was the thing that should matter most.

"Okay." My mom nodded. But not like she thought anything real had happened. More like, *Okay, you're crazy, but I'll be nice.*

"So?"

"I'll tell him he's making you uncomfortable."

But not, I thought, *that he's doing anything wrong.*

"He's doing it, I swear." Wanted to scream at her, "You want to be with a guy who's ogling your daughter? How is this okay with you?"

My mom must have seen something in my face, because she took a huge breath and said, "Baby, I'll watch. And you tell me when you think it's happening again. But—"

"But."

"I'll be really honest and say, I think when James

looks at you, what he sees is my daughter—and that's all."

It took me a while to figure out that it isn't only that my mom doesn't want to believe anything about James; she doesn't believe what I say, period. She thinks I'm just making it up. That I'm crazy or something.

Daisy

Later that night the phone rings. I'm working on an essay about girls who choose to wear head scarves when my mom calls, "Daisy." I know it's Max, because nobody calls me this late except Max, so I pick up the phone in my room, say, "Got it." Then when my mom hangs up, I say, "Hey . . ."

A weird voice says, "Hey, Daisy Stubbs. This is Leo Thayer."

Is he kidding? I'm about to say I'm sure he has the wrong number, as I know he wouldn't be caught dead talking to someone with such loser scores, when he says, "So, I was a jerk."

Things you do not expect from Leo Thayer. Top of the list: apologies.

Still, I say, "Really? No kidding."

"Yeah, no kidding," he says, playing right along.

I hesitate. "So, enlighten me. Why were you a jerk?"

I guess Leo didn't expect that one, because there's

silence for a while. Then he says, "Do you know when your Crowley meeting is?"

"Not a clue."

"Well, I went to him to find out and . . . I don't know. It's all kind of garbage, you know?" He says it in this rush, like he had to say it before he stopped himself. "I mean, the guy's such a jackass."

"You just figured that out?"

"*No.* But sometimes it bugs you. How much they want."

I can tell from his voice it really is bugging him. "Well, you don't have to give it to them."

"Yes, you do. If you want . . ."

He doesn't say what he wants, but I know. What I don't know, what I sort of want to ask him is, Do you want it because you're into it, or do you want it because if you don't get it, you think the whole world is going to laugh its ass off and call you a loser?

Then Leo says, "So, will you come back? To the group?"

I hesitate. "You know, midterms are coming up, and the team has a lot of away games—"

"Come on."

"What do you care?"

"Group looks good on my college résumé." I can't help it. I laugh. "I'll call that a yes. Hey . . ." Then he stops.

I say, "What?"

"Nothing. Good night, Daisy Stubbs."

> The joke is how everybody goes on and on about merit. Give me a break! Getting into college is all about who you know. Are you one of us? Are you related to people like us? Face it, people, legacies are just affirmative action for rich white kids. Sure, they sprinkle a few "different" types in there for appearances. But in the end it's all about connections.
>
> —Bill's College Sucks Blog

MAX

What I need is a plan. Telling your best friend you like her is not something to be undertaken lightly. Risk of humiliation high, chances for doom near certain.

First thing to consider is the method. Is this a face-to-face thing, a phone thing, or maybe even an e-mail thing? I pretty much think if you're telling someone you think she's a goddess, it should be face-to-face. I mean, for one thing, that way physical contact can ensue. But that's assuming the person likes you back.

"Hey, Daisy? It's me. Say, you know how we've been friends for, like . . . ever? Yeah, well, here's the thing. I'm sort of madly in love with you—"

Click.

Dear Daisy,

I am writing this e-mail to you so you will not laugh in my face when I say that for some time now I've been aware of the fact that while I value our friendship enormously, I also want to touch your breasts. . . .

Forget it. Face-to-face is the only option.

I need an occasion. Something special. Something almost, maybe, sort of like a . . . date.

A date. An event in which traditionally a male-type person and a female-type person pursue a mutually pleasurable activity with the ultimate goal of pursuing a . . .

Seriously mutually pleasurable activity. Oh, God, I don't even know if I can kiss her.

If this were any other girl, I would call Daisy up and say, "Okay, I really like this chick. Tell me what to do." And she would. She'd make sure I didn't end up looking like a doof.

Here's the thing: How do you say to someone, "We've known each other for forever. And I still want to be who I was with you—only, I also want to be something entirely different"?

Jane

It's weird when I see them at school. It's like, since we're not in the group, are we still friends?

On Monday I see Leo in the hallway hanging out

with some of the guys from lacrosse. He's leaning against the wall, laughing. He looks like a totally different person, so I just keep going.

Wednesday I see Max as I pass by the newspaper office. He's in a meeting, but he waves at me. Then says to someone, "Come on, we don't need another article on school cleanliness. . . ."

And Friday I see Daisy having lunch with Luisa Martine. I don't know Luisa at all, but I sense she's the kind of person who wouldn't like me. So I don't try to get Daisy's attention. I couldn't stand it if Luisa said something like, "You know her?" and Daisy said, "Not really. She does this dumb SAT group. It's lame, but I feel bad for her."

Daisy

Pardon my ego, but this team is kicking ass.

Maybe because it's Luisa's last year and we want to get as far as we can for her sake, but man, we're pretty damn good.

It's totally about chemistry. Last year we had too many prima donnas. Like, hello, you're not Becky Hammon, chill out. This year we have some good role players. And Luisa and I have been playing together for so long I don't even have to look to know where she is. I throw it, she's got it. Connect. It's like dancing.

And, I am proud to say, I have not argued with a ref all year. (Well, except that one time when they were totally wrong—even they admitted they were wrong—and I don't think it's arguing if everyone admits you were right.)

After practice I hang around. I like having the gym to myself, imagine I'm playing Becca Petrovna, who's the guard for Cormier. She stands five feet ten inches in bare feet, is an all-state semifinalist, and scores fifteen points a game, even when she has cramps.

But I can beat her. When I'm really on, I can beat Becca Petrovna. So I play Phantom Becca in my head to make myself work harder. As I do layups I think:

Move it, Becca, I'm coming through.

Keep the ball moving. Palm to floor, palm to floor. Slow it down.

Slam . . .

Coming through . . .

Oh! Becca, weren't you watching?

Speed. I want to go fast, run flat out, keep the ball going. Charge the basket, go up and . . . in.

Pound back down the floor. Circle under, go up and . . .

Oh, yes.

Hurts, doesn't it, Becca? Sucks to lose.

I know trash talk is jerky. I know I shouldn't do it, probably shouldn't think it. But it's like the slam of the ball. A rhythm in your head, a beat that says, *Go, go, go, go.*

LEO

On the stairs I hear a basketball clang against the backboard, then I listen as it makes its way downcourt. Other than that, silence. Someone shooting hoops, fooling around.

All the stairway doors have a glass pane in them, so I go up, have a look, in case it's Tobin or any of the guys from lacrosse.

It's Daisy. And she's not fooling around. She's going full tilt, up and down the court, faking, shooting, switch dribbling. She goes up and misses. Catches it, pounds down the court, puts it in.

I go in, yell, "And it's two points for Dewey. Becca Petrovna has no clue what to do with Ms. Daisy Stubbs. . . ."

Daisy stops. Immediately. Then starts slowly dribbling the ball. Her face is all red, a hank of hair is hanging in her eyes. There's a dark triangle of sweat on her T-shirt. She swallows, tries to catch her breath.

I say, "How's it going?"

"What?" *Slam.*

"Anything."

Slam. "Anything's okay." Fast, she pitches me the ball.

I catch the ball, hold on to it. It bugs her, I can tell. She thought she was getting it back.

I ask, "How're the practice tests going?"

"How 'bout I have finals coming up and a million other things?"

She holds her hands up for the ball, and after a second I pass it back to her.

MAX

"To connect."

"Joigner."

"Conectar."

I take French. Daisy does Spanish. So when we study for our language finals, we swap books and test each other in different languages.

"Conjugate *conectar* in the subjunctive."

Daisy gets as far as *he would have connected*, then falls over onto the floor. "I think it's time for food."

"It's only four thirty."

"It's time for caffeine."

I point. Daisy's Diet Coke is right in front of her.

"Then, I need music." She gets up, goes to my CD collection. She finds an old Green Day CD and puts it in. It's both perfect music for studying, as it makes you hyper, and no good at all, as it totals your concentration. Daisy spreads her arms, swings her hips to the music. She looks sort of . . . incredible.

Watching Daisy jump around, I have an idea. "The Foosballs are playing at the Beacon over winter break. I was going to try and get tickets."

Daisy nods her head in time with the music. "Excellent."

To make sure, I say, "So you want to go."

"*Yeah*, I want to go."

"Cool." There's something I want to make sure of, though, before I set this up. "We could ask those guys if they want to come. Like, if you want to ask Leo."

Daisy looks scornful. "Leo? To a Foosballs show? No way." The song changes, and she turns the music down.

She says to me, "You know I could never date Leo, right? I mean, he's a jerk. No more jerks for Daisy."

I nod. "Cool."

Daisy

Max and me study for a few more hours, then I really do crash and go home.

After dinner I take a bath. Something's bugging me and I can't figure out what it is.

Yes, I can. It's Max.

Well, not Max—Leo. Or not Leo, but me telling Max that I wouldn't date Leo.

I wouldn't. Date Leo. The guy's a jerk. Particularly about women. But what bothers me is that I said it because I felt like it was really important to Max that I say it. Like it was a test of some kind, and if I didn't say, "Leo Thayer, no way!" it'd be like, "*Bzzz!* Wrong answer." And that sucks. Friends shouldn't test you, it's obnoxious.

I felt like Max was saying, "Hey, Daise, you know you have rotten taste in men. You know you get in over your head. You're not getting in over your head again—are you?"

No. I am not.

"Yeah, but remember what happened with Kyle. . . ."

Yeah, I remember. Believe me.

One thing I learned with Kyle . . . well, I learned a lot of things with Kyle, but the *primary* thing I learned with Kyle is never ever tell your friends you're in love. Because when it goes sour, everybody remembers what a schmuck you were, and that makes it a thousand times worse.

Except I thought I was in love. Correction: I didn't think. But I was in love.

Kyle was so funny. Yes, he was really cute, and that was another thing, but man, he was hilarious. He could make you laugh at anything. He'd always say to me, "You are too serious, Daise. We gotta lighten you up." Then he'd lift me up and down, and as I started to laugh he'd say, "Yeah, I think she's getting lighter. Oh, yeah, lighter now."

Most guys get funny when they drink—at least, they think they do. But that was when Kyle got unfunny. He'd still be making jokes, but they had a really nasty edge. We'd be hanging out with friends, and he'd go around the room and insult every one of them. Something personal, something you wouldn't forget— or forgive, except it was Kyle. Then the next day he'd be frantically looking for people to apologize. And I always thought, *Well, he says he's sorry. . . .*

That's what I told Luisa when she asked me why I never told him where to get off. "He says he's sorry."

Then at his senior party he took off after Bobby

Finnegan. Bobby worshipped Kyle, would laugh at anything he said. That night Kyle told Bobby that he had looked into Bobby's future and it was pathetic. Bobby laughed. He told Bobby he was going to have a lousy job, an ugly wife, and kids who couldn't stand him. Bobby laughed. He told Bobby he was going to be the kind of loser that when he called his old high school buds, they'd pretend they weren't home.

That's when I said, "Cut it out."

Kyle stared at me. "What?"

"You're being obnoxious."

"Obnoxious?" He said it like he didn't understand the word. "Ob*nox*ious?" He took a step toward me, and instinctively I stepped back.

But I said, "Yeah, as in jerk."

"I'm a . . ." His hand closed into a fist, I saw it. "I'm a . . . sorry, what was that word again?"

"Jerk," I said.

People said later that Kyle never meant to hit me, that he was always aiming for the wall. But I was there. If I hadn't ducked, it would've been my face that was shattered, not the plaster.

Of course Kyle said he was sorry. Said he didn't mean it, that I *knew* he didn't mean it. But I was numb. Whatever he said, it didn't matter anymore. I went from feeling everything to . . . nothing.

Leo Thayer is a jerk. That's not a big secret. Nonetheless, a lot of girls think he's hot. Luisa once said she wouldn't mind cradle robbing if Leo was the baby in question. But I've seen him in action at too many parties. Always different girls. Stupid little freshmen who are like, "Ooh, Leo." Most of them go home crying. All of a sudden he'll decide they're boring and tell them to get lost. Usually by making out with one of their friends.

So I know Leo Thayer is a jerk.

I just never thought it was something I had to worry about.

Jane

On Tuesday I'm in the lobby and I see Daisy coming out of the administration offices with some pamphlets in her hand. At the door she turns, says, "Yeah, okay," to someone I can't see.

I'm not sure whether to say hi to her or not. For a moment I think about it, how to say hi in a way that doesn't sound like, *Hi, I'm pathetic, please talk to me:* "Hey, Daisy." "What's up?" "Daisy, hi!"

"Hello, Jane." Daisy waves her hand in front of my face.

And then, just like that, she asks me if I want to have lunch.

For lunch Daisy has a pita smeared with peanut butter and an apple. To me, it seems like the healthiest, sexiest lunch you could have. My tuna in water seems sad and uptight.

I say, "Why were you in Crowley's office? Did you have your big meeting?"

"Oh, God, no. He's only seeing Ivies now. He won't get to a charity case like me for forever." She takes a bite of her apple, says with a full mouth, "Financial aid stuff," and rolls her eyes.

I'm happy I can say, "He hasn't called me, either."

"Oh, he doesn't call. You get a *letter*." Daisy rolls her eyes. "'I command you to come to my office and hear your fate.'"

"Your parents have to come, right?"

"Oh, yeah." She must see something in my face, because she says, "Can your parents keep it together for school meetings?"

"No, they're okay. Just doing anything with my mom can be a . . . thing."

Daisy nods. "Yeah. What's her guy like? He lives with you, right?"

"Yeah." For a second I desperately want to tell Daisy everything. But I couldn't stand it if she thought I was making it up, that I was some insane loser. Also, when I told Lily, I think she told other people. I couldn't stand it if Daisy was that kind of person. If she is, I'd rather not know.

But I really want to keep talking to Daisy, to not have her think I'm boring. Now she's waving to someone a few tables away. She knows everybody.

Because it's the first thing that comes into my mind, I say, "Do you think Leo's hot?"

"*Leo* thinks Leo's hot."

"I know, I don't get it."

"I get it. I just don't happen to agree."

I can't believe it. She isn't telling me, "This is totally none of your business. Why are you asking me this, you freak?" She's just talking to me like we're friends.

I say, "But you and Max . . ."

Daisy starts. "Oh. God, no. It'd be like incest. No." Then she smiles slyly. "So, by all means, feel free to ask him out."

The thought of asking Max out—asking anybody out—was so far from my consciousness that I have no idea what to say.

Daisy waves her hand. "Sorry, that was obnoxious. Only, I feel like I scare girls off of Max. One time he dated this girl, Chelsey Hobart? It was over in, like, three weeks. Then one day she comes up to me in the hallway and snaps, 'Thanks a lot!'"

"Why?"

"She said, 'You should know there's not a lot of point in *anybody* dating Max.'" Daisy frowns at her apple. "She claimed he was obsessed with me. I was like, 'Hello, we're friends.' Females can be so jealous sometimes, it drives me nuts. Max dumps her and it's some dark conspiracy? Please." Daisy finishes her pita. "So, for the record, if you have any interest in Max, I thoroughly approve."

I smile like I'm saying thanks. But privately I think Daisy wants me to date Max because deep down she knows she should, but she doesn't want to, and she doesn't want to feel guilty.

Everybody knew about her and Kyle, even someone totally out of it like me.

I look at Daisy. Wonder if she's heard about James. Wonder if she knows I know about Kyle. Think how weird it is how we know all this stuff about each other but we can't talk about any of it.

I'd like to tell Daisy, "This lunch was the nicest thing that's happened to me since I got to Dewey." I'd like to ask her, "Does this mean we're friends—and not just because of the group?" But you can't. Someone would think you were totally pathetic if you did.

I have to think of something we can do that has nothing to do with the SATs. Because I don't think I could stand it if we just all took the test and it was like, "Okay, bye."

I try to think of some other big event that's coming up. But all I can think of is my birthday, and who cares about that?

LEO

When I see Jane and Daisy come out of the lunchroom, I have that weird feeling of, *Wait, something's going on without me?* Which is dumb, so I get rid of it.

As they pass, Jane doesn't even see me, she's so into whatever. But Daisy glances over. We see each other, then she goes back to Jane.

Since I don't even know what it is, I should leave this whole thing with Daisy alone. Yeah, it's a little fun to tease her, but come on. We're not . . .

Whatever. Like I said, I don't even know what this is.

That night I'm sitting in the kitchen with Zo, trying to help him with his homework. If he waits for Dad or Jenna to help him, he'll be old enough to flunk out of high school. I point to the box in his workbook. The big question is "4 + 4." What Zo needs to figure out here is that an eight goes in the box.

"Zo . . . what goes here?"

Zo drives his monster truck over his workbook. I put my hand on it, say, "Figure out what goes in the box, and I'll let you jump the truck over me."

While Zo thinks about what goes in the box, I think about Daisy. Wonder if she's working on the SATs. Or telling herself, "I'll play catch-up during winter break." Less than thirteen weeks till the test, Daisy. And how much work does anybody get done over winter break?

I'm going to be at my mom's in Santa Fe. No work gets done then. It's called survival.

Zo yells "Eight!" He looks up, all excited. He loves getting things right.

I slap hands with him. "Put it in the box."

While Zo works on the next problem, I pick up the phone. As it rings I think, *If her mom or dad answers, I hang up.*

But Daisy's the one who picks up. Hearing her go, "Hello?" I say, "Hey."

"Hey," she says. Then, "Who is this?"

"Leo." She doesn't say anything. "Just making sure you're doing those practice tests."

"Hey, I did one."

"Yeah?"

"Half of one."

"Whoa, I'm blown away. How'd you do?" Long silence. I say, "Want to go over it?"

"Well, the meeting's the day after tomorrow, we could—"

"Who cares? Let's do it now."

I wait, thinking the next thing I'm going to hear is, "Thanks, but no thanks."

Which is why I'm surprised to hear, "Okay. Hold on. . . ."

We go over the first few questions. The word stuff completely freaks Daisy out. It's like watching Zo figure out 4 + 4. Except he's seven.

Finally I say, "There's actually an easy way to remember it. Just think about the root, the first part of the word—*hydro*—which means 'water,' so you just look for the one word that's got anything to do with water."

There's a long pause. Then I hear, "Okay. Thanks."

"I've got a whole list, Greek and Latin words, what they mean. It helps."

Daisy laughs. "I can barely speak English, now I have to learn Greek?"

"Yeah, girl, you gotta learn some Greek."

Another silence. I just used a voice I never thought I'd use with Daisy Stubbs. I don't know why, how it came out. I'm about to switch back to Leo Basic when she says, "Yeah, well, why not?" Then: "What else do you have?" Like, *Bring it on. . . .*

So I do. I start telling her—*ab* for "out" or "away," *magna* for "big," *voca* for "call." She plays along, saying, "Oh, like *MAGnitude* and *magnanimous* and *vocation* and *wocka-wocka-land. . . .*" I'm not really sure which voice I use for this one. Somewhere in between the Leo Basic and the other Leo.

But it's easy. I like it.

MAX

December 5

Dear Mr. Bastogne:

I am writing in order to set up a time when you and I can meet regarding Max's college future. Based on your child's performance to date, I have drawn up a list of prospective schools that might be suitable. But I would welcome the opportunity of discussing his/her needs and wishes in this area, as well as any concerns you may have.

Please have your child stop by my office or contact my secretary at 555-0838 to make an

appointment for the beginning of the next semes-
ter. I look forward to meeting you.

> *Sincerely,*
> *James Martin Crowley*
> *College Admissions Guidance Counselor*

The second I get the letter, I call Daisy. "I got my Crowley letter."

"No way. What does it actually say?" I read it to her. "'Schools that might be suitable.' What a pompous ass."

"I know, right?"

"Are you psyched?"

"About what?"

"Come on. Being in the early group."

I look at the letter. "Am I?"

"Sure. You're almost an Ivy," she teases. "We might have to stop hanging out together."

"Shut up. Hey—I got the Foosballs tickets."

"Excellent! We'll celebrate."

"Celebrate what?"

"I don't know. Think of something!"

Over dinner I tell my dad, "We have to set up a meeting with the college adviser. To talk about what schools I should apply to." My dad nods. He's not a big fan of Crowley. He's not a big fan of anybody in authority. "I can set it up if you want."

"Anytime after work's good."

I think, *This will be easier if my dad doesn't go in there with a big chip on his shoulder*—"Who are you to tell my kid where he can and can't go?"—so I say, "Supposedly, if you get the letter this early, it means they think you're a good candidate. Like, you can get into the top schools."

"That we know," says my dad. He puts down his napkin. "How's the SAT stuff going?"

I say, "Good," and wonder how my dad always finds a way to say something that makes you feel great, then follows it up with a big fat *but*.

I wonder if anybody else got the letter.

Jane

I'm finishing my paper for *Hamlet* in the living room when my mom comes in with a letter in her hand and asks, "Who's Mr. Crowley?"

"He does college admissions. Why?"

"He wants to meet with us. Talk about your future."

This is it, then. The big Crowley letter. I hold out my hand. "Can I see it?"

My mom gives it to me. Weird little phrases jump out at me: "college future," "based on your child's performance to date."

I hand the letter back. "Hey, Mom? You know my birthday?"

She smiles a little. "Yeah, I seem to remember it."

My birthday is February 14. Valentine's Day. Only the most embarrassing day anybody could have a birthday. But it's the only thing I can think of to get people together.

"I know it's two months away, but I was wondering if maybe I could have some people over."

"A party?" My mom looks seriously excited.

"I don't know so much about a party," I say. "I was thinking something—"

I'm about to say "smaller," but my mom interrupts. "We could really do it up, maybe have some of my friends over, really make it a Valentine's thing." She looks puzzled, like she can't figure out what she's supposed to be feeling here, and there's no director to tell her. "Wouldn't it be fun for you?"

She looks so hurt that I don't want this great thing that she's offering. Well, even at a big party we could go off and do our own thing. And maybe it'd be better if it wasn't so much about me.

So I say, "Yeah. That'd be great, Mom, thanks."

"Great!" She starts to leave, then stops, holds up the letter. "What am I supposed to do with this?"

"Make an appointment."

"Right. Got it." She spins out of the room.

Hey, did you hear Jane Cotterell's having a party?

Cool! Is her mom going to be there?

LEO

The second I see Max headed to Crowley's office, I know. He got the letter.

Mariah Fredericks

I wait till he comes out. As he does he says to Elinore, Crowley's assistant, "Okay, thanks." Then he turns around, sees me. "Hey, Leo."

"Got your letter."

"Oh . . . yeah. Making the big appointment." Max shrugs, like it's no big deal. "When's yours?"

"Don't have it yet."

This surprises him. "Yeah, you and me both," I want to say. Except it's not me and him both. It's him and Kyra, and a few other chosen Ivies.

Damn it, damn it, damn it.

"Jane got hers," he says, like he's trying to figure this out.

Big surprise. Crowley sucking up to the movie star. That's probably under direction from Frank, the principal: "Treat her nice, Jim, let's see if we can get a new lunchroom out of her."

Shouldn't be pissed, but I am. Jane makes it in ahead of me. Man . . .

"It doesn't make any sense," says Max, and I know he's trying to be decent. "I mean, it really doesn't. There probably isn't a reason."

I shake my head. "There's always a reason."

I start walking away, then remember something and turn around. "Good luck with finals."

"Yeah, you too. Have a great break."

I nod. "See you at the SAT thing."

And that's all I can do before I have to get out of there.

Daisy

I know when Leo calls now. He doesn't call every night. But when he does, it's always around ten. So when the phone rings at ten fifteen, I yell, "I got it," and pick up.

"So," he says, "your guy got in."

There's something weird about his voice. Not just being pissed about Max, something else. I say, "Yeah, well, he's really smart."

I'm about to say, "And so are you, and don't worry about it," when Leo says, "Yeah, is Jane really smart? Or is her mom really famous and has a lot of money? You know, 'cause I don't mind, I just like to know the rules."

And I know what it is I'm hearing. "Are you . . . bombed?"

"I'm happy. Although my dad has crap taste in rum. You want to come over?"

"For crap rum? No, thanks."

"No, not for that, man . . . never mind. What're you doing over the break?"

"Stayin' right here. You?"

"My mom's in Santa Fe. Santa Claus in Santa Fe. Yo-ho-ho and a bottle of rum. It's gonna suck."

"Why?"

"Because it usually does. Do you really not care?"

"About what?"

Leo groans. "You know . . . the whole thing. Do you really not care? Because if you don't, I want to know how you do that. I want to know what you know. Give me the secret, babe."

Tonight over dinner my parents got into one of those stupid arguments that isn't about anything because it's really about money, which we're not allowed to talk about at the table. My mom busting my dad's chops for forgetting to pass on a message. "How could you forget?" Which, translated, means: "How can you forget when you've got nothing else to do all day?" Means: "Maybe this is why you lost your job, if you can't even pass on messages."

"There isn't actually a secret," I say.

"Ah, I knew it."

"What?"

"You do care."

Leo giggles. That dumb drunk giggle that cuts right across my nerves like broken glass. *Let's have fun, we're the happy people, it's a joke, man, come on, Daise, lighten up. Oops, there goes my fist. . . .*

I say, "Have a nice time in Santa Fe," and hang up.

Jane—
An excellent and original essay on <u>Hamlet</u>.
I can't agree that the text supports all
of your conclusions about Gertrude.
Perhaps you are being a tad harsh? Fine
work overall. Have a good winter break!
—A

From: KYGal@earth.net
To: leo345@world.com
Hey, you! Have fun in sunny Santa Fe! I'll
be skiing *avec la famille*. Beats bonding,
right?
  Call me. If you feel like it.
  When is your Crowley meeting, anyway?

Message on Daisy's Answering Machine:

"Uh, hey, it's me. Jane. I just wanted to say have a
wonderful holiday. I'm going to be in Connecticut with
my dad, but if you wanted to meet up in the city sometime, that could be really cool. Otherwise, I guess . . . I
guess I'll see you when I get back. And uh, oh, say hi to
Max. And happy holidays. Bye. Oh, you can reach me at
203-555-8769."

Daisy

After finals, two losses, and holiday shopping at the last
minute with no money I am so ready for some serious
headbanging, it's not even funny.

The other day my mom said, "Maybe on your
break you'll have time for a little SAT practice." In
other words, "Because I'm sick of busting your dad's
ass and getting nowhere, I'm going to bust yours
instead."

Gee, thanks, Mom. Merry Christmas to you, too.

When Max arrives, I don't even give him time to say

hi to my parents, I just pull him out the door and yell, "Later."

In the elevator I say, "Like, a hundred years later."

Max laughs. He has a new jacket. It's dark, looks good. And he did something with his hair. I'm about to say, "Do I detect . . . gel?" but decide not to. Guys get uptight when they're caught trying to look good. Especially Max, who *never* tries.

Instead I say, "Looking sharp for the holidays."

Max says, "Yeah, well."

MAX

Okay, definite plus was the comment on looking good. For one thing, it means the gel stuff is not a total disaster. Which, at eight thirty this evening, I was pretty much convinced it would be.

However, list of missed opportunities so far:

1. Failed to kiss her on first meeting, which would have established that this was absolutely a *date*.
2. Failed to pay for both drinks, which would have done same.
3. Failed to initiate any intimate contact before concert, such as putting arm around her shoulder, or touching arm or other appropriately designated body parts.

Did manage to dorkily step on her foot while dancing. Twice.

Daisy

Max dancing cracks me up. The guy has got zilch sense of rhythm, but he's got crazy energy. For a while we just flail and bump and kick and scream. The band pounds everything else out of your head, everyone's nuts. Everything's red and green for Christmas, people have tinsel wrapped around their necks, Santa hats all cut up and spray-painted. It's great.

At one point Max stomps on my foot, yells into my ear, "Sorry! Are you okay?"

And I'm like, "Right now I feel nothing. And it's great."

I think: *That's what's great about Max. You can be with him and not think about him at the same time.*

MAX

I'm leaping in the air, getting closer to Daisy with intent to collide and possibly kiss, when a guy works his way over to us and starts dancing with her. No big deal, just one of those "Hi, I'm drunk" concert things. But to say I want to kill him would be an understatement.

Only, Daisy doesn't look like she minds. She's dancing with the guy, responding to his goofy-ass moves with far better moves. She catches my eye, and I give her a look like, *Who's the loser?* But she just laughs.

Mariah Fredericks

So, fine. There's a girl kind of bobbing around me. She looks sweet, has glasses, so I turn and start pogoing in time with her. Like, *Hey, I'm cool, I dance with other people too.* I see Daisy glance over, but I pretend I don't.

Then after a while I turn a little, try to say to the girl, "Okay, that was nice, thanks." But she turns with me. Argh. Nice girl with glasses, it's time for you to go back into the crowd now.

Finally I just turn my back on her. Not a great thing to do. But I've had it done to me a million times.

"She was cute," Daisy yells.

"Who?"

Daisy points to the girl.

"Oh. No." Then: "Not my type."

Meaning: "I do have a type, and if you ask me what that is, I will give you a very close description of . . . you."

But Daisy's dancing with someone else again.

Daisy

I'm like, *Hello, you're looking cute. Wearing gel. I'm giving you all this room . . . hook up if you want to!*

Next break I'm going to tell him.

But at the break, when we're getting something to drink, he says, "This is so great. We gotta seriously do this . . . all the time. It's great. I . . . uh . . ."

He hesitates, looks at his drink with a big, crazed grin. I say, "You, uh, what?"

He shakes his head, toasts me. "It's just great."

MAX

I couldn't do it at the bar. It wasn't the right moment. Like, "Hi, here we are, with a million drunk people around us. Oh, by the way, I'm insane about you."

But now the night's almost over. The concert's finished, we're walking home because we're both way too high to sit on the subway. Daisy's going on and on about the lead singer, how his mouth can stretch to beach ball proportions, and I'm thinking, *What would Napoléon do?*

Napoléon would never be in this situation. He'd be off conquering Poland or something, and women would just naturally flock to him.

But I have to do something.

So I stop. There in the street, right in front of the Athens Diner, where we always go.

And say, "So, speaking of mouths . . ."

Daisy

Immediately I know exactly what Max is going to say. And all I can think is, *Oh, God.*

But you can't say no before someone does something. Can't go, "Wait, you're about to say you like me, and you so shouldn't because I'm not there and you're going to feel dumb, which is going to be awful, and . . ."

And while I'm thinking about all this, Max says, "At this particular moment in time I would like to kiss you. If that wouldn't be too weird."

Um, yes, that would be way too weird.

But then I look at Max, and I think, *This is your best friend. He's an amazing guy. Do you know* absolutely *this will not work?*

My arms are folded. I unfold them. Say, "Okay."

MAX

As I lean in I think, *This isn't right. This should be easier. If it's not easy, then it shouldn't be. . . .*

But I'm not one of those guys for whom anything is easy. So if I feel like a total jerk right now, it's probably not a sign of anything.

Probably.

I'm just about at Daisy's mouth when it occurs to me that I should take hold of her somehow. Her arm or head or something. So I put my hand on her arm, and she sort of moves like, *Oh, okay,* and puts it around my neck.

She knows so much more than I do.

It feels really weird being this close to her, so I say, "You know what? I'm just going to get this first one over with."

She laughs. "Okay."

"Okay?"

"Yeah, sure. Go for it."

So I do. I put my mouth on hers, just on the top. . . .

It's like two fish bumping into each other. *Hey, watch where you're going!* You pull back, go, "Oh, sorry, 'scuse me. . . ."

Daisy

I think, *Max, calm down. Nothing's going to happen here.*

Then I realize Max wants something to happen. That is, in fact, the whole point.

Which makes me feel so unbelievably sad, I give him a full kiss. A real one. I guess to make up for not liking him. I hold it, thinking, *You are such a great guy . . . why is this not happening?*

But it's not.

Max says in his Cockney voice, "That was nice, madame, may I have another?"

I step back, say in the same accent, "No, I think you've had quite enough."

"No, I don't think I have. . . ."

He steps toward me, and I put my hands between us. Say, "Seriously," in my own voice.

Bad moment. Really, really bad moment.

I can't stand how awful it feels, so I start talking. "I . . . love you. You know that. And if I was going to date anybody, it probably would be you, but I can't be with anyone now. . . ."

MAX

I get it immediately. This is the brush-off. What's sad is, it feels much more right. It feels real. Totally and unbelievably sucky, but real.

For a split second, when Daisy kissed me back, it was like a different world, a different me, and it was probably the greatest split second of my entire life.

And even though I get it, even though I accept the brush-off, I want to say, "There was something in that, you know, in the kiss. Not the first one that I did, that sucked, but the one you did, that was . . . sort of good. That wasn't fish, it was people."

It was us.

There was an us. For that split second. So, what was that, that us?

Then I look at Daisy's face, how embarrassed she is. I think, *That wasn't an us. That was a sexy girl who knows how to kiss. That's biology.*

I say, "It's okay."

Daisy sighs. "It's not. This should be happening and it's not because I am very screwed up about guys." We start walking, neither of us looking at each other. I hear her say, "And I don't want to screw this up. I haven't, right? Totally wrecked it?"

I glance over. She's looking at me in this way that gives me the smallest, smallest sense of what it might have been like to be her boyfriend.

I say, "Don't be dumb. It'll take a lot more humiliation than that to wreck things."

Daisy laughs. And I know the worst is over. Along with everything else.

LEO

The flight back from Santa Fe takes forever. It's like, where's Concorde when you need it?

On the drive back from the airport I ask my dad, "Did you get anything from school?"

He frowns. "Don't think so." He laughs a little. "Why? Should I be worried?"

I look out the window.

Jane

I have made a deal with myself. Over the holidays I decided that I wasn't going to be the one to set the next SAT meeting. That if everyone wants to do this, then they'll say they want to do it, and if they don't, then . . . that'll be fine.

But on the train ride back from Connecticut I started making a list of food that I think would be nice to have at the party. I can't remember if Daisy's a vegetarian or not.

Daisy

It's really weird how you can wake up one morning and think, *Oh, I have no friends.*

Then as I say hi to everybody on the first day back at school I think, *Come on, you have friends.*

Only, I can't really talk to any of them right now.

With Max everything is fine, but nothing's . . . good. He won't pick up the phone to talk, won't say, "Let's hang, watch a game, whatever." It always has to be me.

Which is a total pain in the ass. How many times do I have to prove, yes, I want to be your friend? Even if I don't want to be your girlfriend. (And by the way, when did *that* become such a crime?)

Luisa I can't talk to because over the holiday I got so frustrated with Max I told her the whole thing. Let's just say she had the *wrong* reaction.

When I told her about Max asking me if he could kiss me, she grinned and said, "Yeah, go Max!" And I was like, "Excuse me?"

"Oh," she said. "This wasn't a good thing."

"No." I looked at her like, *Why would you think it was?*

She did a slow, elaborate shrug. "No, I just thought . . ."

"What?" Like, did the whole world think this was happening except me?

Luisa put her hand up, her cue for *Hold it.* "I don't happen to think it's the most heinous thing in the world if the little guy thought about moving things along. I'm saying, I can see why he had the idea."

"I did not give him any signals whatsoever that this would be okay."

Luisa sipped her smoothie.

"I didn't!"

Luisa slid her hand through the air: *Anyway.* "It's your call. But if you're avoiding Max because you're holding out for some other bad boy who will mess with your head . . ."

And that's when I said, "Thanks a lot, and you can go screw yourself." Which I really shouldn't have said.

So, no Max. No Luisa.

Leo I don't even want to think about.

So at lunchtime when I see Jane, I wave her over to my table. As she sits down I say, "Hey, I'm sorry I didn't call. The whole holiday thing got away from me totally. How was Connecticut?"

Jane smiles, rolls her eyes. "You know. Like you say, the whole . . . holiday thing."

"I know, right?" I can't believe it. Suddenly Jane is my best friend.

Another thing I can't believe: I say, "So, when's our next meeting?"

MAX

It's really weird being around Daisy right now. On the one hand, I want to see her to make sure everything's cool. On the other hand, I feel so desperate about it, it makes me feel even more pathetic.

So when Jane tells me we're all getting together on Thursday as usual, I think it'd be good to hang with Daisy in a group. But the fact that Leo is also in the group makes me want to forget the whole thing. Because I have a feeling something's about to happen, and I don't need to see it in slow-mo.

I keep reminding myself of what Daisy said: that she doesn't want a boyfriend right now—any boyfriend.

And that even if she did, she wouldn't date Leo because she knows he's a jerk. I keep reminding myself that I have to believe her.

LEO

When I walk into Jane's apartment, it's like everything's exactly the same. Jane's got the cookies and pretzels out. Max and Daisy are sitting on the couch like always. Everybody's SAT book is on the table.

Only, something is different. I can't figure it out.

Well, for one thing, two of us have our Crowley letters, and two of us don't.

And I can tell from the way she's not looking at me, Daisy's still pissed over that last phone call. I want to say, "Babe, I'm more than happy to forget the whole thing—whatever it was."

Another thing that's different is the scores. All of a sudden Daisy's well into decent territory, while Max bombed out totally. He shrugs. "I kind of blew it off over the holidays."

No kidding. I say to Daisy, "Not too shabby."

"Well . . . ," she says, "I got a little help on my verbal."

And like that, I know we're past it. Again, whatever it was.

Jane went up a little bit. Writing down her score, I say, "Max, man, she's passed you. Gotta catch up."

In a chorus Daisy and Jane yell, "Shut up, Leo!" and Daisy throws a pillow at me.

Because the scores are so loopy, we decide to write them off as holiday craziness and forget them.

Then Jane says, "Good, because I have my Crowley meeting tomorrow, and I need serious advice. What should I do?"

"Boycott," says Daisy.

I throw the pillow back at her. "Don't let your parents take over," I tell Jane. "They'll be all like, 'We want this and this and this'—everything they didn't have. Like if they went to Ivy League, they'll want some laid-back granola school for you. If they did the flaky art school thing, they'll want you to do MIT. You have to get Crowley to see what you want."

There's a long pause. Then Jane says, "I don't know what I want. I hate stuff like this."

"Like what?" asks Max.

"Things where people just decide who you are by looking at some letters and numbers. Like they're looking at you, but not really. You might as well not be there at all."

Jane

That Friday, Mom and me meet my dad on the steps of the school. He reaches out and hugs me, "Hi, little girl," then says, "Hello, Julia," to my mom, who says, "Hi, Steve." Then she walks up the steps. Dad and I follow behind, his arm around my shoulder.

While we wait outside Crowley's office, I think about what Daisy said. How I should talk about restaurants. I remember what Leo said, how I shouldn't let my parents take over. And how Max wants me to remember everything and tell him, so he'll know what to expect. He has his meeting next week.

"Mrs. Cotterell, Mr. Cotterell . . ." Crowley comes out, starts shaking my parents' hands. Then he brings us in, points to the chairs where we should sit down.

He looks only at my mother the whole entire time. He speaks only to my mother the whole entire time. As he talks about my grades and my PSAT scores, whether I want to go far away or stay close to home, a big school or a small one, he talks only to my mother.

My dad reaches out and puts his hand on mine.

After a while I just zone. Forget about remembering things for Max or not letting my parents take over. It's fine if they take over. They seem to care about it all a lot more than I do.

Then I hear my mother say, "Maybe we should ask Jane these questions. It's her future."

Reluctantly Crowley looks at me. "Jane? Do you have any sense of the kind of school you'd like?"

Oh, great. Ignore me for forever, then go, "What do you want, Jane, *right now*?"

I say, "I don't know."

My mom jumps into the silence. "I think Jane might be happy at a smaller school—," but my dad says, "Julia," and she stops.

And then there's this long, weird silence. I have Daisy's voice in my head, *"Tell them you want to open a restaurant."*

I say, "I think . . ."

Everyone looks at me. All these expectations. That I know will turn into disappointment the second I say anything.

"Nothing."

Crowley says, "I think our goal in the coming months is to develop a slightly more well rounded vision of Jane Cotterell. I know this is only her second year at Dewey, but it would be a good idea if she started taking part in some extracurricular activities. Drama, maybe?" A smile for my mother. "She needs to make a stronger impression. Stand out more."

"What about the SATs?" my dad wants to know.

"We need to get her scores up."

Then Crowley holds up a piece of paper. "Shall we go over the list?"

Daisy

The mail usually comes before I get home, so I pick it up on the way. In the elevator I look through it and find something from school, addressed to my parents. In the corner of the envelope someone has handwritten "J. Martin Crowley," just above the school's name.

Well, well, well. My Crowley letter at last.

I open it, half expecting to read, "Dear Mr. and Mrs.

Stubbs: Normally at this time of year I invite parents and students to discuss their college options. However, as you are poor and your daughter is unable to cope with standardized tests, this will not be necessary in your case."

It doesn't say that, though. Just the basic blah, blah about call or come in to make an appointment. My dad can do that. All he's got to do now is write his book, which I'm starting to think is just an excuse not to look for a job.

In the kitchen my dad is making a cup of tea. That's the other thing he does now: drink tea. By the end of the day his tea mugs are everywhere.

He asks, "Anything in the mail?"

I hold up the letter. "Big Chief Jackass wants to talk about college." My dad smiles, a little, and takes the letter.

Sitting down, I ask, "How's the book going?"

He nods this way and that as he pours out the water. "Slow." Which has only been his answer for the entire year.

While my dad gets me a mug, I say, "Greatness takes time."

"That it does," he says, and we clink mugs. "How's the studying going? The test stuff."

Smooth move, Dad. Letter comes about college, all of a sudden you're interested in the SATs again. Didn't see that one coming.

I almost hate to tell him. "Okay. The group is helping, I get it better now."

He smiles. "I'm not worried."

For a weird second I feel furious. Like, *Why don't you worry? Why don't you deal with this instead of . . . making tea all day?*

I don't want my dad to see what I'm thinking, so I go to my room. I pick up the phone to call Max, tell him, "Hey, me too . . ."

And end up calling Leo.

When he answers, I say, "Hi."

"Oh, hey. What's up? Word probs?" He's teasing me.

"Uh, no. I got my letter. I was kind of wondering if you did."

"Uh, no. No, I did not." He swears.

"Well," I say, "I think we've pretty much figured out that the best don't go first here. If I get the letter before you do—"

Leo interrupts. "Don't say that."

"Why? You're, like, Mr. Perfect College Material. I'm, like, Ms. College Nightmare."

"Stop it. You got a lot of things I don't have." A pause. "You shouldn't put yourself down."

"I'm not."

"You are."

This is getting dumb, like a kid's game. I say, "Not."

"Are."

Oh, man.

I say, "Well, look, I think the whole thing is obviously rigged and a total joke. So"—Leo's about to say something, I can feel it—"see you Thursday, okay? Bye."

LEO

The second I hang up with Daisy, I pick up again and call my dad at the office. "Did you get a call from school?" Because now I'm thinking, *Maybe Crowley calls some people?*

"Zo's school? No, why?" My dad sounds all panicked. He's thinking Zo fell off the jungle gym, cracked his skull.

"No, *my* school. From the college adviser. Did he call, send a letter, to set up a meeting?"

"Oh." I hear the flip of my dad's date book. Get a Palm, already, Dad. "Yeah . . . I have to call him."

A huge surge of relief. I am not last. Actually, who knows? I may even have been before Daisy. My dad's such a freaking flake, I'll never know where I really was in the ranking.

I say to him, "Okay, could you do that, please?"

"Sure. What's this about?"

"College. It's my list meeting." Total blankness from the other end. "Where I get my list of colleges."

"Oh." Long pause. "Well, then, I'll be sure to call him."

What my dad is saying here is, "You care way too

much about this stuff." He's saying, "Why can't you be all cool and laid back like me?"

And what I'm saying is, "I don't care what you think I should care about. Just. Call."

Jane

On Thursday they all want to know how my Crowley meeting went. And they all want to see my list.

Then Daisy says, "No, come on, that's creepy. What are we going to do, sit around and compare? 'Ooh, I got Brown, but you didn't'?"

But she wants to see it, I can tell. I say, "I don't care," and put it down on the table. They all crowd in to look.

Leo points to one of my safeties and says, "Out in the middle of nowhere, people get constantly high just to stay sane."

Max nods over my reach schools. "That's a really cool school. My cousin goes there."

"Yeah?" Because I don't care about any of them. There's nowhere I think, *Wow, I want to go there!* I say to Max, "Maybe your cousin's school will be on your list. Maybe we'll have some of the same colleges on all our lists."

Daisy looks at each of us. "Uh, I don't think so."

I think, *Why not?* The same school could take us for different reasons.

Then I ask, "Hey, is anyone doing anything on February fourteenth? Because my mom's having a party.

Sort of for my birthday, but not really. But I thought maybe you guys could come. If you wanted. I know it's, like, three weeks before the SATs. . . ."

Daisy grins. "I think we can forget about the SATs for one night." She looks at Leo, who rolls his eyes at her.

Max says, "Yeah, definitely. Is it going to be, like, fancy?"

"No," I say immediately. "I mean, some of my mom's friends'll be dressed up, but don't worry about it. Just come any way you want." I can't believe it. I'm so happy. They didn't make excuses, say they had to check or anything. Just said, "Of course we'll come." How amazing is that?

Later, as they get ready to leave, Leo asks Max, "Are you nervous about Crowley?"

"No." Max shakes his head. "Except I've felt like I had to throw up since Tuesday."

MAX

That wasn't true, what I said about having to throw up since Tuesday. It's been much longer than that. Ever since I realized my dad and Mr. Crowley were going to be in a room together. Talking about me.

My dad will not like Crowley, I know that. He doesn't like anyone who's in charge of what you can and can't have. But he thinks it's your job—my job—to outsmart guys like Crowley, to get the things they don't want to give you. So if Crowley doesn't put top schools on my list, my dad will be mad at him—but he'll wonder what I did wrong, why I wasn't smart enough to get around him.

I don't think there's a way I win here.

"What's the absolute worst thing that could happen?" Daisy asks me at lunch that Friday.

"I have no good schools on my list. My dad realizes I'm the Mets, not the Yankees . . . and I hurl all over Crowley's office."

"Well, that would be totally excellent," says Daisy. She squeezes my arm. "Those other things are not going to happen. Nobody is not going to want you."

You didn't, I think. But I say, "I'll try not to miss Crowley when I puke."

At four thirty, I'm sitting on the bench outside Crowley's office when he opens the door and looks at the empty space next to me.

"My dad's a little late," I say.

"Oh," says Crowley. He opens the door wider. "Well, would you . . ."

"No, that's okay, I'll wait here for him."

There is, of course, a clock on the wall. A clock that tells me just how late my dad is, just what degree of screwed up we are. I know my dad will get here. I know when he does get here, he will be okay. But he won't apologize for being late.

In fact, when he does come at 4:42, all he says is, "I'm here."

I go knock on Crowley's door. He opens it. "We're here."

The first amazing thing is when Crowley says, "You must be very proud of your son, Mr. Bastogne. He's a terrific writer. I really enjoy reading his columns."

My dad says, "Yes." Tense, like he's waiting for the *but*.

Crowley looks at me. "What are you thinking, Max? Sportswriter?"

I say, "That's probably what I'm best at." Then think, *I should have said "good," not "best."*

"*Daily News* or *SI?*"

Okay, Crowley just named both of my dream jobs. "Either would be pretty cool with me."

Crowley goes over my transcript, which is mostly good except for a few screwups in math and French. When he mentions those, my dad nods grimly. Then Crowley says, "Overall, Max is an extremely appealing candidate for any number of excellent schools. In terms of places like Columbia or Harvard, there is the small drawback that he's from New York, as the top schools want to maintain regional diversity. . . ."

Columbia. Harvard. Crowley is talking Columbia and Harvard and me. In the same universe.

"But I don't think we have to worry too much about that at this time. Max, what were you thinking?"

That I'd kill to go to Columbia. "I just want a place where people are kind of smart and into stuff. You know. Like politics and sports and . . ." *A place where not all the guys are rich, blond god types.* "A good journalism department. That'd be cool."

My dad breaks in, "What about the B minus in trigonometry?"

"Grades are always a factor, but when someone demonstrates strong talent and passion—"

"What about the SATs?"

Crowley checks my file. "Max's PSATs were satisfactory. I'm assuming they'll go up. They actually should go up," he tells me. "You did prep?"

"Yes, he did," says my dad.

"Well, then, we'll wait and—"

My dad says, "But they have to come up. The scores."

"Ideally."

"No, not ideally," my dad says, his jaw tight. "You tell us what we have to do and we'll do it."

I say, "Dad . . ." Because he's acting like Crowley's hiding some secret thing we have to do. Then when I don't get into Columbia, he'll say, "Oh, sorry, Max, if only you'd . . ."

Crowley says, "Shall we go over the list?"

Daisy

When the phone rings, I pick up, go, "So?"

"It was okay." Max sounds breathless. "It was seriously okay. Crowley thinks I can get into Columbia."

Something I did not expect: a weird drop in my gut. Max is going places. Like, the top places. The kind of school I would never ever get into in a million years. No one will even tell me to apply. For an intense second I miss him and I hate him.

Shake it off. . . . "That's great. Told you."

"Yeah, and all these other places." Pause. "My dad's not so sure I can get in, though."

"Yeah, screw your dad."

"No, he has a point. Everybody wants to go to these places. Competition's insane."

"Uh, who knows more about it? Crowley or your dad?" No answer from Max.

"He was okay," Max says slowly. "He reads my columns. I was like, *You're kidding.*"

Okay, now we think Crowley is a human being. I think of James Butrinsky, who, yes, is a stoner, but an amazing artist; of Luisa, dying to get into U. Penn., with her bad SATs; of Ava Sandler, who is one of the sweetest, kindest people you'll ever meet, even if she'll never win an award for anything in her life. I think of Leo. All these people Crowley doesn't have the time of day for.

Max interrupts my thoughts. "What?"

"No, nothing. I still think Crowley's an ass." Silence. "But at least he recognizes your genius."

"Yeah. Look, I gotta hit the old SAT book a little. See you tomorrow, okay?"

"Yeah, okay."

When Max hangs up, I think about calling him back, saying, "Okay, wait, that was dumb, let's back up here. . . ."

But like the man said, he's busy. Gotta hit that SAT book . . .

Jane

It's funny. You'd think since his Crowley meeting went so well, Max would be happy.

But he's a nervous wreck. When he gives his score on Thursday, he apologizes for it being so low—even though it's not that bad. And when we go over the problems, he has a lot of trouble with the ones he got wrong.

"I can't get it," he says. "I don't know what's going on."

"You're stressing," says Leo. "Relax. Be like Jane."

I look at him like, *What?*

"No offense." Leo puts his hands up. "I'm just saying you never let the test wig you out."

"Yeah, guess what," says Daisy. "She'll probably get a higher score than any of us."

MAX

Given any two real numbers m and n, which of the following is never true about the quantity $nm + mn$?

Mariah Fredericks

Okay, right away I can eliminate *c*. And *a* doesn't look too likely either.

B, *d*, or *e*. *B*, *d*, or *e*.

Oh, wait, *e* can't be true; *e*'s out. So it's down to *b* or *d*.

If you can get it down to two, and you don't know, guess.

Fine, I guess *d*.

Ordinarily I don't look at the back of the book until I'm done with the test. But this time I want to know, did I get it right? Did the trick work?

What do you know? It did.

Leo has his meeting tomorrow. Daisy still hasn't scheduled hers. Which is a little dumb, but I'm not going to tell her that.

Funny if Leo has a lot of the same schools. If we were, like, competing. I mean, we're so different, I don't see how you could say, "Oh, this guy's obviously better."

If you can get it down to two, and you don't know, guess.

LEO

You're supposed to bring both parents to your Crowley meeting. But with the number of psycho divorce cases, the school understands if you bring just one.

I meet my dad on the steps after school. Before we go in, I tell him for the ninetieth time, "Let me handle this."

He nods, like it couldn't matter less. "What is this meeting again?"

"It's for college. They tell you what you should be doing, tell you where you can think about applying, stuff like that. . . ."

"Shouldn't you get to choose where you want to apply?"

Argh. Hello, Dad, reality! Barely holding it together, I say, "Yeah, but they help you by giving you this list so you can narrow it down. You know, where they think you have a good shot of getting in."

"What if a college you like isn't on the list?"

This, ladies and gentlemen, is my dad. If, in any given situation, there is a *wrong* question to be asking, you can be absolutely sure he will be asking it.

Which is why I say again, "You don't have to do anything. Just . . . I know Crowley, let me deal with him."

"He's the adviser."

"Yes, he's the adviser." My dad gets hung up on the mural in the lobby, but I nudge him ahead, and finally we get to Crowley's office.

Once we're there, I feel like we're okay. My dad does pretty much as I asked, and shuts up. Smiles, nods, goes, "Um-hm." But basically lets me take over.

Crowley says, "The one gap I can see in your résumé, Leo, is the extracurricular. Some students wait until their senior year to load up on Drama Club and student government. But I think it would be ideal if you could do some things this year. Participate in a few events, write articles for the paper, do community work."

I think: *Yeah, tell me when I have all this free time.* "Sounds good."

My dad stirs in his chair, says, "Maybe this is crazy, but I'd like to see Leo less busy."

Yes, Dad, that is crazy. Shut up and let's get to the list. But of course Crowley has to say, "I understand your concerns, Mr. Thayer. The pressure of junior and senior year can be daunting for parents and students. Leo has always seemed to have a very clear idea of what he wants, and a willingness to do what it takes to get there. Of course, sometimes that willingness can be misconstrued."

You don't want to be seen as a grade grubber, Leo. Not just some test monkey . . .

"Which is why, ideally, he should find an activity or group that would show he has interests outside of academia."

My dad smiles tightly. "I believe the term is *well rounded.*"

"So it is," says Crowley.

Then he hands me the list.

I hesitate before looking. Because what if Yale's not on it? What if I've been thinking I can get Yale, and all along everyone has known it's way out of my league?

If Yale is not on this list, I'm handing it back and saying, "I think you forgot something."

I unfold the piece of paper. Look.

There it is, right at the top, where it belongs.

My dad is out of there as fast as he can be. As I leave I say to Crowley, "Well, glad we had this meeting."

Crowley looks blank. "Did you think we wouldn't have this meeting?"

"No, but I know . . ." You probably shouldn't admit to the college adviser that you're on to his game, so I try to finesse it. "That there are certain kids you see earlier than other kids."

Crowley shakes his head. "I don't know what you mean."

Okay, so he's not admitting it. "Guess I misunderstood."

Then all of a sudden Crowley smiles. Like he's just figured out what I'm talking about and he's decided to come clean.

"It's alphabetical, Leo."

Jane

What's really weird is, we have to ask.

We all know Leo had his Crowley meeting. We all know how much he wants Yale. But on Thursday he doesn't say anything about it until Max says, "So?" And even then all Leo says is, "It went okay."

I say, "And?"

"Oh, yeah. He put Yale."

Mariah Fredericks

I say, "Well, that's great," and Max says, "Yeah."

Daisy doesn't say anything. Just smiles.

Somehow I think she already knew.

"Work time," says Leo. "We've only got six weeks to go till the big day."

MAX

On the way home I say to Daisy, "Did you know about Leo?"

"Did I know what about Leo?"

"Crowley. Putting Yale on his list."

"Yeah, Leo said something . . . why?"

"Nothing." *Uh, when did he say this something?* "Weird how he and I both have Yale on our list. We're . . . sort of different people."

Daisy doesn't say anything. Once she would have said, "Uh, just slightly different."

Shut up, Max. Do not say it. Whatever it is, don't say it.

But I'm still wondering when Leo talked to Daisy.

I say, "It doesn't really matter. I don't think I'd apply to Yale anyway—"

And I'm about to say "because I'd never get in," when Daisy turns on me. "You know, can we not talk about this?" I step back. "Because some of us are not going to have Yale on our list. Or Brown or any other stupid Ivy school. And, like, yay for people who do, but just sometimes, can we talk about *something else?*"

And before I can say, "Wait, this was just about me being dumb about Leo," she stalks off.

LEO

I call Daisy the night before she has her Crowley meeting. The first thing she says is, "My parents are making me insane."

I laugh. "That's the deal. Just ignore them."

"They're like, 'What should we say? What should we do?' I keep telling them *I* don't know." She pauses. "*You* should come and talk to them."

"If you want."

"I know what it's going to be. 'You're going nowhere, Daisy, unless you get twenty-two hundred on your SATs.' It's like, just say it already."

"Crowley is not that bad."

"Shut up. You just love him 'cause you got Yale." She's quiet a moment. "I feel like everyone's going someplace but me."

"I'll find you a place," I tell her. "We'll get you in."

Daisy

I am not allowed to say anything. I am forbidden to speak.

Well, not really. But after the last crack I made about Crowley while we were waiting outside his office, my dad said, "Okay, Daisy," and I knew that was it. No more comments. God forbid we offend the great Crowley.

When Crowley finally lets us in, I take the seat farthest from his desk, while my parents crowd around it. Crowley picks up my file, holds it in front of him like a shield, and says, "I see no reason Daisy should have any difficulty getting into a fine school."

My mom smiles. "That's good news. Hardly surprising . . ." This time I get the smile. *Chill, Mom, this is the good part.*

"We're interested in the possibility of scholarships," says my dad.

Crowley nods, says smoothly, "There are many student loan programs."

My parents look at each other. I know what they're thinking: Loans mean debt. My mom says, "There are also scholarships, aren't there?"

"Ye-es." Now Crowley's all cautious, like we think he's got the money in a drawer and we're going to mug him. "Generally they're awarded to students who are more . . . in need than Daisy. The competition for them is extremely tough." He coughs. "This is an area where Daisy's SAT scores could be an issue."

Now he opens the file. "You're taking the SATs next month?"

"Yep."

"And have you taken a prep course?"

"Nope."

My mom says hastily, "She's been part of a study group."

"Has it been helpful?"

I shrug. I don't know why, I can't stand giving the guy what he wants.

My dad says, "So she needs to get the scores up? If we're thinking about scholarships."

"Substantially," says Crowley.

Both my parents look at me. I say, "Yeah, okay, I'll try. But you know, I don't think we need to get our hopes up. Let's face it, I'm average."

Immediately my mom says, "Daisy," and my dad shakes his head. Crowley waits for it all to die down, then says, "Actually, Mr. and Mrs. Stubbs, Daisy is right. While *we* know perfectly well that she's an exceptional individual, on paper, to colleges, she is . . . well, average."

He doesn't have to say it: No money for average kids.

"Her grades are good, her extracurricular is outstanding, and I'm sure her recommendations will be persuasive. But if you look at it with a points system—"

"A points system." My mom looks like she's going to leap across the desk and pound Crowley into the floor. My dad puts his hand on her arm.

"Which is how many colleges look at students"—the gloves are off now—"it would be helpful if Daisy didn't have a weakness in the test area. The SATs don't count for as much as many people think they do. But you want to have all your bases covered. The competition is simply too high not to."

Then he pulls out a piece of paper. "It was a little difficult to make up a list for Daisy, given the uncertainty of her scores and financial aid requirements, but . . ."

He puts the list on the table. My parents lean in to look, while I think: *Points, scores, financial aid. It all comes down to numbers.*

My dad looks up from the list. "Berkeley?"

"In many ways it's an ideal school for Daisy. However, if the SAT scores don't come up significantly, we have very little chance. But we're hoping they come up." He looks at me. "I just wanted to give you an idea of your options, Daisy. What you have to gain."

And, of course, lose.

You are invited!
To the celebration of Jane Cotterell's birthday
and the festival of St. Valentine.
No discussion of the SATs, colleges, or anything
remotely serious allowed!

Jane

I make Daisy show me her list. Because I want to see if we have any schools in common. We only have two, but I put little check marks next to them anyway.

She says, "Hey, did you get your notice of where you're taking the test?"

"Yeah, it's somewhere on the East Side."

"I'm downtown," says Daisy. "At the design school. Max got P.S. Forty. Leo's at I.S. Nine."

"So none of us are in the same place?" I don't know why, somehow I thought we'd all be taking them together. "That sucks." Then I say, "You're still coming to the party this weekend, right?"

"Yeah, of course."

I relax. If Daisy's coming, Max and Leo will definitely come.

"My mom's turned it into this big thing. She kind of needs a job right now. . . ."

Daisy laughs. "Whoa, my dad, your mom. That's funny."

"Yeah, right?" I'm thrilled; we have this in common, sort of. "So she's invited all these movie people, but I figure we can hang out in my room."

My vision is this: While all the craziness goes on outside, me, Daisy, Max, and Leo will be in my room, talking and laughing about our stuff. I'm going to stash food there so we don't even have to come out for that. It'll sort of be like *Little Women*—only with two guys.

LEO

There are a lot of reasons not to go to Jane's party tonight. I have an English paper due Tuesday and a calc exam on Wednesday. And frankly, I've blown off the practice tests lately. With the Crowley madness going on, I couldn't concentrate. My scores are still okay. But after the Crowley meeting I'm thinking I need better than okay. I'm thinking I need perfect.

The big 2400. Kids get it every year. No reason why I shouldn't be one of them.

Twenty-four hundred doesn't guarantee anything. I know that. But in that one area you're foolproof. No one can find fault with you there. Hey, you're perfect.

Only, I'm not. Not yet. My essay needs work, and the math should go up. So I really shouldn't go to Jane's party. Except . . .

For a second I think of calling Daisy, saying, "Are you going to be at this thing or what?"

Then I think, *Don't be an ass. You can't plan these things. They happen or they don't.*

I generally avoid things I can't plan.

Generally.

MAX

Friday morning I say to my dad, "I'm going to be out tonight."

He looks surprised. "Oh. Lakers are on."

"Who're they playing?"

"T-Wolves."

"Should be a good game."

"Yeah, I was thinking we'd get some Chinese food, but . . ."

For an insane moment I think of saying, "Screw Jane's party." Because the thought of my dad sitting here alone with Kobe and a carton of lo mein is just way too sad.

My dad waits that one extra second, then says, "But you're going to be out, so. Have a great time."

"I'm going to a party at Julia Cotterell's," I tell him, like he'll understand better.

And he pretends he does, saying, "Oh, well, then . . ."

That night as I head off to meet Daisy I call good-bye as I pass by the living room. My dad's sitting on the couch, and he raises his hand as I pass. On the TV they're calling the starting lineup for the Lakers.

One thing I've thought of: If I go to Columbia, I may have to live at home. And I'm not sure I want to do that.

Three weeks from tomorrow I will have taken the SATs.

We all will have.

Daisy

I'm not looking for Leo. What I want to happen is this: Whether I see him or not, it becomes very obvious that whatever was or was not going on between us was nothing but SAT craziness, and we can forget it now.

Which is why I told Max I wanted to go to the party with him. Of course when he sees me, he says, "You look good," in a way that makes me wish I'd put on jeans and not this short skirt.

I look over at him. He hasn't done the gel thing since the night we saw the Foosballs. I want to tell him he should. But I can't tease him like that anymore.

I miss that. Teasing him.

Jane

I am so excited. Nervous. But seriously excited.

Normally I hate parties. This one I can't wait to start.

My mom hired a whole bunch of caterers, and before the party I hang out in the kitchen with them. I figure, hey, maybe I can learn something. I tell one of them I'm thinking about going into catering, what do I need to know? He says, "Prep." He hands me some limes and a knife and shows me how to cut them up.

As I chop up the limes James comes into the kitchen. He says, "Just here to get a drink of water."

Then he looks over at me. "That's a pretty big knife."

I ignore him, dump the ends of the limes into the garbage can. I slam the lid shut, and James says, "Easy."

I knew it. *Oh, I just came in here to get a drink of water.*

I do not look at him as I leave the kitchen. I get to my room fast and shut the door. Then I get up on my bed. He is always there, that's the thing. Always, always there. He's not supposed to be, so why is he?

I can't wait till those guys get here.

MAX

Certain nights you have a feeling. Something's going to happen and it's not going to be good. As we go up in the elevator I want to say to Daisy, "I'll give you twenty bucks if we go watch the Lakers instead." But if I say that, it's like, "Don't hang out with Leo, hang out with mee-eee."

She looks really good tonight. Like *Look at me* good. I worry about who she wants to be looking, but then she says, "I bet this thing is going to be really fancy. I couldn't figure out what to wear. You think this is okay?"

"It's . . . great."

The elevator lands on Jane's floor. As the door opens Daisy says, "The Lakers are on. Is it heinous if we ask Jane to turn on the TV?"

I laugh. Maybe some nights you have the feeling but you're wrong.

We ring the bell, and a total stranger lets us in. Inside it's a mob scene. People you can tell are seriously rich. As we push our way inside Daisy whispers to me, "Oh, man. Look at this. . . ."

She's actually nervous. I whisper, "Nobody here looks as good as you, believe me." And it's true.

"Yeah, right." She runs a hand over her skirt. "Okay, anyone famous, tell me, because I'm not going to have a clue."

I point out a guy who's on a cop show. Daisy strains to see, then slaps my arm. "Man, I missed him."

For a while we prowl around, half looking for famous people, half looking for Jane, but not really, because sometimes Jane's so intense she puts a damper on things. Like, we can't do celeb spotting around her, obviously.

At one point I say to Daisy, "Okay, you go that way, I'll go this—," but she grabs my arm and says, "No, seriously, you are not leaving me."

I think something I really shouldn't. To cover, I say, "Are we the youngest people here?"

"Definitely the poorest," says Daisy.

"Would madame like a drink?"

"Oh, madame most certainly would."

While we're at the bar, Jane appears. "*There* you are." She looks a little pissed off.

Daisy

I grab Jane, give her a big hug. "Hey, gorgeous gal. Happy birthday." I hand her my present, say, "It's nothing, don't get excited. . . ."

Jane stares at it like no one ever gave her anything before. "You didn't have to do that."

"Of course I had to. It's your birthday." I look around the room. Don't see Leo anywhere. *And that's a good thing, Daisy.*

I tell Jane, "So, you need to explain who all these people are."

"Oh . . ." Jane shrugs. "Friends of my mom's."

I think of my mom's friends. They don't look like this. They don't look like they own the world and you're just renting space here.

There's so much money in this room I can't breathe. I bet all these people went to great schools because their mommies and daddies went to great schools, and all their kids'll go to great schools, and so on and so on. . . .

I never want to be a part of this world. But I hate feeling shut out of it.

I notice that the living room opens onto a balcony and say, "Hey, let's go outside."

Jane

We have to pass by James on the way to the balcony. But because Max and Daisy are with me, I feel safe. I don't really know why Daisy wants to be out here when it's so cold. But I guess it's better than being inside with all those people. I just hope Leo can find us when he comes . . . if he comes.

When we get out onto the terrace, Max says, "Man, what a view." And I guess it is, if you haven't seen it a million times.

I'm about to say, "Okay, done that. Why don't we go into my room?" when Daisy says, "Monsieur Le Max? I am in need of another drink."

He says, "Right away. Jane?"

I say, "No, thanks," and he goes back inside.

Daisy watches him go, then nods to the crowd. "Kind of funny that everyone thinks this is what they want. Like if they get a great SAT score, somehow it all leads to this."

"What do you mean?"

"Oh, like money. Being famous. Amazing place." She

looks at me. "Must be something, living in the middle of it. Like, it's all just there."

It's like Daisy's asking me a question I'm not sure how to answer. "Sometimes."

"If you could pick anywhere in the world to live, in any way, what would it be?"

Small, I think. *Quiet. Only people I like around me.* I ask, "What do you think will happen? After . . ."

"After what?"

"I don't know, all of it. The test, college . . . do you think we'll know each other?"

Before she can answer, there's a knock on the sliding door. My mom's voice, saying, "You two must be frozen! Jane, there's someone I want you to meet. Her daughter just got into Brown, and—"

"Could I do it later?"

"Later you'll be frozen. Come on."

There's no saying no, so I head toward the door. My mom says, "Daisy?"

Who says, "I should wait here for Max."

Daisy

God, poor little Jane. You just want to drag her out of this whole scene. Her mother yanking her around, "Go here, do this, be that. . . ."

Still, I don't think I can go in there again. Not without Max. I keep seeing the price tag on this skirt, and I feel like everyone else can see it too: "My God, who let her in?"

I always thought when I actually saw these people up close, I'd be cool about it. Now I just feel tacky.

Screw Leo, man, for not showing up.

The door slides open, and the noise from the party surges. I turn around, expecting to see Max. Max, who can make this all seem funny instead of horrible . . .

But it's not Max. It's Leo.

LEO

All this time I've been waiting at the bar, watching the three of them on the terrace. When I see Max and then Jane come inside, I think, *Okay, here's my chance. I'm going to go out there and say* . . .

Who the hell knows? Now that I'm here, I can't remember.

I call out, "I actually hate heights."

Daisy looks like she was startled out of saying what she was going to say. "You're kidding."

I take a step out, shut the door. "No, seriously."

Daisy leans against the railing, spreads her arms out, and looks down. "Well, these are definitely high heights." She bends backward a little.

I say, "You need to stop that."

She smiles. "Why?"

"Because you're freaking me out. Seriously. Please . . ." I wave my finger. "Come here."

"What if I don't want to?"

"Be nice."

Daisy glances above my head. Looking for Max. But there's a big crowd at the bar, and Max ain't coming back anytime soon. She folds her arms. With what she's wearing, she's got to be feeling the cold.

She says again, "What if I don't want to?"

"You want to," I tell her.

Daisy

It is seriously cold. I'm right in the wind here.

I take one step away from the railing. Since Leo doesn't look like he wants to move too far from the door, I think we're safe.

"You're really scared of heights?" Because I didn't see Leo as scared of much.

"Bad fall on the jungle gym when I was three."

I nod toward the room beyond the glass door. "That's what freaks me out."

He looks. "Them?" I nod. "You just have to act like you're one of them, it's easy."

"But I'm not."

He smiles. "Big secret: Nobody is."

Oh, God . . . I look back toward the view. "Just so you know, Max is coming back."

"You going to hang with Max all night?"

"Gee, I don't know. He's only my best friend."

"He *is* only your best friend." He takes a step forward.

I say, "Go hit on some freshmen."

"No freshmen here."

He smiles, and I can't help it, I smile back.

"Go hit on Julia Cotterell, then."

He looks through the glass doors at Julia on the other side, like he's thinking about it. Then shakes his head. "I think that would kind of freak Jane out."

Which makes me think of freaking Max out. But I can't not do things because Max would freak out: "Hi, life—I'm not having you because Max would freak out."

You said you'd hang out with him. You said nothing would change. You said you weren't into being with someone right now. . . .

Then the lights go out inside and I hear, "Happy birthday to you . . ."

Thinking we should be in there, I head toward the sliding door. But Leo catches my hand, pulls me back. For a split second I think the obvious is going to happen.

But he just whispers, "Now would be an excellent time to leave."

MAX

From the bar I see Leo and Daisy tiptoeing back inside and around the edge of the crowd. They're not singing "Happy Birthday" with the rest of us. They're headed straight to the door.

I watch as Leo gets their coats out of the closet. He puts his finger to his mouth like, *Shh*, and Daisy tries to stop herself from laughing.

I could tell myself it's not happening. What I know is happening. I could say, "Get real, Daisy isn't going to fall for a jerk like Leo Thayer."

But since I know that's not true, it's kind of beside the point.

Jane

It was all just a ploy. There was no woman with a daughter who got into Brown. It was all about getting me inside for the cake. Then we had to do the whole song thing and blow out the candles.

When that's done, I look around for Daisy, but I don't see her. I do see Max, holding two drinks, and say, "Where's Daisy?"

I expect him to answer right away, "In the bathroom," or, "Talking to your mom"—but he says, "She left."

"She left." I say it because I can't believe it, say it so Max will say, "Left? No, *leapt*, onto the phone, somebody called." I mean, we only talked for, like, two minutes. We barely even hung out. She just came, had a drink, looked at the famous people . . .

And left?

I say, "She didn't say she was leaving."

Max sighs. "Well, she did. Leo, too, by the way."

MAX

Sometimes Jane can make you a little crazy. I tell her about Leo, and she's like, "Huh?" It's like she's so hung up on her own crap she doesn't notice anything else that's going on.

Now she says, "I can't believe they just left."

I want to scream, "Breaking news, Jane: Daisy's gone, Leo's gone. They didn't say bye to you? Well, gee, that sucks, but you know what? So do a lot of other things."

LEO

The thing that is such a pain is getting the first kiss over with. Like, "Hi, I like you, you like me, could we just do this, please?"

I should definitely have had one last beer.

The thing is, I didn't feel like it. There was just a point when I wanted to be out of that party and alone with Daisy, and . . .

And now I am and I don't have the first clue what to do. We've been walking for blocks now.

The light changes and we have to wait. There's no real traffic. We could go if we wanted to. And then what? Home? What if it's just "Well, good night"?

I'm thinking about that possibility while we cross the street. Then Daisy says, "Hey . . ." And then we're kissing.

I mean seriously.

Like . . .

I did not think she would be like this.

We break for a second because someone's gonna start tearing clothes off if we don't, but I keep kissing her face because I just like the feel of it, her skin and the way she smells.

Then I say, "We could go to my house."

She smiles. "I don't think so."

"Nobody would care. I swear." *Please, Daisy, so seriously come to my house.*

She pushes me away, just a little. "My parents wouldn't be so into it. I'd have to call them."

She's still kissing my neck, so I don't think I'm being dumped.

I say, "Well, this sucks."

She laughs. "It doesn't suck."

She lets me go, starts walking away. But backward, so she's facing me.

I say, "So, I'll call you tomorrow?"

"It's today already."

"So, today."

Jane

I'm not angry. That's not it.

I'm not angry that Leo and Daisy left and Max was like, "Yeah, bye, see you."

I just think it's really rude.

If I'm going to be totally honest, I am disappointed.

Because this was kind of supposed to be our night. Our big "Who Cares About the SATs?" night. Instead everybody just left.

I should have known. Right when they came in and were like, "Who is everybody? Point out the famous people." That's all they cared about.

Here's what I wish: that there was a test you could give people and it would tell you if they were

    a. a nice person
    b. a jerk
    c. neutral, doesn't matter
    d. your friend
    e. a traitor

Because people are really good liars, and a lot of the time it's hard to know.

My mom keeps saying, "Wasn't it a wonderful party?" and I keep saying, "Yes." James sits on the couch next to her. He's pretending to listen to her, but he's not really. As far as he's concerned, she's not even in the room. You'd think she'd clue in: Who is he looking at, Mom? I mean, why can't anybody see this?

MAX

That night in the bathroom while I brush my teeth, I take a good look in the mirror. Because I think I have to realize something here.

I am not handsome. I will never be handsome.

Women will never like me. Not in that way. I will always be their friend.

And I just have to face that.

I know Daisy probably thinks she was being nice not to tell me it was just me she didn't want to date. But it's not nice to do that to someone. If someone is undatable, you should tell them. You should say, "Sorry, on a personality scale you score a ten. But looks, you're in the bottom percentile." Otherwise someone could go through life thinking they're okay and have no idea why they're alone.

I guess with love you're always looking for someone who's more amazing than you. But the problem is, that person's looking for someone more amazing than they are.

Sorry, I only date twenty-four hundreds.

Juniors Taking the SATs
Please assemble in the auditorium at 2:00 p.m.
to hear senior Tory McEwan discuss her
successful test-taking strategies.
Attendance is mandatory.

Daisy

I know I should feel awful. I should feel really, really bad for what I did to Max. And to Jane—walking out of her party like that was sucky. The party was so important to her, and I blew her off completely.

But as much as I yell at myself and tell myself what a jerk I'm being, I can't feel it. Like nothing's real except, *Oh, my God, he's incredible.*

Leo's IM-ed me ten times this morning. He's definitely a boy who likes to chat. The last time I said, *"Stop. U'll get sick of me."*

Besides, I have to talk to Max. I called him three times over the weekend, but no answer. I can't decide: Have I done something ultimately crappy? Or something I had the right to do? Or both?

Right before lunch I find him in the study cubes, this row of desks that are walled off so you can get some peace and privacy. I pull up a seat next to him, say, "Hey."

For a moment he keeps working. I peek at what he's doing. SAT stuff. Of course. He carefully fills in a dot, then says, "Hey."

He puts the pencil down, looks at me.

I say, "It's weird. I totally admit that."

"It's not weird."

He says it in a cold, flat way that tells me it's a diss, but I guess I deserve it. The only thing I can't stand to hear is, "He's just another Kyle." Because Leo's not, and Max knows it. But he might say it anyway out of hurt.

I say, "I'm really sorry."

"Why?"

"For . . ." *Not liking you, not admitting I liked Leo.* "Well, for one thing, running out on you at the party."

Max could say anything here. What he chooses to say is, "Oh."

I wait. "So?"

"So?"

"This is going to make me crazy if we can't make this okay. I'm not going to be happy."

Max raises his eyebrows at some unseen third person, like, *Do you believe her?*

"Please, please tell me how we make this okay."

Max laughs a little. "Uh, I don't know. We act like it is and hope for the best?" He looks at me, and I see he's just as scared as I am that this won't work.

I say, "Are you going to that dumb SAT lecture?"

"Sort of have to. They claim they're taking attendance."

I point to the floor. "Meet you here in two hours?"

"Okay," says Max.

LEO

One thing Daisy said over the weekend was that she didn't want to be one of those obnoxious supercouples. What she really meant was "Cool it in front of Max," but I said, "Check. No pink teddy bears at your locker."

So I'm not surprised when I see them at the SAT assembly, sitting in the back like always. Put in your time with the little guy, fine.

Still, I get out my cell, send her a message: *"Free l8tr?"*

Then I see Jane come in, and I wave her down. She hesitates for a second, then comes over. As she sits down I say, "Great party."

She looks at me, then back at Daisy. "I thought you guys would be sitting together."

I go blank. "Why?" Because I know Jane'll be too shy to say why and drop the subject.

Which she does, glancing up at the stage, where they've got Tory sitting on a lone chair. "I don't even know what this is about."

I yawn. "Tory got, like, the highest score in the history of whatever. Got her into Stanford on full scholarship, blah, blah. Crowley thinks we can learn something."

Jane smiles. "Like what?"

"Who knows? I mean, if she took the test for you, maybe that would help. Otherwise it's gonna be all, 'Oh, relax, don't forget to breathe, eat a good breakfast. . . .'"

Then Crowley comes in and we all have to shut up. As he introduces Tory, I check my cell.

It says: *What time?*

MAX

Daisy's trying to be cool about the messages. While Tory's talking, Leo sends her three more. But she answers only the first one.

I know what she's doing, sitting with me instead of

Leo. "See, we're still friends, even though I am boffing a major cretin. We're still friends, even though you totally humiliated yourself by thinking I could ever be physically attracted to you." Part of me hates it. And part of me is relieved she still wants to have anything to do with me.

I hate that, too, by the way.

I try to focus on Tory. You can sort of like Tory and sort of hate her too. She's very smart, and her family doesn't have money, so she's worked for everything she's got. But if she says one more time how the SATs aren't about you as a person, that they're this totally false image of who you are, so you shouldn't worry, I'll puke.

Like, yeah, Tory, easy for you to say when you've already got your perfect score.

Jane

I feel bad for Tory. Having to get up there and speak while everyone ignores you or thinks you're this big suck-up. Now she's trying to tell us that no matter what you get, it doesn't matter because it's not a real reflection of you—and they're all rolling their eyes. At least, Leo is. When he's not IM-ing Daisy.

Tory should just say, "You know what? Screw you all. I got what I got, and I'm not sharing with you losers."

Daisy

After the meeting I try to get over to Jane, but she splits before I can reach her. I ask Leo if she seemed pissed, but he says, "About what?" Some things guys don't get.

But that afternoon I'm in the library checking out a book on the Sudan when I see Jane at one of the tables. I slide in opposite her and wait for her to look up.

And wait . . .

Finally I say, "If you want to slap me, that's totally okay. I won't hit back or anything."

She closes her book. Gives me a long look like she's debating what to say. "Guess I missed something."

It's weird, the way she's talking. You're not really sure what she means. It's not like her, but I guess this is Jane when she's mad. "Uh, if you mean me and Leo, I didn't really know it was happening until it happened. So you didn't miss it."

"No, I'm not good at noticing. I don't know why, somehow I don't see things right."

I don't know what to say. It's true, but I don't think Jane should be beating herself up while I'm apologizing to her. To change the subject, I say, "Did you go to the Tory thing?"

Jane smiles. "I sat with Leo. Didn't you see me?"

"I couldn't see him," I lie. Jane nods, but I can tell she doesn't believe me. "I felt kind of bad for Tory. Crowley using her as his little tool."

"I thought people were really mean to her," says Jane softly.

And I know what she's saying is "People are really mean, period." Quickly I say, "I think Tory's way cool. I mean, she doesn't have a lot of money, and she got all these scholarships. . . ." Then I realize this is the opposite of Jane.

I finish, "And she's a seriously sweet person. . . . Jane, I'm sorry."

She looks up, and for a second I see the old Jane.

Then all of a sudden she snaps out of her mood, and she smiles. "Oh, God, it was just a dumb party. I'm psyched for you and Leo, that's great."

It feels too good to hear someone who doesn't hate the idea of us. "Really?"

"Totally."

I want to give her something back, so I say, "We're on for Thursday like always, right?"

She says, "You still want to?"

"Of course. I mean, the SATs are in a few weeks, right?" Jane nods. "Are you feeling okay about them or . . ."

Jane looks thoughtful. "I feel like I know what I have to do, I just don't know if I'll be able to." She shakes her head like, *Does that make any sense?*

"Yeah, me too. I feel like there's all this stuff I should be doing, but real life keeps getting in the way."

LEO

"It's *b*."

"Come on, now." I tap the right answer with the pencil. Daisy grins. "*C*, then."

We're sitting on my bed with the SAT book open. Daisy's sitting in front of me; my chin is on her shoulder. Probably not the most efficient way of studying.

She says, "I like your little brother." She met Zo today. They had a monster truck race around the couch.

"Yeah, he was pretty crazy about you. Next question."

She looks. "Do you honestly care if we learn from this paragraph that lung cancer rates are higher in high-density populations?"

"Yes, I care deeply."

"I don't," she says, and kisses me.

MAX

Okay, the answer is . . .

Please let it be *a*. Please let it be *a*.

Crap. Not *a*.

That's three in a row I've gotten wrong. The most wrong in a row I've ever had.

This is not a good time to be screwing up like this. I keep telling myself I'll be okay with the essay. Then I remember I don't write well under pressure. That my essay could be "Uh . . ."

What I need to do is find a way back to that point when it all made sense. When it was almost . . . easy. When I was the guy who knew what was going on.

Basically before this whole thing with Daisy and Leo happened.

The two things are not connected, they're not. I

Mariah Fredericks

keep telling myself, *Who cares? Just because they're . . . whatever . . . doesn't mean you can't pass this test.*

Gah. There's only fourteen days left. To stop myself from freaking, I switch over to essay practice. Usually I kill here, but I can't concentrate on the question of whether individuals or the masses affect the course of history. So, instead, I make up my own essay question.

Would you agree that Max Bastogne's life sucks?

Okay, opening paragraph. Take a position . . .

Yes, I would agree that Max Bastogne's life sucks. It lacks the things necessary for an unsucky life.

Support your position with five points . . .

1. Love is essential to life. Max is incapable of inspiring love.

2. A happy family is essential. Max does not have much of a family and what he does have drives him crazy.

3. Health is essential. Max is healthy, which means he will live his sucky life longer.

4. Friends are essential. Max does have friends—but that is all they will ever be.

5. Success is essential. Max might have once

had some delusions that he would be suc-
cessful. But after he flunks his stupid test,
he will be a pathetic failure for the rest of
his days.

Concluding statement . . .

Without doubt, Max Bastogne has a sucky life.

Jane

The closer we get to the whole thing, the more I really don't care. I'm still taking the practice tests, although really, what does it matter now? It's not like I'm suddenly going to change. But I am doing what I have to do.

I don't care what I get. Which is weird. Even as I do all this stuff, I don't expect to get some wildly high score out of it. It'd be nice, but . . .

Anyway, it'll be interesting to see how we do. After all this.

Sort of hard to believe the test is just a week away.

Daisy

At our last meeting of the SAT support group I almost say, "Guys, let's be honest and change the name to the SAT Freak-out Group. Because that's all we're doing here."

Like, for the last ten minutes we've been arguing over whether the answer could be *e*, even though the book says it's *c*. Max and Jane are both saying it could be *e*; Leo says it doesn't matter. What the book says goes.

"What are you going to do?" he asks them. "Write the SATs a letter that says, 'Dear Sir: Your test is all wrong'?"

"Why not?" Max throws his pen on the table.

"Yeah," says Jane. "Wouldn't that be wild? If they canceled the whole test because *they* got it all wrong?"

Leo looks at me like, *Help*. I look at the books and tests sprawled all over Jane's living room. "Maybe we need to take a break."

Max shakes his head. "I feel like if I take a break, I'll lose it." He picks up the book, starts flipping through it.

I reach over, try to take the book away from him. "If you don't, you'll *definitely* lose it. Come on, guys. The sad fact is, we're not going to get any better in the next two days. We are what we are, you know? I vote pizza and videos, anybody with me?"

Leo and Jane both raise their hand immediately. I look at Max.

MAX

I don't want to take a break. I want to keep working.

I want to explain to them, "You don't get it. I have to do well on this thing. I have to go to Columbia, and I have to get away from all of this—my dad and Daisy—and I have to be around other weird people. Who do well on tests even if they can't do life stuff. Because that's the only way I have a shot."

But everyone's voting for a break, so I do too.

LEO

Immediately I vote me and Daisy get the videos. I know it breaks the whole "We are not a couple" thing, but I don't care. I need some air.

In the elevator Daisy sings that goofy old song, "'Ahh, freak out, nuh, nuh, nuh, nuh . . . *le* freak, *c'est* chic . . .'"

"Let's not go back."

"Stop it."

In the store I go and find every single one of Julia Cotterell's movies. Daisy makes me put them back. Then I turn toward the porn, but she says, "Uh, no."

As we head back I say, "Just, I got my own problems. I don't feel like hand-holding."

"No?" Daisy takes my hand.

"Come on, you must be freaking a little."

She lets go of my hand. "Yeah. Sure. But here's the deal. I'm me. I'm gonna do how I'm gonna do. I worked hard, I tried. I can't get all into 'Oh, what if I don't get such and such?'"

I can't help it. I ask, "What if you don't get such and such?"

"Then, my parents flip out and we go into debt for the rest of our lives or . . . I don't know. Maybe I don't even go to college. It's not like that's the *only* choice."

Anybody else, I would think this was a major cop-out. I'd be like, "Yeah, what are you going to do, hang out on a beach somewhere?"

Daisy, I have this weird feeling that whatever she does is going to be cooler than going to Yale.

Sort of sacrilege on my part. Hope the SAT gods don't punish me.

Jane

I can't tell if Max is upset over the test or because Leo is out with Daisy. I say, "You're going to do great, I know it."

He smiles a little. He's trying not to open the test book, I can tell. "Thanks. I'm worried I'm going to lose it on the actual day."

"So you just take it again, right?"

"Yeah, if you bomb out once . . ." He shrugs. "Sort of feels like you'll always bomb out."

I don't know what to say. Max is so obviously smart and talented and everything a college should want—and here he is talking about bombing out for the rest of his life. I say, "I think it's really crazy how we're judged on who we are for those three hours. You can't let them define you like that."

He says, "People define you all the time. Usually in a way that sucks."

"That's why you have to keep some things secret," I say. "If people don't know about it, they can't judge. It stays yours."

When Leo and Daisy get back, we all go into my room, where I have a TV. I get out the phone, say, "Okay, what does everyone eat, not eat?" Immediately they all start talking. Pepperoni, no meat, extra cheese, mushrooms, gross, who eats mushrooms? Somebody says anchovies as a joke, then anchovies and pineapple both.

Later, when we're watching this guy survive a plane crash, I think, *This is what I wanted.* How weird that it all kind of worked out. I'm glad I didn't make a big thing over the party. For a second I think about the test on Saturday. Then put it out of my head. What will be will be.

When we change the DVD, Daisy prowls around my room and finds a stack of old games I keep in my closet—Chutes and Ladders, Monopoly, that kind of thing. My mom's been on me for forever to get rid of them. But I used to play them all the time with my dad, and I don't know, I just can't throw them away.

Daisy takes down Chutes and Ladders. "Oh, man, I remember this." She sits down on the bed, opens the box. "Oh, my God . . ." She takes out the little people, makes them walk across my pillow.

Max takes out what I used to call the spinner, the board with the arrow that you spin to find out where to go. He spins it. It points to Daisy. "You win," he says.

She laughs, spins it again. It points to Max. "Nope, you do."

I sit down on the edge of the bed and flick the arrow lightly with my finger. It turns, faces me. Then Leo spins. For a while we make a little game of it, each person spinning the arrow, seeing who it lands on, and calling out their name.

"Max . . ."

"Daisy . . ."

"Leo . . ."

"Jane . . ."

Daisy spins. It hits me, and she says, "Jane. You're it. No, wait, you win. Sorry!" She laughs at her mistake.

"Leo . . ."

"Daisy . . ."

"Daisy again . . ."

"What do we win?" asks Leo.

"Who cares? Keep playing."

Part

I II **III** IV

Put Your Pencil Down. Turn Your Test Booklet Over.

MAX

One month until I know my SAT score.

I keep telling myself, *This isn't final. No matter what happens, I can always take it again.*

It's like, "That wasn't me. You're actually going to hold me responsible for all that?"

I just hope it turns out okay. That's all I ask: that I not be totally and utterly humiliated.

LEO

I think I got it.

I go over it in my head, what I did, chose this, chose that. Overall, I think it'll be okay. If I made a mistake, people are never going to know. The final number is what matters. Nobody looks and says, "Wait a minute, what about this?" I seriously do think it'll be okay.

Actually, I think it'll be really good.

Another thing I tell myself is that even if this isn't perfect, I'll have a solid baseline. A good basic score I can fall back on if everything else fails. And next time when I take it, I can push for higher without worrying.

Jane

It's funny. I have absolutely no idea how I did. Not a clue. At the end of the day I was like, "Well, that's over."

Daisy

I could be wrong. But I'm pretty sure I screwed the whole thing up.

MAX

When I get home, my dad says, "So?"

LEO

What's hysterical is, my dad doesn't even ask. No phone call from Mom, either. It's not until Jenna asks, "Hey, how'd it go?" that my dad says, "Oh, yeah. The test."

Jane

My mom is waiting when I get home. The second she sees me, she leaps out of her chair and gives me this huge hug. Then she says, "We're going out to dinner. Anywhere you want."

Sort of the last thing I want to do is go out to dinner. I'm exhausted. But you have to pretend and do these things, so I say, "Sure."

Daisy

My mom and dad know better than to ask. But the minute I walk through the door, I can feel it, the questions: *How'd it go? Did you ace it? Are we safe?*

They're both in the kitchen, so I stop and say, "It totally sucked from beginning to end. Don't ask me how I did, I have no idea."

My mom says, "When do you find out?"

I recite, "A month by phone or Internet. Five weeks by mail."

"Well, we'll do the phone," my dad says. My mom nods. Like, *Yeah, gotta find out how the kid did.*

"Whatever," I say, and go to my room. I pick up the phone and start dialing.

MAX

Daisy says, "Hey, it's me."

"Hey. Did you survive?"

"Sucked, man."

I laugh. "I know."

LEO

The first time I call Daisy, her phone's busy. So I go to the computer to send her an e-mail. While I'm on, a message pops up.

> From: KYGal@earth.net
> To: leo345@world.com
> So? How do you think you did?

I message back: *"Fine."*

"Bet I did better."

"Is that a bet?"

"100 bucks."

I hesitate. There's something about messaging with

Kyra that feels like a no-no. But it's just messaging. A stupid little bet. What's the harm?

Ah, but would I tell Daisy?

No reason to tell her. I don't tell her every time I hang with Tobin, either.

I message back: *"You're on."*

Daisy

The second I get off with Max, I call Leo. When he says hello, I say, "Hey, Mr. Perfect."

He laughs. "Cut it out."

"What are you doing?"

"What do you mean?"

"Like, is there any reason I can't come over?"

"I can't think of one."

"Excellent."

MAX

"Hi, you've reached Julia, James, and Jane. We're not home right now, but leave a message at the dreaded beep, and we'll get right back to you. Thank you."

Jane

For Monday I make little bags of Hershey's Kisses and put them on everyone's locker. Just so they'll know I'm thinking about them. As I'm trying to balance a bag on the handles of Leo's locker I hear Daisy say, "Hey, your phone was busy, young lady."

I turn, let the Kisses fall on the ground. As Leo picks them up Daisy says, "We're going out to lunch, you want to come?"

It's funny. Once they're away from school, Leo and Daisy don't hide that they're a couple. In the pizza parlor Leo puts his arm around Daisy's shoulder, and she drinks from his cup. I'm happy they feel like they can be like that around me. Every couple needs a friend, like a confidant.

I'm imagining them having a fight and both talking to me about it, and what I'll say that'll help them make up, when Daisy says, "So?"

I don't know what she means for a second. Then I remember—the test—and say, "I think it went okay. I mean, you don't really know until you get the scores."

Leo says, "Are you calling?"

"Yeah, my mom set it up." He puts red pepper on Daisy's slice. I guess he knows she likes it that way. "Are you?"

"Internet." He looks around the table. "So we'll all find out at the same time."

Some seniors go by, and Leo scoots away from Daisy a little. I say, "You guys shouldn't have to hide. . . ."

"I just want to not be an official school couple," says Daisy. "Like, friends can know, but otherwise . . ."

I know. I am a friend.

It's going to be okay.

MAX

I'm on the steps of the school, interviewing a senior about his college letter expectations, when I see them all come back. Leo, Daisy, and Jane.

And I think: *Okay, so that's how it is.*

I pretend to be writing down the senior's big fears about not getting into Amherst. That way, nobody has to do the "Oh, hi, Max" thing. When I look back, I see Leo has his hand in Daisy's back pocket. Which pisses me off. Could you advertise it a little more?

Some people at school will think this is weird. Anybody who really knows Daisy will think, *Uh-huh. Another jerk.* But most people will be like, "He looks good, she looks good—why not?"

I don't think anybody would say, "But she should be with Max!" More people would have found that strange than will find this strange.

The senior says, "You're just up against so many good people. Sometimes I feel bad for the schools, you know? Like, who do you pick?"

Yeah, I think. *You won't feel so bad when they don't pick you.*

LEO

Okay, it was jerky of me to put my hand in Daisy's pocket. And yeah, I did it so Max would see. But the guy's gotta know. I mean, how long are we going to keep pretending?

Mariah Fredericks

Daisy

Between SAT scores and college acceptance letters, the school is completely crazed. Everybody's waiting to hear: *How'd I do? Did they pick me? What score did I get? Where'd I get in?* Like everybody's future is on the line all at once. In the hallway, the classrooms, the bathrooms, the cafeteria, it's college . . . SATs . . . college . . . SATs. I've told Luisa to call me the instant she gets her U. Penn. letter.

I'm sitting in the kitchen, wrestling with Spanish, when my dad comes in and picks up the phone. One look at me and he says, "Expecting a call?"

"Just, Luisa might be getting her letter today, and . . ."

"You want to keep the line free. No problem." My dad smiles and puts on the kettle for tea. "Everyone's stressing out these days, huh?"

"Yeah."

"What a lousy time," my dad says, and I laugh because it wasn't what I expected him to say. "You know, I was thinking the other day about all this. Colleges, scores, all these tests. You know what I remembered?"

"What?"

"How when I was in high school, the thing I most wanted in the entire world was to go to Berkeley. To me, that was the center of the political universe. If I wasn't there, forget it."

I think. "You didn't go to Berkeley."

My dad smiles. "That's right. Didn't get in. I thought that was it—good-bye, future."

"So . . . what happened?"

"I went to NYU instead. Found out there's more than one center to the universe. Oh, and I met your mom. That was pretty good."

I smile. "Yeah, I'll give a thumbs-up on that one."

My dad turns the teaspoon over on the table. "So, what I think I'm trying to tell you is that no one place is going to make you into something you're not. And no place can stop you from being what you're destined to be. It's what you bring." He smiles. "And you bring an awful lot, honey."

"Oh, gosh, Dad, thanks." I say it goofy, but I hope he knows I mean it.

"Oh, gosh, Daisy, you're welcome."

Then the phone rings, and I leap for it. All I have to hear Luisa say is, "Daise?" and I know.

You don't cry like that when you're accepted.

I tell Luisa to meet me in the park, and when I get there, she's already sitting on a bench by one of the entrances.

I say, "What happened?"

Luisa shrugs. "You know what happened. I didn't have the SATs."

No. Everything in me rejects this. Luisa turned down over a bunch of numbers? No way. "You should talk to Crowley. He's a total ass, but he does have connections. Maybe he can call his buds at U. Penn."

Before, Luisa looked sad. Now she looks bitter. "Oh,

yeah, I went to Crowley. A few months ago, 'cause I was thinking of applying early. He 'explained' that wouldn't be a good idea. He 'explained' that competition for the top schools is very high this year and that there were 'stronger candidates' than me."

"Like *who*?"

"Like Andrew Fraser. Like Tara Keminicki. They both got in."

Andrew and Tara. Yeah, they probably did well on the SATs. But they're not remotely as amazing as Lu. I guess there's no test that measures "amazing human being."

I hate Crowley. Crowley sucks out loud. If Luisa were one of his little Ivies, some rich girl with perfect everythings but no brains and no opinions, he'd be all over U. Penn., going, "You gotta let this girl in, she's fantastic."

Luisa was so excited about U. Penn. She even bought the stupid sweatshirt. How can you want something so badly, and they don't want you?

But there's something upsetting about that, a little tug of guilt from something I don't want to think about, so I say, "Crowley sabotaged you, man."

She shakes her head. "Come on. I wasn't good enough."

"That's crap," I tell her. Luisa holds her hands out like the facts are in them and she's showing them to me. "Well, U. Penn. sucks."

Luisa laughs. "Hey, I can't say I love a place and then say they suck when they turn me down."

"Why not?"

Luisa laughs again. "I guess maybe I will burn the sweatshirt."

As we leave the park she says, "When do you get your scores?"

"Next week."

A chill settles in my stomach. I can see it now, all these schools crossed off my list. "Sorry, Daisy, with your low SATs, these schools are simply out of reach."

Jane

By this time tomorrow I'll know. I'll have this number and I'll be able to show it to people and say, "Yep, that's me."

My mom is completely freaking out, of course. Why miss an occasion for drama? I'm watching TV in the living room, and she's asked me about twenty times how early I can call and find out my score.

Even James says, "Calm down, Julia."

She sits down next to me, tries to focus on the television. "What're you watching?"

"Actually, it's boring." I pick up the remote, start flipping. All of a sudden my mother's face is on the screen. She has weird feathered hair and is wearing the most awful clothes.

Apparently my mom agrees, because she shrieks,

"Oh, my God," and leans forward. "God, I look hideous."

"*Summer of Love,*" says James, setting aside his book.

Some old actor with a ridiculous mustache comes on, and my mom laughs. "Oh, he was the biggest nightmare. Jane, I've told you a million times not to be an actress, right?"

I say, "Yes, Mom," because she has.

"Well, make it a million and one."

We watch for a little while just for fun, with my mom groaning and hiding her eyes whenever her screen self speaks. James says, "Actually, you look a lot like Jane."

"Oh, I do not," says my mother. "Jane is a thousand times prettier."

James looks at me like he's trying to decide. Because my mom is right next to me, it's okay. I concentrate on the screen. I have to admit, my mother and I do look alike—although I am not pretty. It's strange, watching her on screen, with her real self here, and then me, another part of her. Like, who are we, really?

"What time can you call again? Sorry, sorry!" My mother puts her hands up as I hit her with a pillow.

"Maybe I won't call at all," I tease her. "Maybe I'll just never know."

MAX

The night before we get our scores, the Mets are on, and my dad and I eat dinner in the living room. The

Mets aren't going anywhere this year. They lost a lot of good players last year because they sucked so bad. That's the thing: When you suck, no one wants to play for you. They want to play with guys who know how to win . . . like the Yankees.

There's one thing my dad would never ever forgive me for: rooting for the Yankees. He's a psycho Mets fan. Even though they don't win like the Yankees—well, nobody wins like the Yankees. Some years the Mets can drive you crazy, they're such screwups, but he still roots for them.

Once when we were watching a game, I asked him how come, when he's so focused on success and doing well, he doesn't root for the Yankees.

My dad shook his head. "Anybody can win when you have that much money. That's not winning, that's just buying talent. When you beat the guys who have an unfair advantage—that's winning."

The A's get a hit off the pitcher and my dad swears. The coach comes up to the mound; they're taking the guy out. I say, "They left him in too long."

My dad waves his hand. "He blew it in the second inning. Should have taken him out sooner."

During the commercial he asks me if I'm going to call in the morning. He knows I am, he just wants to make sure. I say, "Yeah."

He says, "You feeling good about it?"

I nod. "Yeah, not so nervous. You know, it's just . . ."

What does Leo always say? "Just figuring out the tricks."

"That's right." My dad points at me. "That is absolutely right. The whole thing is just tricks and games. But you have to be smart enough to get around them."

I'm not sure who "them" is, but I nod.

Sometimes, times like this, I wish we had a bigger apartment. Sometimes my dad just feels too big, and you want to be away from it. His feelings become this big balloon, like one of those crash pillows that blow up and take up all the air. Like now. He's sitting there thinking, *My kid's smart. My kid works hard. My kid's going to beat the Yankees.*

And I want to say, "Uh, Dad, I'm gonna get taken out in the fifth inning."

But we don't really need a bigger apartment. Not for the two of us. We moved here when I was five, once my dad figured it out that my mom had left and she wasn't coming back. That all we needed was one bedroom, because he could sleep in the living room on a foldout couch.

I never thought my mom was coming back. Like, once you're gone, you're gone. A few years ago, when we got a call saying she was dead, her car had crashed, it was like, *Well, that's sad, but I didn't really know her.*

That's what I told Daisy. She said, "She was your mom. I think you're allowed to freak out here."

Which was nice, so I thought about it, if I wanted to

freak out. Part of me did, just to get it over with. Then a part of me was like, *Why? For her?*

I said, "Yeah, but she didn't want to be my mom, so I'm not gonna waste a whole lot of time going boo-hoo."

And Daisy said, "Okay," and that was that.

Dad turns the mute button off and the game blares back into the living room. The crowd's cheering for the relief pitcher, and they sound really stupid. I want to yell at them to shut up. But my dad's right there, and this place is too small to yell.

That's what it feels like when I think of my mom being gone: too small.

LEO

I don't check first thing. Everyone does that, and all that does is jam the system. You can imagine all across the country kids going, "Come on, why's this stupid thing so slow?"

So I wait. Until after breakfast, when I'm good and ready. I go into my room, shut the door, and log on to the Princeton site.

Of course I mistype the address. *"Site could not be located."*

Come on, don't screw with me. Type it again. Duh, put in a colon.

Come on, Leo, get it together.

Banging at my door. "Lee-ooo . . ."

I yell back, "Not now, Zo, okay?"

"What're you doing?"

Agh, Zo, go away. "Nothing. Just . . ."

The thing asks for my social security number. The door rattles; Zo trying to get in. I yell, "Quit it," and screw up.

Furious, I go to the door and yank it open. Zo steps back, but not far enough. I shout right into his face, "I said *later*, all right?" and slam the door shut.

With one finger I stab out my number. Think, *There, you happy? Now give me my score, you . . .*

And there it is.

Not perfect.

Good. High. Fine.

But not perfect.

Crap.

Jane

It's weird. How little it means in the end.

I mean, I'm looking at the numbers and thinking, *There it is. My score.* But I don't really care. It's a bunch of numbers. How am I supposed to care about that?

I try. For a second I think, *With those numbers you could maybe get into Yale. Or Brown. Or anywhere you wanted. You can do all these things. . . .*

Then I think, *All what things?*

That's the thing about these numbers. They don't answer questions like that.

Daisy

I pick up the phone, put it back down.

It's stupid. Whatever I got, I got. Not knowing isn't going to change anything.

Of course, in three minutes I could know that I'm stupid and doomed to failure.

My mom knocks on the door. I say, "Yeah," and she pokes her head in. "How's it going?"

I look at the phone. "Can't quite do it."

"Then, don't. There's nothing that says you have to know today."

"Yes, there is. You and Dad will have a heart attack if you have to wait."

"Eh, one little heart attack, we can handle it." She smiles. "Seriously. We can wait."

"Yeah, well . . ." I pick up the phone. "I can't."

As I dial, my mom starts to leave. But I put out my hand, and she takes it. I wrinkle my nose, like, *I know I'm dumb.* And she squeezes my hand, like, *No, you're not.*

When I hear the number, I almost can't believe it.

I shriek the number at my mom, who all of a sudden is hugging me like crazy.

MAX

When I hear the number, I think, *Not good enough.*

Then I think, *Shut up. It's good. It's fine.*

Also: *You'll do better next time.*

Two voices in my head. I can't figure out which one is right.

I really, really hope Daisy did okay. I call, but her line is busy.

LEO

When I pick up the phone to call Daisy, a little part of me knows I'm hoping she didn't do well. Then I can say, "That sucks, babe," and focus on her screwup instead of mine.

But I know the second I hear her voice, she did just fine and I have to be happy for her. When she says, "1890," I say, "Congrats, you deserve it."

"Well, hey, you had something to do with it." She gets all shy, and then I do feel really happy for her.

Then she says, "So?"

I echo, "So?"

"Cut it out. Come on, tell me."

I lean back in my chair. "Ah, not what I wanted." I really, really don't want to say it. I know it's fine. I know it's good. Just with everything I did, it wasn't what I expected. But she told hers, so I have to tell her mine. Blah, blah. "2300."

"That's pretty okay."

I snap, "I didn't want okay." I know I shouldn't take it out on her, but I don't get why no one understands this. No one thinks it's okay not to want to be just okay.

"I know," she says slowly. "But does this mean we can't celebrate? 'Cause you only did, like . . . okay?"

I laugh. I don't know why this girl has the power to make me feel stupid. And why that's somehow all right.

Jane

I pick up the phone and call Daisy. But her line is busy. So I try Max. He's busy too. I even try Leo, but guess what.

They could just be checking their scores, I think. *It's not necessarily that they're all talking to one another and not to you.*

I do get it. I'm not first on anybody's list. Daisy's going to call Max or Leo before she calls me. They're going to call her first, me second. That's fine.

I sit down on the floor, hit redial.

Daisy

The second I get off the phone with Leo, it rings again. I pick up and it's Max. Immediately he asks what I got, and I tell him. "That's pretty good," he says.

Pretty good . . . "Yeah, I know it's not, like, the highest ever, but . . . how about you?"

"Only okay," he says.

When he tells me, I say, "That's only okay? That's, like, great." I can't helping thinking: *If you think that's only okay, you must think my score is doo-doo.*

For a weird moment, I feel guilty. Like, when did I start caring so much about a test?

Then he says, "Hey, were you just trying to call me?"

"No."

"Oh. Your phone was busy."

"Oh, yeah." Then I stop because I don't want to get into the whole Leo thing with him.

But then I think, *Lying is lame*, and say, "Yeah, Leo called."

"I figured."

I can hear he's pissed, and I want to say, "Hello, I don't control the phone lines. I have no power to decide who gets through first."

There's this long, ugly silence. This should so not be happening right now. We should be happy, we should be . . . me and Max.

Maybe you can't be Me and Max. You're You and Leo now.

But that's so wrong, so not true. . . .

Then Max says, "So, we should celebrate."

"Yeah, totally. Uh, my parents are taking me out tonight." And then I'm seeing Leo. . . .

I say, "Hey, I have an idea. After we do the parent stuff, why don't we all meet at the all-night diner?" Max hesitates. "You know, like, me, you, Jane, and Leo?"

I can tell Max is a little bummed we're not doing something that's just us. But he says, "Okay. Cool."

Next I try Jane. But her phone's busy. Probably still getting her scores.

MAX

2070.

I repeat the numbers in my head, trying to get a feel

for them. 2070, 2070, 2070. I am 2070. Not as good as 2100. Better than 2000. I am ten points better than all kids who got 2060.

I can't put it off any longer, so I go into the living room. My dad's not even pretending to be watching TV or reading or anything.

There are two ways I can do this. Be all happy and say, "I did great!" and hope my dad agrees. Or downplay the whole thing and hope he says, "Are you kidding? That's really good."

I want to say "I did great!" because I think I did pretty close to great. But close to great and great are not the same thing. Not when you have great to choose from.

So instead I say, "I did okay."

He nods. "Yeah?"

"I did . . ." I give him the score. Wait for him to say, "Hey, way to go!"

But he doesn't. He's waiting for me to say if it's good or it's bad. Like my judgment of my score is as big a test as the test itself. You did great if you think you did lousy, lousy if you think you did great.

I say, "I think for the first time it's not too bad."

He immediately nods. "No, not too bad."

"I mean . . . next time I'll do better."

"That's right."

I think for a moment: How much would I give not to have to do better next time? How much, to be able to say, "I did great. I don't have to do better next time.

There doesn't have to be a next time for me. I got it, I did it. *I can stop trying now!*"

A whole, whole lot.

Jane

When Max calls to tell me we're all meeting in some diner later tonight, I say, "Great, thanks."

He laughs. "For what?"

"Uh, for letting me know."

It's not until the afternoon that my mom bursts out with, "I'm sorry, honey, I can't take it anymore. Please call."

I say, "I did call."

Her eyes widen. "And?" I tell her. "*Honey!* That's . . . that's . . . aren't you proud?"

"I guess. It's just a test."

"You know what? It isn't. It really isn't just a test, because it means a lot to colleges if you do well, and you did well, and honey, I am so *proud of you.*"

Then she gives me this incredible hug. Like I've proved something to her, done this thing she had no idea I could do. Suddenly I'm a different person, someone she has to take seriously.

For a few seconds I finally feel what it is to do well.

Then James comes in, and she yells out the good news. He nods, says, "See? Told you prep was worth it."

My mom turns on him. "Hey, this isn't prep. This is

Jane." She hugs me, rubs my arm. "She's a pretty smart kid, you know."

I can't believe it. My mom has actually taken my side. I lean into her a little bit to say, *Thanks,* and she rubs my arm harder, like, *You're welcome.*

That's when I decide I'm not going to tell anybody. Before I thought I would. But I feel so good about my mom and how she's reacting, it's like, *You know what? Nobody else needs to know.*

The group, though, I'll tell. That's only fair.

LEO

I go out to the living room, where Zo's playing with his monster truck. I say, "Hey, guy." But he ignores me.

I put my foot in front of the truck, an invitation to run me over. Zo swings around, pushes his truck under the coffee table.

I think of Zo's face when I slammed the door on him and say, "Sorry."

He just keeps pushing the truck.

I wish I could explain to him about the test, about having to do well. Really well, and how I'm not sure I did well enough. How I'm not sure I can.

But I don't want to put all that on a little kid, so I say, "Okay. See you around."

Before I meet up with Daisy by the park, I grab a full bottle of Bacardi out of the liquor cabinet. If my dad complains, screw it. You have to celebrate somehow.

Daisy

I see Leo before he sees me. He's already sitting on one of the benches by Central Park, so I have a second to think, *He is actually a pretty amazing-looking guy.*

I approach, put a foot on the bench. "You can be arrested for loitering, you know."

"I'd rather get arrested for something more interesting."

He pulls out a bottle in a paper bag and two cans of Coke. "Let the celebrations begin. Rum and Coke for the lady?"

Drinking's not really my thing, but I know Leo's into it, and hey, special night. So I say, "Sure."

He takes a chug of my can of Coke, starts pouring in rum. I say, "Whoa, enough. I'm a lightweight."

"You? Give me a break." But he stops pouring, hands me the can. Then he pours out half his Coke into a garbage can, starts refilling. When he's done, he takes a quick swig from the bottle.

I tell him, "Don't pass out on me, now."

"Nah." He holds up his Coke can, and I clink mine against it. "To, uh . . . well, to you." He smiles. "I can't think of anything brilliant, you make me stupid."

I feel myself go red, kiss him to say thanks.

That goes on for a while, then he breaks off, takes another slug. There's something about the way he does it, like, *Phew, made it through that, better have a drink,* that makes me say, "You're bummed, aren't you? You wanted a perfect score."

He takes another quick sip. "Eh, you know. There's always next time."

"Yeah, but you wanted it now."

Part of me is worried he's going to be pissed at me for pushing it. Or pretend he doesn't care. Instead he nods, and all of a sudden I feel how bad he wanted it. I want to say, "You are so much more amazing when you're *not* being Leo the Lion," but that's probably too heavy.

I say, "It's not . . . it's not so important, you know? To be perfect?"

"Oh, yeah?"

"Yeah." I put the can down and slide onto his lap so I'm facing him. "Perfect is . . . pretty boring. Now, imperfect . . ." I kiss him. "That could get a girl really crazy."

"You're already crazy," he says.

Looking down at him, I tell myself, *You cannot fall this hard. You have got to be way more careful than this. You cannot get stupid.*

The problem is, I'm telling myself all this . . .

But I'm not listening.

MAX

They're late. Daisy and Leo. For a while it's just me by myself drinking a soda and wondering, *Is this what my life is going to be like?*

For no very good reason I think of my mom. When

she left, she left big-time, went all the way to Dallas. She didn't know anybody in Dallas, just wanted to get away from us, I guess. You can imagine her sitting in a booth like this one, thinking, *Well, this sucks, but at least they're not around to bug me.*

I don't get it, though. How being alone is better.

When Jane comes in, she stands by the door a second, looking for "us." But there's only me.

LEO

I'm feeling good. But not so good that I don't realize I'm feeling good, if you know what I mean. Like I know I have to chill out a little. Anyway, there is no more rum.

Daisy says, "You're okay, right?" It's the third time she's asked it. I'm like, "Yes, obviously." I even walk an imaginary line for her. Walk it very slow and steady.

She pulls me along, laughing. "We're late."

I say, "I am late for no man." Which makes sense to me.

I wonder if they'd sell me a beer at the diner.

Jane

It's nice. Sitting here alone with Max. Like, "Hey, if Daisy and Leo can go off together, we can too." Not in that way, but . . . we don't miss them is what I'm saying.

Max must be thinking the same thing, because he says, "You know, we don't have to wait."

I smile. "You think we should leave?" We both know we're not going to do it; that's how we can even talk about it.

"Sure." He looks at his watch. "In . . . five minutes if they're not here, we leave."

And all of a sudden it's real. I say, "Okay."

Then: "And then what do we do?"

"I don't know. What do you want to do?"

He looks me in the eye, and I think: *Daisy is really stupid for picking Leo over him.*

But before I think of what I want to do, Max points to the door. "They're here."

Daisy

Max and Jane at the diner. *Our* diner.

It's not something I like to see.

Oh, great, Daisy. You don't want him, but no one else can have him. Who was it who said to Jane, "Oh, you should ask him out"?

Maybe because I feel like such a jerk, I make a big thing of hugging them. Hug Max: "We suck, we're late. . . ." Hug Jane: "You so need call-waiting." Because it occurs to me, I don't even know how Jane did.

I ask her, and she says, "Oh God . . . uh, 2250. Big deal, right?" And I can't help it. I think, Jane got higher than Max? Yeah, that makes sense. But it does. Jane is a really good test taker. She might not care, she might blow it off, but she gets this stuff. It's like the less you really think, the better test taker you are. Which is nasty of me, and I need to stop.

"Congratulations," I tell her. "You deserve it."

MAX

Leo is definitely a little trashed. What's funny is, he's nicer trashed. He puts up his hand, and after a second I slap it.

"Hit me, man," he says, "What'd you get?"

So I tell him.

"That's pretty decent."

"Not really. What about you?" I'm already braced for him doing better, so when he tells me the score, it doesn't feel so bad.

"Congrats." But that isn't enough. "Seriously, man, that's great. You should feel good."

LEO

Personally, I think clearer when I'm trashed. God's honest truth. Like now. All of a sudden I get that I didn't used to like Max. But he's an okay guy.

At this moment he's thinking, *Crap, he got higher than me when I should've got higher than him, but I'm not going to be a jerk about it.*

Frankly, I would have been a jerk. Max, you're a better man than me, or however that goes.

I say, "The thing is, guy like you, it doesn't matter."

He smiles. "Matters for everyone."

"No. Seriously. You have something that's yours. Any schmuck who tries hard enough can get a perfect score. Big deal. Not a lot of people can write like you can. That's what colleges want. It's not like in the alumni newsletter they go, 'Hey, so-and-so aced his medical boards.' They say, 'Our guy Max Bastogne won the Pulitzer.'" I take a slug of coffee. "Tests are kind of meaningless once you get to real life."

Jane says, "Well, what's this?"

Jane

"Absolutely," says Daisy, dipping a french fry in ketchup. "And wait, doesn't that mean that tests are . . ."

"Meaningless?"

Max laughs. "But they're not. I mean, they are, but they're not."

Leo raises his hand. "I have a brilliant suggestion." Daisy looks skeptical. "Why don't we . . . shut up? About the whole entire test thing? The letters S, A, and T cannot be mentioned in that order again for the next six months."

"That is a brilliant suggestion," says Daisy.

But I do want to say one more thing. "Doesn't this prove, I mean, our scores, and who we are, that the test has so little to do with you? Like, you definitely don't have to be that smart to do well?"

Leo grins. "Hey, Jane, you ever think maybe you are that smart?"

MAX

Later you realize how many things you didn't see. How much you missed. Later it all seems so obvious.

That morning I actually see Tory McEwan sitting on the bench outside Crowley's office. But I don't think anything of it.

Later I wish I had said something. Talked to her, maybe even stopped her. I wish I had said, "You might think this is the right thing to do. But this is going to have a huge effect on everybody. This is going to screw a lot of people up."

But I didn't say anything to Tory, so I don't actually find out what's going on until math class, when Steffi Kleinberg leans over and whispers, "Did you hear?"

I keep my eyes on the blackboard, where Ms. DiMitri is writing out a problem. But I shake my head.

Steffi hisses, "About Tory McEwan?"

I shake my head again.

"She went to Crowley . . ."

Ms. DiMitri turns around. Steffi sits back up, folds her hands in front of her. Ms. DiMitri goes back to the blackboard.

Steffi comes back. "She went . . ."

But she's whispering too low and I can't hear her. I shake my head. She leans in closer, "She went to Crowley and she told him . . ."

Ms. DiMitri looks over at us. For a few moments we both act like she has our complete attention. For some reason I'm feeling freaked. Like I have to know, right now, what Tory told Crowley. And I also really don't want to know. Most rumors you hear are a joke. He likes her, she's with him, she's lying about her dyslexia. . . . Stupid. Doesn't matter.

I can tell from Steffi's voice: This does matter. This is not a joke.

When Ms. DiMitri's back is turned, I look back at Steffi. But she's not going to risk whispering again. Instead she's writing on a clean page in her math book. I watch her as she writes, but I can't see it all. Just the words *"She went to Crowley and she told him . . ."*

Steffi lowers the cover of the book and turns it toward me.

"That someone paid her to take the SATs for them! And she did!"

Jane

At first when I hear it, I can't believe it. How could anybody be that stupid?

What was Tory thinking?

Everybody's looking at everybody now. Trying to remember who took the SATs in March. Was it you? Was it you?

Because Tory didn't tell Crowley who it was. She felt like she had to admit what she'd done, but she didn't want to get the other person into trouble.

I don't know how they're ever going to find out who

it was. I mean, the school telling whoever that they have to "come forward." Who's going to do that?

I think, really, they don't want the person to come forward. I think they don't want to know. Because the score is high; it'll get you into a good school. And Crowley doesn't want to blow that. Another Yale or Harvard or Brown . . . he's not going to screw that up.

I bet after a while they act like nothing ever happened. Pretend it was all just nothing.

That's usually what people do.

LEO

I'm running to meet Daisy when I hear, "Leo!"

I turn, see Kyra. She comes up to me, puts her hand on my arm. "Just tell me it wasn't you."

"What wasn't me?"

Her eyes gleam. "You don't know? Tory McEwan just confessed to Crowley that she took the SATs for someone else."

"Man . . ."

"And it was someone who took them in March. Didn't you take them in March, Leo?" She tilts her head like it's the most innocent question in the world.

"Oh, ha, ha, Kyra." But she's not laughing. I say, "You took them too."

"But I know I didn't cheat."

"Tory isn't saying who paid her?" She shakes her head. "Why'd she open her mouth?"

"She was afraid she'd get caught, that someone might have seen her at the test center and thought, *Wait, that's weird.* So she thought it was better to confess, not screw up her chances later on."

I can't help it. Someone would say I'm supposed to admire Tory for speaking up. But it's like, *Girl, you took the money, keep your mouth shut.*

"What's Crowley going to do?" I'm going to be late for Daisy, but I gotta know.

"He's going to hold what he calls a town meeting."

I roll my eyes.

"I know, hysterical, right? And he's going to demand that the perpetrator turn himself—"

"Or herself."

"Or herself—in."

"Who would be stupid enough to do that?"

"I guess Crowley's hoping they crack under pressure. A lot of people are really pissed off about this, Leo. They want to know who it was. Everyone's worked too hard to be jumped in line by some cheater. So, for your sake, I hope it wasn't you. Or anyone you know."

She smiles, starts walking away. Then all of a sudden she turns back. "Hey, didn't your girlfriend do, like, really well? And wasn't that kind of a . . . surprise?"

Daisy

"So, who was it?"

When Luisa asks me this at lunch, I think it's a

joke. Like, "Knock, knock, who was it?" "Who was it who?"

Then she tells me about Tory.

After I register what she's saying, I say, "Are you sure? People are always saying, 'Oh, he cheated,' or whatever."

"Totally," says Luisa. "Someone saw Tory coming out of Crowley's office. Tears, the whole bit."

All I can think is, *Cheated? Somebody took this crap seriously enough to* cheat?

"Why'd she do it?"

"Somebody offered her a lot of money."

Of course. Some rich kid figures, *Hey, no problem, I'll just get Tory McEwan to do it. Perfect.* That's these tests in a nutshell.

Then Luisa says, "Or their parents did."

"God, you think somebody's parents . . ."

"Look at the lunatics in this place. 'Oh, my little Peter's going to Hahvahd.' Hell, yes, I think somebody's parents would do that."

I can't help it. I think of Max's dad. Or Jane's mom. I mean, who'd turn down Julia Cotterell?

Luisa shakes her head. "All I can say is, they better find out who it was, and they better kick their ass. That person should never see the inside of *any* college."

I say, "They'll find them. Nobody keeps secrets in this place."

"They better." Luisa looks at me, all intense, and I

remember how she wanted to go to U. Penn. so bad. How she didn't because of this stupid test.

As we walk out Luisa says, "Look, I don't know if I should tell you this or not."

"But . . ."

"People are already picking their favorite suspects. And your guy Leo is tops on the list."

MAX

We don't have the SAT meeting anymore, of course. But after school we all somehow hook up and head straight for the diner. Jane and I sit down next to each other, before Leo and Daisy force us to, and Daisy catches it, looks at me like, *What's that about?*

I don't know. I don't know what it's about. But leave it alone.

Daisy sits down. "I can't believe it. I can't believe somebody would do that."

Leo says, "Why not?"

"Yeah," says Jane. "People get crazy."

"People are crazy now," I say. And it's true. All day all anybody could talk about was who it could be and what they'd want to happen to that person. None of what they wanted to happen to that person was very nice.

Jane says, "How'd they do it?"

Leo shakes his head. "People are saying Tory and whoever it was were both in the test room, but they switched tests at the last second."

Daisy said, "I heard they just sat next to each other and copied the pattern of dots."

"Who knows?" I say. "Maybe Tory just showed up, took the test, and signed the person's name."

Jane shakes her head. "They're never going to find out who did it."

"Oh, they will," says Daisy. "There are no secrets."

"Yes, there are," I say. She looks at me. "I mean, if the kid is rich and their parents give a lot of money to the school. Or they're an Ivy, and Crowley's already talked them up to his buds—you think they're really going to expose that person?"

"Or they're a minority, and the school'll be scared of being accused of racism," says Leo.

"Shut up," says Daisy.

He glares at her. "Oh, what? We're only supposed to think a rich kid did it? Or an Ivy? Why would people like that need to cheat?"

"I don't know why," flares Daisy, "but they do."

Jane says quietly, "Come on, guys. It's bad enough."

Jane

In fact, it's horrible. It's like we all were when we first met in that stupid prep class. Each of us thinking we were so different from one another, most of us not liking one another.

Almost to myself I say, "It shouldn't matter."

Leo says, "Of *course* it matters."

LEO

I say, "You think colleges don't hear about this stuff? You think it won't make them look at every one of our applications differently? Man, I don't get why Tory had to have her big attack of the guilts."

"Gee, I don't know," snaps Daisy. "Maybe she felt bad."

She is seriously annoying today. I know she's all upset because this confirms everything she thinks about the big bad system, but give me a break.

Daisy

I know Leo didn't do it. I absolutely know that. He has way too much pride to cheat.

I just really wish he would shut up about Tory and why she had to open her big mouth. I want to say to him, "You do realize a lot of people think you did this, right?"

But I don't want to have a big fight about it in front of Max and Jane, so I say, "When's the stupid Crowley meeting again?"

"Tomorrow," says Max.

MAX

Lots of people blow off big school meetings. They hang out in the bathroom, go have a smoke, whatever. Not this meeting. It's packed.

As Daisy and I wait to get into the auditorium someone behind us says, "I heard Crowley's going to say who did it."

Someone else says, "What? Cheated?"

"Yeah, like, he's going to expose them in front of the whole school."

Daisy rolls her eyes at me. I roll them back. We both know that's not how Crowley works. But it's the possibility, the smallest chance, we might find out *who did it*—that's what's got everyone crowding into the auditorium.

For no very good reason I think of the Roman spectacles. Where they threw people to the lions and everyone watched as they were ripped to shreds.

Daisy

It's a total freak show. The room is packed, nowhere to sit, kids are lining the walls, craning to see the stage, wanting to know the second Crowley comes in.

I hate to admit this, but part of me wants to ask Max who he thinks did it. I don't want to get caught up in all this madness—Who was it? What'll happen to them? God, they should be expelled!—but it's hard not to be. Even if it is totally gross.

We find a place at the back and sit on the floor. When Max isn't looking, I glance around, see if I can see Leo. I spot him sitting with Tobin a few rows from the very front. I smile, give him a look like, *You suck-up.* He does sucking motions with his mouth. I see Jane come in, and wave to her, but she doesn't see me and goes and finds a free seat somewhere in the middle.

Then Crowley comes on stage and absolutely every-body shuts up.

LEO

Right away you know: This is not a joke.

Crowley grips the sides of the lectern, glares at the crowd. Like each and every one of us paid Tory to cheat and we're all equally guilty.

"As you have no doubt heard, a student has come to me with a very disturbing story. In March a junior paid her to take the SATs in their stead. The student who was paid has since realized what a grave mistake she made and has given me the money for safe-keeping."

I think: *Gave you money? Ah, that explains the sharp new suit you're wearing.*

"This student did the right thing and brought this matter to my attention. But she would not tell me who it was who paid her. So now it is up to that person to come forward.

"I would like to say to that person, that score is not yours. That achievement is not yours. You have under-taken none of the effort and deserve none of the reward. If you do not come forward and word of this gets out, the scores of every one of your classmates will be in doubt in the eyes of colleges."

Everyone's looking around now. They hadn't thought of that. Morons.

Jane

For no reason at all I feel like laughing.

I mean, this is just so insane. Crowley up there like some judge: "You shall be punished, you evildoer."

All for a stupid test.

Crowley says, "I strongly urge the student who paid Tory McEwan to admit what they did, out of consideration for their classmates and respect for the truth."

And that's when I do laugh. The guy whose business it is to tell colleges that this kid's a genius and that kid's a saint, all of a sudden he's big on the truth. I want to shout, "What about all the times you've told us to do things just so we could tell colleges we did them? How is that not a lie?"

The girl sitting next to me gives me a dirty look, and I shrug, like, *Sorry.*

Which is, of course, another lie.

MAX

After the meeting the four of us hang behind in the auditorium. I don't know about anyone else, but I'm feeling flipped out.

I try and make a joke. "Gee, I actually thought they'd chop someone's head off. I'm disappointed."

Jane laughs. "I know, right? I don't see why everyone's making such a big deal out of it."

Maybe because the past two days have been so intense, there's a weird moment where I remember that

Jane is rich and that her mom is a movie star and that she probably won't have to do much in her life if she doesn't want to—and that she may be the kind of person who doesn't want to. In that moment I really, really don't like her.

Because to that kind of person, it doesn't matter if someone cheats. Because they've been getting by unfairly all along. Even if they don't know it.

Then I think: *That's jerky and unfair, the kind of thing you start thinking when the competition gets out of control.* "I'm so much better than her. He doesn't work as hard as I do. I deserve more. . . ."

I start to say something to hide what I was thinking, but I can see from the expression on Jane's face, it's too late. And whatever started at the diner the night we got our scores may not be anymore.

Daisy and I walk home together. It rained during the day, and for a while Daisy avoids the puddles because it means she has to concentrate on where she's going and doesn't have to look at me.

Which is probably a good thing, because I'm thinking about something I don't want her to see.

Then all of a sudden she stomps through the next one in her path. "So?"

I echo her. "So?"

"You think they're going to figure out who it was?"

"I don't know." Because frankly, that isn't what I've

been thinking about. If *they're* going to figure it out. I've been wondering if Daisy is going to figure it out.

In this fake-casual voice she says, "Who're your top three?"

"I don't have them."

"Sure you do. Everyone does."

I say quietly, "I don't have three."

Daisy skirts around the next puddle. For a while I think she's not going to ask. Then as we wait for the light to change she says, "You know what? I think you should just say it."

"No."

"If you think it, you should say it."

No, because you'll hate me if I say it. "I could be wrong. I probably am wrong."

"But you totally assume it was Leo." Her voice is flat.

I don't say anything.

Daisy says quietly, "That's mean. That's really nasty. I . . . I don't even know where your head's at on that one."

That pisses me off. Like it's *so* impossible to think Leo might have done this? We can't even talk about it, she just immediately takes his side?

I say sarcastically, "Uh, well, my head is at that he's psycho to get into Yale and he may have thought, *What the hell, why take chances?*"

Daisy is staring at me. "Do you have *any* idea how hard he worked for this?"

I can't stand it, Daisy defending Leo over something

she so totally doesn't respect. "Because what else does he have, Daisy? It's not like he can play sports or—"

"Write," she says nastily.

"He said he needed a perfect score. . . ."

"Which he didn't *get!*"

"Came close enough." *Don't say it, Max, shut up, shut up.* "I don't know—maybe the check bounced, so Tory decided to lower it a little."

Daisy's hands open and shut, and I know right then that if she had something, she'd throw it at me. I didn't mean to make her that mad. I thought there'd be enough of her that wasn't tied up in Leo that she could see that it's not insane to think he might have done this.

But Daisy never sees that stuff, not until it's too late. . . .

Not meaning it, I say, "I'm sorry."

Which was the exact wrong thing to say. Daisy shakes her head slowly in disgust. "Are you kidding me?" She takes a step toward me. "This is not about the SATs, don't even *think* I don't get that, okay?"

Even though at this moment I hate Daisy for being stupider than I ever thought she could be, I can't ignore the fact that this is as close as we've been since that night with the Foosballs. It's like she's rubbing the whole thing in my face: *Want to kiss me now? Still think we should get together?*

I wonder, *For how long has she thought I'm a jerk?*

Another thing I wonder: Did she ever tell Leo? Like, is it something they laugh about? Feel sorry for me about?

Of course she told Leo, Max. Of course they feel bad for you.

And all of a sudden I get it: *We are one kind of person. You are a different, sadder species. You don't dare question us.*

At least this time Daisy doesn't get to walk away first.

Daisy

"What's wrong?"

"Nothing." I roll over so my back is to Leo. He puts some fingers on my waist. It tickles a little and I smile.

He says, "Come on, what's bugging you?"

Did you cheat?

"Nothing. Seriously. Just . . ." Maybe sometimes a little truth gets to the bigger truth? "The whole thing with Tory bums me out."

Hand gone. Leo gone. Big sigh.

I sit up. "What?"

"No, nothing." Then, "I wish you'd let it go."

Why?

"Doesn't it bother you?"

LEO

Lot of things are great about Daisy. One thing I can't stand: Everything's gotta be fair.

Why is she obsessing about this?

Another thing I can't stand: If she's obsessing, I've got to obsess. Like now she wants to know, does it bother me? Don't I care about little starving babies in Africa?

I say, "No . . . yeah. You know, who cares? Let Crowley handle it."

I reach up so we can go back to the things we both really, really agree about, but she snorts, "Crowley's not going to deal with it."

And back to the lecture.

"Guy looked like he was breathing fire to me."

"Yeah, like he's upset someone got a fake good score. What's Princeton Review? A bunch of fake good scores . . ."

I'm about to say, "Yeah, and what was me on the phone talking you through prefixes and suffixes?" when someone knocks on the door, and we have to do the whole fix-the-clothes, get-off-the-bed thing.

Jane

I never pick up the phone when it rings. Basically because it's never for me. So when I hear James call, "Jane . . . ," I think, *What?*

I yell out the door, "Who is it?"

"A boy," he calls back. "Max?"

I pick up in my room, say to James, "It's okay, I got it. . . ." I wait for the click, then say, "Hi, Max."

"Hi . . ." He sounds like he called the wrong number by accident and now he's not sure what to say.

I prompt, "What's up?"

"Oh, I was thinking of writing an article on the whole cheater thing, and I thought I'd get some student reaction. Quotes, that kind of stuff. I don't have to put your name, I could just put, 'One student said.'"

I laugh. "You can put my name, I don't care."

"Oh, well, I'll put your name, then. So, uh, what do you think of it all, Ms. Cotterell?"

"I think it's being blown way out of proportion."

"So, you don't feel like your college chances are seriously threatened by someone's fake scores."

"No, I don't. But I guess I don't have anywhere I'm dying to go, so it doesn't really matter to me." I hesitate. "You don't have to put that in, right?"

"No. But it's an interesting angle. Like, do we all care so much because we think it's morally wrong, or do we just feel screwed by someone who played the game better?"

What do you know? I came up with an interesting angle. "Right. Although, I guess if they get caught, then they didn't play the game so well."

"Well, that's why we want them to get caught," says Max. "That's why we want them punished. So we don't feel stupid."

His voice trails off, like all of a sudden he's thinking of something else. I want to say, "Hey, you want to go back to the diner sometime? Just us?"

But then he says, "Well, anyway, thanks for the quote."

As I hang up I have the weirdest feeling he called to tell me something else but decided not to.

I'd like to think he was about to ask if I wanted to go

back to the diner with him. But I don't think he was. Which sucks, frankly. I guess he's still hung up on Daisy.

For a second I feel a surge of rage: *Why does everyone adore Daisy? Why is she, like, the only woman in the universe? She's not that amazing. . . .*

Then I remember she's my best friend and feel really, really horrible.

Grafitti in the fourth-floor bathroom:

Vote for your American Cheater!

1. Leo Thayer
2. Danny Chin
3. Kyra Fleming
4. J. Martin Crowley
Guys, THIS IS NOT FUNNY.
Yeah! Whoever it is should be shot!

MAX

I walked by Mr. Davidson's class today. He's got a huge white board. Usually it's covered in numbers.

But today it was totally clean. Except for four words:

who is the cheater?

The latest rumor is that some kids are cooperating with Crowley. Giving him names, telling him who they think might have done it. When I heard that, I thought, *This is going to get ugly real fast. . . .*

Now the parents are involved. I heard a lot of them have called Crowley's office, demanding to know why he isn't putting more pressure on Tory to say who paid her. Poor Tory. Ever since she confessed, people have been hassling her like crazy. Which is probably why when I approach her in the hallway, she jumps like a gun went off.

I say, "The newspaper wants me to interview you. But I'll understand if you think that's a bad idea."

She shakes her head, pulls her books closer, like they're a shield. "I really . . ."

"I know you can't say who."

She puts her head down, starts walking. "I don't want to talk about it at all. I don't . . ." She turns around, yells, "Leave me alone!"

Daisy

Luisa and I are in the lunchroom when she says, "There's your girl."

I turn, see Jane. I wave to her; she waves back but doesn't come over. Which is good, because then Luisa says, "I can't quite decide if I think our little cheater is her or Kyra."

I'm annoyed but try not to show it. Luisa has gotten very bitter over the whole SAT thing. Anyone with money is a suspect, as far as she's concerned. On the one hand, I totally understand. On the other, she's gotten a little crazy. Like everybody else these days.

Still, I say, "I thought you thought it was Leo."

"I said other people thought it was Leo."

"Well, I'm telling you, it's not."

Luisa raises an eyebrow.

"It wasn't, Luisa, and you better not say it was. In fact, why don't you leave Jane out of it too?"

Luisa's eyebrow goes higher. "Excuse me, didn't mean to insult La Princessa."

"Yes, you did, and you don't even know her. I hate it, how this whole thing has become a way for people to bash people they don't like. 'Oh, she's a spoiled brat, she must have done it. He dumped my friend, he must have done it.' I mean, the people who are sneaking off to Crowley's office? You know some of them are just pointing the finger at anybody who did them dirt."

"Well, *I* would hope if people knew something, they'd let Crowley know."

From the way she's looking at me, I can tell she means: "You know your boy cheated, and you're covering up for him."

LEO

There are, of course, people who think it's cool. That somebody cheated on the SATs and got away with it—so far. Near the cheater poll in the bathroom someone's written, WASN'T ME, BUT I WISH I'D THOUGHT OF IT.

My friend Tobin came up to me and was like, "Dude, why didn't you let me in on it?"

And I was like, "Dude, because I didn't do it."

He pounded me on the shoulder, said loudly, "Disappointed in you, man." But I couldn't tell if that was because he thought I had or hadn't done it.

I don't take it too seriously that a lot of people think it's me. I mean, yeah, it sort of pisses me off when some self-righteous sophomore gives me a dirty look, but what can you do? That's what happens when people know you're ambitious. Crowley hasn't called me in, and that's all that matters.

Daisy's very quiet when I meet up with her after school. As we head to the park I say, "What's up?"

First she does, "Nothing." Then she says, "I had an annoying lunch with Luisa. She's pissing me off these days."

"Still angry over the whole U. Penn. thing?"

"Yeah, and . . ." She shrugs.

"What?"

"No, you know, this whole stupid SAT hoo-ha. I wish whoever did it would just say so, so we could all get on with real life."

"Well, maybe everyone should just get on with real life anyway, you know? Because it's not like anyone's coming forward."

I know I sound irritated, but that's because I am irritated. It's like, lately every conversation I have with people is about this. Even every conversation I have with Daisy.

Actually, especially with Daisy.

I say, "Let me guess. Luisa thinks I did it."

From the way Daisy hesitates, I can tell I've hit it. Then she says, "No, she thinks Kyra. Or Jane."

I laugh. "Give me a break. Like Jane would ever have the guts to pull that off."

"You think that took guts?" She looks at me.

"Yeah, sort of." Daisy's still watching me, and I say, "What?"

"I guess I don't really know what you think of this."

"Oh, come on."

"No, seriously. Every time we talk about it, you're like, 'Who cares?' Or you even think it's cool . . . or want me to think it's cool. . . ." She breaks off.

I stop walking. Say, "You know how I know *you* didn't do it?"

"Because nobody would cheat to get 1890."

"Because you're a rotten liar. There's no way you could have done this and it wouldn't be all over your face. But you know what else I know, just because you happen to be a rotten liar?"

Daisy shakes her head.

"That you think I did it."

Give the girl credit, she doesn't deny it. She's quiet for a long time before saying, "I know you didn't, but I'm scared you did."

Which pisses me off so much I say, "What if I did?"

"Stop it."

"No, seriously, what if I *did*?" One thing I'll never get is how you can go from thinking someone's the coolest person in the world—someone who actually *gets* you—to thinking they're the enemy. I want to scream at Daisy, "What the hell are you so scared of? Why is this so important to you? Why is this more important than me?"

She looks straight out in front of her, like I'm nothing she even wants to look at. "You *didn't*."

She goes and sits up on the park wall. I follow her, saying, "You think the whole thing is a joke, Daisy, so *what do you care?*"

Now she's looking at me. Staring at me. Her jaw's hard, and her eyes are bright. Tears or something else, I can't tell.

Because I figure I may as well let her in on what really annoys me, I say, "You don't even wonder about Max, do you?"

"Wonder *what* about Max?" We're fighting now, no question about it. I broke the big rule: Never say anything bad about Max.

I shrug. "If he was the one. I mean . . . no, it couldn't be Max. Max is such a genius, Max is such a great guy. He'd never do anything like this, even though his dad's on his ass twenty-four–seven and the guy looked like he was going to have a nervous breakdown before the test."

"Max didn't do this."

I take a step closer. "How do you know?"

Daisy shouts, "Because I know. I. Know."

She jumps off the wall, starts heading down the street. I run and catch up with her, say, "But you don't know that about me."

"Not anymore."

She doesn't even break her stride, just keeps moving. I have the worst urge to shove her, wrench her arm, throw her off balance any way I can.

Instead I stop. Let her go on. I don't know if she looks back or not. Because I don't wait to see.

Which, I think, means I win.

I'm not upset. I'm really not. I'm angry, which is something totally different.

But I also feel good. Like, *Hey, you think that about me, screw you. You're so hung up on Max, be my guest.*

And that's why I have a drink. Because I want to celebrate. Which is what you do when you realize, *I never needed you anyway.*

Jane

James asks who the boy is who called the other week. I say, "A friend."

"Boyfriend?"

If she were here, my mom would say that James is

just being nice, showing an interest. For a second I try to see it that way.

But I can't. I look in his eyes and I know.

Daisy

I haven't spoken to Leo for three days. Not since our fight in the park. I miss him bad, but I don't know what to say. "You know, I actually didn't think you did it before we had the fight, but the way you flipped out on me makes me wonder."

I know on Friday lunch he hangs out with Tobin and those guys in the park. I'm wondering if I should head over there, when I hear, "Daisy?"

I turn, see Crowley smiling at me. Not a Crowley smile, but really smiling. Almost . . . human.

He says, "I was wondering if, later today, you could stop by my office," like I'd be doing him this big, big favor if I stopped by.

For a second I feel flattered. So this is what it's like to be one of *those* kids. Like maybe there's an award or scholarship I'm eligible for.

"Sure. What time?"

"Any time after three is fine. Great. Thank you, Daisy." And he walks off, grinning like I made his day.

I decide not to look for Leo. Maybe today after my Crowley meeting I'll call him, use it as an excuse to talk.

★

That afternoon when I go to his office, the door is closed. I can hear Crowley talking inside, and I listen for a second to see if there's someone else in there. "Yeah, I have a pretty fair idea." There's a pause. He's on the phone. I knock. "Hold on a minute. Yes?"

I open the door. Crowley nods, waves me in. "I have a student here, Frank. Call you back?"

Frank. Frank is Frank DiPesci, the principal.

"Yes, I certainly will. The moment I know."

He hangs up and I sit down. "Does the principal want the Ivy figures for this year?"

"What? Oh, no." Crowley laughs. "No, that was . . . something else. Always something. So." He puts his hands on the desk, leans in. "I'm, uh . . ." He sits back in his chair. "Gosh, you know, this is tricky. This is a tricky thing."

I nod. "Okay."

Crowley frowns. "What I'm about to discuss with you I wouldn't . . . necessarily discuss with most students. It's sensitive. But you've always been an important part of Dewey, and well, let's face it"—Crowley smiles, a signal: *Real me here*—"you're a lot more mature than a lot of our kids. More mature and more intelligent. People here think a great deal of you, Daisy."

"Thanks, Mr. Crowley."

He looks surprised. "You didn't know that?"

I laugh. "Uh, no . . ."

"Oh, well, my bad, then. I should have made that

clearer a long time ago." The hands are back on the desk again. "So, Daisy, here's my problem."

All of a sudden I get it. This is Tory McEwan. I sit very still.

"As you know, one student came to me a few weeks ago and told me something . . ."—he shakes his head like he still can't believe it—"very upsetting. You know what I'm referring to."

"The SATs. The kid who cheated."

They must be talking to every kid who took the test in March, trying to find out if we know who it is. Who we think it is. Immediately I think of Leo. I'm really glad Mr. Crowley can't read minds. I am not saying anything.

Crowley nods. "Exactly. And as you know, we had hoped that that individual would come forward, that they would be honest enough to . . . well, that hasn't happened."

"They're probably pretty scared," I say, trying to offer him something, because I have no intention of giving him what he really wants.

"Yes, I imagine they are."

"You were a little intense in that meeting."

Crowley nods quickly. "I was." Then he looks me in the eye. "But this is a serious matter, Daisy. There are no secrets in this world. If colleges hear that one of our kids cheated—and they will—it casts doubt on all of our students. And I can't have that. It's not fair."

I think of Luisa. "No, it's totally not."

"No." Crowley's nods slow down. He's giving me time, an opening to say, "You know, the rumor is . . ."

More time.

Finally I say, "Look, I can't tell you who it is. Because I don't know. I really don't." I think of saying, "You know, we all pick who we think it might be, but that's because we don't like them, not because we know anything." But then Crowley will say, "Well, who do you think it might be?" and I'll be stuck.

Crowley's face goes blank. "You can't tell me."

"I really can't."

"Because you don't know."

"Right." Leo. He thinks it's Leo.

Crowley makes a face and looks away like he wants to say something really ugly. We're way past the "We think so highly of you, Daisy." It's weird when you've always known someone was evil, then you see it, and you think, *How are you in charge of anything? Don't people see what a piece of slime you are?*

Crowley looks up, laces his fingers so his hands are one fist on the table. "How do you want me to say this, Daisy? Your scores went up pretty dramatically."

Before I understand what Crowley is saying, I feel it. Everything I have ever known about this school, and the way it works, is suddenly revealed as true. If you are rich, you are fine. If you are not, you're screwed. Over and over it keeps slamming in my head: *No, no, no.* I don't even know what I'm saying no to.

Finally I manage, "I did not do this."

Crowley says evenly, "You can see why I have my doubts."

Yes, I think, *yes, I see why you have your doubts.* Because Jane is a movie star's daughter and Leo has money, and all the other kids who took the SATs in March, their parents give money to the school, and I'm just the dumb jock who shouldn't have done well, but I did, and it's easy to say I did it, and everyone will go, "Yeah, we knew it all along."

I look in Crowley's eyes, and I swear he knows I did not do this. He knows exactly what he's doing. And he doesn't care.

I have never in my life hated anyone this much.

"I did not do this."

"It's something we need to talk about, Daisy."

"I did not do this." My voice rises, and I see Crowley wince. Good, I hurt him.

And all of a sudden I know. That's how to fight him. Shout, yell, do anything but go quietly. I get to my feet and scream, "I didn't do this."

I can hear people murmuring outside in the hallway. Good, let them hear. I throw open the door as violently as I can. Crowley gets up. "You are not leaving."

"Screw you," I scream. "Screw you. I did not do this, and you can *not* say I did."

There's a big crowd now. Mrs. Petrie from the middle school, Mr. Zercak, the school nurse. Even Mrs. Lillian, the front-desk secretary. They're all staring.

From the safety of his office Crowley says, "I'll be calling your parents, Daisy."

And somehow the thought that he can call my parents and tell them this lie, that they will have to choose between believing me, who they'll want to believe, and believing him, who they'll think they should, makes me howl. I shut my eyes and try to howl the walls down, the school down, the whole ugly, rotten place.

MAX

When you hear your best friend has been accused of cheating on the SATs, you don't bother with the phone. You just go straight to their house.

LEO

Friday night I hear the e-mail ping, and think, *Finally.* I go to my desk and read:

> From: KYGal@earth.net
> To: leo345@world.com
> Wow, just heard! Did you have any clue? Didn't seem like you did when we talked about it. Or were you just protecting the g-friend?
>
> I heard she really tore the place up when Crowley told her they knew she did it. Went into total denial mode. Very smart, I

think. Unless they've absolutely got the goods on you, deny, deny, deny.

Anyway, if you want to talk, I'm around.

For a split second I think, *Why didn't Daisy tell me?* Then I realize, that's absolutely not what I should have thought. But I did. And I'm not sure what it means that I did.

I pick up the phone, try to call Daisy. But the line is busy.

And even though I know it could be a million things, even her parents talking to the lawyers, I have this gut sense that it's Max.

Jane

When I hear, I can't believe it. It's so incredibly wrong. One of those things where they look at the score, but not the person at all.

I feel like this whole thing is my fault. Like I should never have told Daisy to care about the SATs in the first place. She's right: They're total and utter garbage. This finally proves it.

I call her, and when she says, "Hello?" I can tell she's been crying.

"I just want you to know I think they're total jerks," I say. "And they're not going to get away with it."

She laughs a little. "Thanks."

"Are you okay? Do you want me to come over?"

"That's really sweet of you. But my parents are here, and Max. We're working out our defense strategy."

"Well, if you need anything . . ."

"I totally will. Thanks, Jane."

As I hang up I wish I weren't so useless. That there was something real I could do. Then I think: *There is, Jane. There are lots of things you could do—but you don't have the guts.*

On Monday I'm standing on the sidelines in gym when I overhear two girls talking about it. The reason I listen at all is that one of them says, "I always thought she did it."

"You did?" says the other.

"Yeah, 'cause it made sense. Like, she's going out with Leo—Mr. Total Operator—and it's not like she's a genius, you know. Then all of a sudden she does pretty well on her SATs? Didn't make sense."

"So, you think Leo was in on it?"

"So would *not* be surprised."

I want to yell, "Shut up!" Want to yell, "You don't have the first clue! You're evil, nasty people and all you want to do is rip people apart, when you don't even know them. What you're saying doesn't even make sense."

But you'd have to have guts to do that. You'd have to be someone like Daisy. And I'm not someone like Daisy.

MAX

Matt Locke is the first person who has the guts to actually ask me.

"So, man, did she do it?"

We're in the newspaper office, trying to figure out the front page. Without looking up from the screen, I say, "Give me a break."

"She says she didn't?"

"Yeah, and I know she didn't. For one thing, I know what she got, and if she paid Tory to get her that score, she should have demanded her money back."

"Maybe she told her not to make it too high. Otherwise it'd be a clue. Didn't she, like, totally bomb out on the PSATs?"

I think: *How do we know all this crap about one another? And why do we care?*

I get up from the chair, say, "You figure this out," and leave the office.

Daisy

My mom was like, "You don't have to go to school." But I said, "I'm not letting them stop me."

I'm over the whole crying thing. Now it's like, *Oh, yeah? Prove it.* Because they can't, so screw them. And I'm ready for whatever anybody has to say to me.

So when Hudson Parmentier whispers, "What's the going rate on a good score?" I say, "You will never know," and keep walking.

In the bathroom some girls give me a cool stare, the one that says, *You're trash, but we're too nice to say so.* I choose the snottiest one and fix my eyes on her. The next time she tries the stare, she gets me full force and looks away.

Still, it's a good thing Luisa finds me just before lunch, because I admit, by then I'm cracking up a little. Part of it is that Leo hasn't even called, but I don't tell her that. I feel stupid and pathetic enough.

She says, "You know, I knew this place was low, but I didn't know how low." She gives me a hug. "How are you?"

The thing that sucks about people being nice to you is you immediately get all weepy. At least, I do. I manage, "Okay."

"Want me to kill anyone for you?"

"Yeah, I have a list."

She laughs. Then we see Jane coming over. When she sees Luisa, she hesitates, but Luisa waves her over, says, "We were just headed out to lunch. Care to join us?" Which is really sweet of her because I know she's not into Jane.

We go to this old-people diner where nobody from school goes. Jane and Luisa get salads. I can't eat anything, so I order a bagel and pick at it.

Jane asks, "How were your parents?"

"Well, at first they were worried that somehow they'd made me do it by freaking me out over the money. They kept saying, 'We'll understand, but just tell us if you did this.' Of course I said, 'No.' We're meeting with Crowley on Friday."

Luisa says, "So, where's Leo?"

I sigh. I wish Luisa could be a little cooler about the whole Leo thing. I'm about to explain how this is all so ironic because I suspected Leo, and now I get it, how awful it feels to have people suspect you, when my cell buzzes.

"Hold on."

Jane

You don't even have to ask who the call is from. You can tell from Daisy's face it's from Leo. Luisa and I glance at each other. We're both thinking the same thing: *Took his time.*

Also that we're both surprised we agree on anything.

It's weird. How nastiness brings you together with people so much faster. I guess because then you know you're dealing with what someone really thinks. As opposed to when they're being nice—and are usually lying.

LEO

All weekend I told myself, *You have to call Daisy.* And all weekend I answered myself, *Yeah, she could call you. She called Max fast enough.* Frankly, after that first call it was like, *Man, who needs this? If that's the person you call, fine, but don't expect me to fight my way through a crowd.* Also, I figured, *Okay, I'll just see her at school.*

Then at lunch I run into Kyra. She's all bright eyed, and I can tell immediately she wants the dirt. When she says, "How's Daisy doing?" I almost laugh, she's so obvious.

"She's cool, she's okay." Even though, how would I know?

Kyra looks skeptical. "God, I'd be falling apart."

"Not really her style."

"I don't know," says Kyra. "She was looking a little fragile when I saw her a few minutes ago with Luisa and Jane."

When Kyra says that, it's like, *Wait, Daisy . . . what the hell am I doing?*

And that's when I call.

Daisy

"So I thought you did it, and you thought I did it."

We're in my room. That's one thing I wanted for this discussion: my turf.

Leo says, "I didn't *really* think you'd done it. . . ."

"But sort of."

"Maybe . . . but only for some kind of protest."

"If I did it as a protest, I'd tell people."

"Yeah. You're right. You would." He looks at me like, *Is this over now? I really want it to be over.*

I really want this to be over too. We're this close to

being okay, but there's something I need to say before that happens.

"You thought if Crowley said I did it, then it must be true."

"No . . ."

"That Crowley was for real, and I wasn't." He hesitates. "Come on, you did."

I'm not trying to rub it in that Leo can be an Ivy wannabe. I'm just trying to show him that sometimes he believes that people who have power are smarter and better than those who don't. Thinking that way can really screw you up.

I'm not sure if Leo can admit that about himself. In a weird way it depends on how together we really are.

Then he says, "Yeah, maybe."

LEO

Mistake, right? Never actually admit something like that. The other person never forgets it and you're screwed entirely.

So why did I? Because at that moment I thought, *This is Daisy, you tell her the truth.* I don't know. Somehow, because it was her, I couldn't lie.

Now I'm waiting for her to kill me.

But instead she says, "So, what do you think now?"

"Crowley's wrong, man. I don't get it, but he is."

"Okay." She smiles, really smiles for the first time. "Okay." And amazingly, it seems to be.

Later I ask her, "So, how come you thought I did it?"

"I didn't. At first I was like, no way. But you were such a creep about it. It was like you were defending the person. I thought maybe because it was Kyra . . ."

When Daisy mentions Kyra, I feel guilty.

Guilt is stupid, Leo. Forget it.

But I can't forget it. I never told Kyra, "Daisy could not have done this." I didn't want to look stupid if Daisy had done it. Didn't want Kyra thinking I was dumb. Which annoys me—why do I care what Kyra thinks?

"She's hot for you, you know that," says Daisy.

Automatically I say, "She is not."

MAX

On the day of her second Crowley meeting Daisy and I are waiting for her parents on the steps of the school. A few kids on their way out say, "Hey, Daisy. . . ." They know she's meeting with the Big C. Everyone knows everything in this school—or they think they do.

A lot of people are absolutely sure Daisy did it. Jock, financial aid, it makes sense to them. But a lot of other people are like, "Daisy? What? No way." That makes me think that maybe if you're a decent human being, people remember that.

I ask, "What are you going to say? Anything?"

"I don't think I can speak. I'll just start screaming again."

"What are your parents going to do?"

She grinds the heel of her sneaker on the edge of the step. "They'll try and be polite. Not get in Crowley's face . . ."

"But they know you didn't do it, right?"

"Yeah, they 'know' it. But if Crowley has any so-called evidence, like someone who says they saw me or something, I don't know. They might cave."

I think of the Stubbses. I can't see them ever taking somebody's side against Daisy. No matter what she did, they'd be there for her.

I tell Daisy that, and she shrugs. "They feel really guilty about getting on me about the money."

Daisy

When I see my parents coming up the block, it hits me: We actually have to do this. All of a sudden I don't want Max to leave. Like, I want him to come in and sit with me while my parents and Crowley fight this all out.

He says, "So, you'll call me. . . ." Which reminds me there will be a time after this meeting, a time when I'm just going on with the rest of my life. I give Max a big hug, say, "Yeah, like, the second this is over."

Then my parents and I go inside.

As we walk through the lobby my mother puts her arm around me. At first I'm like, *Oh, don't.* But my mom's like, *I'm doing this whether you want me to or not.* Basically, she's saying she's in control.

All of a sudden I think about how rotten this year has

been for her. How she has to go to school *and* work. How she's the one holding it all together while her husband doesn't have a job and her kid is yelling about college all the time.

I make a vow that I will never ever be mad at my parents about money again.

When he comes out of his office, Crowley's all somber, like a doctor who's going to give us bad news. As we take our seats he slithers back behind his desk and says, "Thank you for coming in to discuss what must be a difficult subject."

My mother glances over at my father. He nods slightly. Turning back to Crowley, my mother says: "This isn't difficult at all, Mr. Crowley. It's not difficult because we have no intention of 'discussing' this with you. We know our daughter. We know she didn't do this. What we would like is an explanation from you as to how you could possibly think she did."

I think: *Wow. Holy crap.*

I mean, I thought my parents would be on my side, but I didn't expect my mom to go for Crowley's throat.

My dad says, "What led you to think of Daisy?"

"The discrepancy between her PSAT scores and her SAT scores was the first thing that stood out."

"Daisy worked extremely hard to get her scores up," my mother said. "So it's hardly surprising that they improved."

Yeah, Mom, I think, *unless you're like Crowley, who*

*thinks the SATs measure natural intelligence and not just test-
taking skills.*

"I had other reasons to believe Daisy was involved,"
says Crowley.

"Such as?" says my dad.

Crowley doesn't say anything for a moment. I realize
he's trying to decide how to put it, so I say, "Did someone say I did this?"

Crowley looks up. "An individual drew certain
things to my attention."

My mom jumps in. "The girl who took the money?"

"No," says Crowley. "Another student. I can't give
you a name."

"Well," says my dad slowly, "if all you have is an
improved SAT score and the word of someone who
won't even come forward publicly, I'd have to say you
don't have very much at all."

"I never said I 'had' anything," says Crowley smoothly.
"Please remember, this is just a discussion, Mr. Stubbs."

"You didn't call it a discussion when you hauled my
daughter into your office."

"I never told Daisy I thought she had done it," says
Crowley. "I only wanted to talk to her about it. But she
became extremely upset. . . ."

I'm thinking furiously. Did Crowley ever say "I know
you did it, Daisy"? Ever?

No, he didn't. He was too smart to say it.

I look at Crowley watching my parents. Waiting to

see if there's any sign that they think I did it, that they'll crack, try to work out a deal. That way he has his cheater, the parents are happy, the scandal's over: "Oh, it was just Daisy. You know, kids like that, what can you expect?"

Problem solved. Never mind who actually did it.

I say, "So basically, you thought, *Oh, I'll try and freak her out and see if she breaks down and confesses?*"

Crowley ignores this, telling my dad, "If a student comes to me with reliable information, it's my job to follow it up. This is a very important matter. It affects the standing of our entire senior and junior classes. However, I'm inclined to agree that in view of Daisy's excellent reputation at Dewey, we can conclude that the individual who gave me her name must have been mistaken."

"Or malicious," says my mom.

Crowley looks from my dad to my mom. Back again. They're not going to crack, and he knows it.

"Let's leave it at wrong," says Crowley.

Afterward we all go out to a Chinese restaurant because, as my mom says, we're too tired to lift a plate. While my parents order drinks, I go and call Max.

"Someone told Crowley I did it."

"Oh, man. Did he give you any idea who?"

"None. I have a few ideas, but you know what's weird?"

"What?"

"I don't even care. I'm so glad it's over, I don't want to spend another second thinking about this."

I hang up with Max, then start to call Leo. Then I remember my parents are waiting, and decide I'll call him when I get home.

I go back to the table, where my mom says, "Your father and I are wondering how rich we could get if we sued."

My dad is grinning, so I know they're not serious. I say, "Well, that'd be one way to pay for college."

"Don't you worry about college," says my mom fiercely.

I play scared and put up my hands. "Okay. Thanks."

Then: "I mean it. Thanks."

My parents look at me. "For what?"

Our egg rolls arrive, and we start eating. As I spread mustard on mine I think, *What it comes down to is this: My parents know me.*

I think about that for a moment. How important it is to have people who know you, who will fight for you. How a lot of kids don't have that.

And somewhere in me I feel something new. A sense of what might be that goes way beyond the SATs or college. A sense of what my actual life could be about. I don't have it in words yet, and I'm not ready to say definitely, "This is my future."

But all of a sudden big-name schools and high scores really don't matter—because something else matters more.

Jane

"I can't believe it."

Ever since Daisy told me that someone anonymously accused her, it's all I've been able to say. "I can't believe it."

"Do you think it was the cheater?" I ask her. We're in the cafeteria, so I keep my voice down, even though it's almost two and the place is pretty much empty.

"You kind of assume, right?" Daisy looks troubled. "I mean, I'm sure I annoy people, but I can't believe anybody would do that just to be nasty."

"Well, it's not like it's so much better if the person did it to cover up what they did."

"No, but that's at least a reason."

I ask, "What does Leo think?" Leo always seems to know how these things work.

"What I think: Thank God it's over."

LEO

Of course, it's not over.

People still want to know who the cheater is. They still want the person punished. Some people still think Daisy did it, that it's all a big conspiracy to hush it up because her parents would sue otherwise.

That stupid list in the bathroom is still there. I try to avoid that particular stall. Now after my name someone's written, WHEN ARE THEY GOING TO CATCH ON TO THIS GUY? I'm like, *Catch on to what?*

When I run into Kyra in the library, she says, "I guess it's good news and bad news, huh?" I shake my head. "Well, like, good that your girlfriend's off the hook. Bad that you're back to being suspect number one."

MAX

Of the letters we get at the newspaper now 99.9 percent are about the cheater. (The .1 percent are about more vegetarian meals in the cafeteria.) Most of them say the same thing: "When are they going to get this guy? Why haven't they gotten him yet?"

Some of them get personal. Like, seriously nasty. Girls evening the score on guys who dumped them, people accusing people just because they're ugly or fat ("You're telling me that tub of lard could even sit through the SATs? They'd break the seat, man!"). Lots of stuff about anyone who gets a time dispensation because of eyesight is cheating anyway, and what are we going to do about that?

Meanwhile, the person who actually did it is just sitting back and watching it all unravel.

Daisy

I'm in the bathroom looking for my hairbrush when I find an envelope in my book bag. Someone's written on it: PLEASE DELIVER TO MAX BASTOGNE AT THE *DEWEY DISPATCH*.

The envelope is sealed. But I can tell there's a letter inside. I don't recognize the handwriting at all. It's all caps, black ink. Can't tell if it's a man or woman or what.

I think: *Who would give me a letter to give to Max?*

Also, *I better not open it.* With things so crazy right now, you don't know what people could do.

Still. I have the weirdest feeling it's from the cheater.

MAX

No one else is around when Daisy shows up at the newspaper office late that afternoon. At first she just hands me the envelope. Then she says who she thinks it's from.

"Seriously?"

She nods.

I turn the envelope over. "You think I should open it?"

"Yeah. I mean, I don't think it's poison or anything."

I sit down on the table, start ripping the envelope open. I should probably be more careful, think about fingerprints or something. Inside is a letter. Plain, dumb white paper. I read the first four words: *I am the cheater.*

Behind me Daisy whispers, "This is . . ." She gets up, walks away. "I can't deal with this." She turns around. "Did they sign it? Do they say who they are?"

"Wait . . ." I read.

> I am the cheater.
> You don't know who I am, but you should
> know who I am not. I am not Daisy Stubbs.
> I know you don't know who I am,

because I hear you talking about me and you never know I am right there listening. I hear everything you say. That I am disgusting. That I'll get what I deserve. That you hope they find me out and I never get into any college anywhere.

Guess what? I don't care.

You all hate the test. You all say it doesn't mean anything about who you are as a person. Well, if that's true, why do you care if someone took the test for me? If you all hate it so much, why didn't you do the same? Why did you take the test at all?

Because you're sheep.

Maybe I am too.

Or maybe I am a wolf in sheep's clothing.

No signature. The only thing at the bottom is "Please print this."

LEO

Of course, that Monday when the article comes out, everyone has a complete freak attack. Forget classes. The cheater's letter is the only thing that's going on at Dewey. In Twentieth-Century History, Mr. Amory says, "People, I need you all to put the newspaper away."

I run into Max in the hallway and say, "Congrats. Quite the scoop."

"Yeah, everyone keeps asking me how I got it. I had this whole big meeting with Crowley this morning. He was *muy* pissed off I didn't bring it to him first."

"Screw him."

"Exactly."

It's weird to agree with Max about Crowley. I kind of envy him being able to sit there and tell Crowley, "No, I cannot reveal my sources."

To get it out of the way, I say, "I know Daisy's happy you ran it on the front page."

Max smiles. He didn't need me to tell him Daisy was happy about it.

Jane

The day the article comes out, I look everywhere for Daisy. I have to know how she feels about it. It must be wild, being on the front page of the newspaper like that.

But she's nowhere to be found.

Finally I find Leo talking to Max in the hallway. Leo explains, "She ditched. Didn't want to deal with the whole scene."

"Do you think she'd mind if I called her?" I look at both of them; I never know which one to ask about Daisy.

Max says, "Sure." After a second Leo nods.

I call her on my cell the second I leave school. She sounds a little cautious when she picks up, but when she hears it's me, she says, "Hey, Jane. What's it like there?"

"Oh, insane. Good thing you missed it. Crowley was looking everywhere for you."

"Definitely good thing I missed it."

"When did you get the letter?"

"Thursday afternoon. Max rewrote the whole front page right before it went to the printer."

"Wow, that's great."

"Yeah, that's my Max." She pauses. "So, what are people saying? Do they still think I did it?"

"No," I say quickly, not telling her about those few jerks who think she wrote it. Or that Max wrote it for her, which is nuts. "I think everyone gets it now. Nobody ever really thought you did it anyway."

"Oh, sure they did." She laughs. "Miss Big Mouth ends up cheating on the test? They loved it. Now they can all go back to figuring out who it is."

"Yeah, seriously." The connection's breaking up a little, so I sit down on a bench outside the park. "Do you ever wonder who ratted you out?"

"Yeah, sometimes. Mostly I'm like, *Waste of time.*" Daisy says, "Actually, I feel sorry for the cheater."

"*Why?* I wouldn't."

"I don't know. It seems so sad, someone caring enough about that number to cheat. And hey, they went to a lot of trouble to get me off the hook, so they're all right by me." She hesitates, then says, "I'm just glad we don't suspect one another anymore."

"What, like . . . us?"

"Yeah. I don't know about you, but I was freaking out, thinking, *Is it Leo? Is it Max?* You know, at one time I thought maybe your mom . . ." Embarrassed, she says, "I mean, you probably thought I did it at one time."

"No. I never did."

And it's true, I never did.

Daisy

You think it's never going to happen, but eventually people do stop talking about it. And even when they do talk about it, they can laugh. Now it's all about graduation; everyone's starting to figure out that a lot of people won't be back next year.

Then there are the parties. For, like . . . everything. The coach and I are putting together a big awards dinner for the team—even though, as per usual, we didn't win any big awards. But with Luisa leaving, we want to do something special.

The graduation bash, the newspaper party that Max gets me into, the junior party . . .

One afternoon I say to Jane, "You should cater the junior party."

She grins. "Hm. Let me think about the menu. Uh, beer. More beer. Some . . . beer. Oh, and how about a little beer?"

I laugh. "Well, it'd be good to have something to wash down."

"Hm. Salmon canapés and some crudités, perhaps?"

"Okay, maybe just the beer."

Lately Jane's got a wicked sense of humor going. I don't know what it is, but she's really up. I remember the girl who always hid behind her hair at the start of the year and think, *Wow, someone's changed.*

I say, "You bringing a date?"

"Yeah, right."

"Jane, come on, now. Our goal for next year—get you a guy."

She smiles like, *Yeah, yeah.* "Are you and Leo coming together?"

I hesitate. "Yeah. Whole thing's kind of out in the open now, so . . ."

But Jane caught it. "What?"

"No, nothing." I don't want my business all over school. But since I know I can trust Jane, I say, "We're not getting along that well right now."

"The end of the year is pretty stressful," she says.

I see Kyra Fleming come into the lunchroom. Try not to hate her, because I have no reason to hate her—I think.

"Yeah," I say to Jane. "Probably just end-of-year boogie-woogies."

LEO

I know Daisy thinks it's my fault we're getting on each other's nerves. But maybe she could get it that she hasn't been around that much.

I mean, the girl always has something going on. This dinner for Luisa, coffee with Jane . . .

And of course, Max. Can't ever forget Max.

Like the other day, I was trying to set up something for summer. I thought maybe we could go to New Haven together, check out the campus. She was like, "Why? I'm not going to Yale."

"Yeah, well, I am. Hopefully."

She got quiet. Started picking at the loose threads on her jeans—which is what she does when she's upset. "Do we have to do this now?"

Have to? Hello, I want to. "What 'this'? I'm talking about a stupid trip to Connecticut."

"Yeah, I know, but . . ." She looks at me like she's waiting for me to say something.

But I don't know what to say, so she ends up going, "Forget it."

MAX

One weekend my dad says, "I'm thinking over the summer you should do another round of SAT prep."

I'm trying to work on an article for the last issue of the newspaper. We always do a list of the year's highlights in a funny way—or at least we try to. When my dad brings up prep, I say, "Maybe." By which I mean "No," but I don't want to get into it right now because this article's due Monday.

He's quiet for a moment. "Only, I looked at the median scores for Columbia, and . . ."

"And I don't quite make it, I know." I hold up my laptop a little. "I've really got to do this, Dad."

That gets him quiet for another few seconds. But then he says, "It's just that if we're serious"—*We?*—"about Columbia, then we need to be thinking about these issues."

I type. "Well, I'm not sure I am serious about Columbia."

"What do you mean?"

I mean Columbia is in New York, and I'm not sure I want to stay in New York, because that probably means living at home, and you know what, Dad? I think maybe the most important thing I could ever get out of college is not being around you for a while.

But now is not the time to say that, so I tell him, "I'm not sure I want to be serious about anything right now, Dad. I've spent the whole year being serious."

I think of something and type it in. "Right now I'm trying to be funny."

Jane

Obviously, I'm not going to cater the junior party. But I'm looking forward to it a lot more than I thought I would. Last year when I went to the sophomore party, Lily spent the whole time talking to some people I didn't even know and it was a total bore. She didn't even notice when I left. It's amazing what people don't see. Or think you don't see.

Like, Daisy doesn't think I noticed the expression on her face when Kyra Fleming walked by.

Like, Leo doesn't think anyone sees how he flirts with Kyra—even when he tries not to.

Or how Max thinks no one has a clue how much he liked Daisy. And how he's still waiting for her to figure it out about Leo and maybe about him, too.

I've decided I was wrong. I do see things correctly. In fact, there's a lot of stuff I see that other people don't. I used to think most people were too busy doing things to watch other people. But now I think I see things because no one thinks to hide stuff when I'm around. They assume I won't notice. Or I won't get it.

Or even if I did, who would believe me?

There's a lot I could tell people, if they'd only ask.

Daisy

One afternoon when I come home from school, I find my dad sitting at the kitchen table like always. But he doesn't have his usual cup of tea going, and the notes for his book aren't spread out all over the place. In fact, there's no mess anywhere.

But I don't think it's some kind of disaster, because my dad is smiling.

I say, "Okay, what's up?" My dad glances at the ceiling. "Ha, ha. Seriously."

"Got a phone call today."

"Yeah?"

"From an old friend of mine at Citizens Rights Watch."

"Uh-huh . . ." I can tell my dad is going to do this at his speed.

"Turns out his boss, the director, just quit."

"And?"

"And he was wondering if I might be interested in the job."

When I've stopped screaming, my dad makes me sit down and says, "It's not the best-paying job in the whole world. . . ."

"Who cares? It beats going to some boring office and doing stuff you don't care about for people you can't stand."

"Yes, it does. But it doesn't exactly solve our college money woes the way a job with a big firm would."

My dad looks at me, and I get it that if I say, "Yeah, what about college?" he might turn down the job, wait it out for something that pays better.

Do I want him to do that? I can't imagine asking someone not to do something they love.

So I say, "Yeah, but that's not what you're about. I mean, it'd be great if I'd gotten a perfect score and was all about grades and you didn't have to worry about scholarships because I was this ideal candidate that any college would love. . . ."

My dad laughs. "Any college I ran would take you."

"But that's not me." My dad puts his hand on mine. "We'll find some place."

He nods, then looks up. "Didn't tell you. The organization has summer intern programs. Kids go to Latin America, build houses, work with kids, do outreach. . . ."

"Are you *serious?*"

My dad starts to say, "And I may have a few connections . . . ," but he has to stop because I'm hugging him too hard.

That night I tell Leo, "I'm going to Guatemala."

"What?"

"Or Brazil. Or Honduras. I'm not sure yet."

Then I tell him about the program. "Isn't that amazing? I cannot wait. You know, all year I've felt like all you guys were going to these incredible places, and now . . . I am just so psyched."

All Leo says is, "Yeah."

"What?"

"No, that's great."

That's when I realize that hearing your girlfriend's ditching you for the entire summer isn't actually the best news.

"You definitely have to visit me," I say.

"Uh, no thanks. Not my idea of a perfect vacation spot."

I know I should be cool, that I just gave the guy ungreat news and need to be nice. But unfortunately, that's the kind of comment that makes me lose it. Like, what do you think, it's all bugs and disease?

"Actually, there are a lot of really gorgeous places. Like terrific beaches and mountains . . ."

"Yeah, yeah, yeah."

I try again. "There are, Leo. You'll see—"

But he interrupts, "You know, my dad's yelling for me, I got to go."

LEO

Let's just run this down here. Connecticut—no way. Can't even discuss it. Way too horrible.

Guatemala or Brazil or Honduras—that we're supposed to get all excited about.

Beaches. Mountains. Right. Because you know, there are no beaches or mountains in this country. There are no poor people in this country. Daisy's gotta go to a whole other country to find people to help. And screw everyone here.

I'm still fuming about it the next day in the library. Then I see Kyra sitting at the next table with an atlas and a guide to colleges in front of her.

She's taking notes as I slide in next to her. "Dear Diary: That Leo Thayer—"

"Is such a lame-ass jerk." But she smiles.

"What are you up to?"

"Just mapping out some college tours."

"Yale's in Connecticut." I point on the map.

"Gee, thanks. I'll remember that."

"When're you going?"

"Not sure yet. I don't really want to go with my parents? But I don't drive."

I think for a moment. Then say, "I drive."

In between Latin and AP chem Daisy waylays me in the hallway with two words: "New Haven."

"What about it?"

"Well, I was thinking. Depending on whether you're into the whole fall foliage thing, we could either go in early June or in September, right before school starts."

"That's okay, I got it covered."

"Or maybe do, like, a Halloween trip." She grins. "Spooky doings in New Haven."

"Really. It's okay." She looks disappointed, and for a second I think, *Screw Kyra*. But then I think, *You know what, Daise? Yesterday would have been nice.*

The Good, the Bad, and the Ugly—This
Year in Dewey History
by Max Bastogne and the staff of the
Dewey Dispatch
Cafeteria's Mushroom Burgers:
Coming to a McDonald's near you—not!
Mr. Weinblatt's Singing Tie: No article

of clothing should be made to sing "Happy Birthday."

Ms. Fornutale Has Her Baby: Dewey community welcomes future Nobel physicist.

Peter Haverford Sneezes Milk: "The horror, the horror!" says custodial staff.

Katie Cartwright Paints Herself Green for Earth Day: Gal's got style.

Luisa Martine's Winning Trey Against Cormier: So, we didn't get the trophy. We got Lu.

Peter Haverford Farts at Mime Show: The shot heard round the world

The Cheater

And to all our graduating seniors— GOOD LUCK! We will miss you!

Daisy

My first clue that I should not go to the junior party? When Leo tells me he's going to hang with Tobin first and he'll meet me there—you know, whenever.

He drops this little bombshell as we're coming back from the movies on Saturday, and I stop dead. Obviously something's going on.

Leo says, "What? You're the one who's always, 'Oh, let's not be a couple.'"

True, I am. I don't want to throw a big hissy over nothing. I want Leo to hang with his friends, and I want to hang with mine. But there's something weird here, and I'd feel better about not going to the party with Leo if I could figure out what it is.

For what feels like the ninetieth time, I say, "I'm really sorry about Connecticut."

Leo looks at me like I'm crazy. "Over it, seriously."

"We're cool?" I watch his face.

"Yeah." He shrugs.

If you ask that question and someone shrugs, you're not cool, no matter what they say. But I'm not going to get anywhere by pushing, so instead of getting into it, I say, "Great."

Then: "I'll ask Jane and Max if they want to go."

LEO

"I'll ask Jane and Max." Oh, wow, Daisy. Big surprise. Like you ever needed me to come anyway.

I'm really not trying to blow her off, that much I'm being honest about. Just, with finals after the whole cheater thing and the SATs, I'm in the mood to get a little crazy. And that's not something you can do with a girlfriend—no matter how into her you are.

I am still into her.

Jane

I'm psyched when Daisy asks me if I want to go to the junior party with her. "Just the ladies," she says. "We'll meet up at my house, okay?"

"Okay, great." Then I have to ask her where she lives, because I've never been there.

On the night of the junior party I get out the clothes my mom bought me to wear to one of her premieres. At first I think, *What happens if someone spills beer on this?* Then I think, *So what? I'll buy another.*

I never think like that, like someone with money. Maybe it's time I did. Maybe I'd have more fun. Like Daisy saying I'm pretty; I never act like it, I never think it. But maybe I should.

When I'm ready, I look in the full-length mirror. If it weren't me I was looking at, I'd say I look pretty good. I think of going to show my mom, then remember she's out tonight. Which is too bad. I wish she could see me like this.

Then I see the door open. See James. Who says, "Well. Where are we going?"

I don't know why, but I instantly feel guilty, as if I put this stuff on so James could see me in it—when the exact opposite is true. I want him out of my room so bad I feel like my heart's going to explode. And yet I also feel like, *You put it on.*

I say, "A party. And I'm really late, so . . ."

He nods. "You look very nice." Like I asked him how I look. But I didn't. I didn't ask.

Then he shuts the door, says, "Jane, can I ask you something?"

I make a little move toward the door. "I am actually late."

"Okay, just one thing. Why do you have a problem with me?"

"I don't . . . have a problem with you."

"Yes, you do. And I'd like us to work it out."

I stare at the floor. I don't want to look at him, don't want to see him looking at me.

I hear him say, "You know, I tried, I've really have tried with you . . ."

Tried to keep my hands off you. Tried not to watch you. But it doesn't work, Jane. It just doesn't work.

I try to edge around him. "Fine, whatever . . ."

"I'd like us to talk about it."

Let's talk about it, Jane. And then when we've talked about it, we can actually do it. What do you say, Jane?

What do I say? I'm saying it right now, screaming it. *Why don't you listen?* I'm screaming, *Stop looking at me! You think it's all nice, all compliments. You're so pretty, Jane, just like your mother, Jane. I'm just looking, Jane, what's wrong with that? But you don't just look; you want and judge and decide—and it has nothing to do with me. I don't want it, but you make it the only thing I can think about. Everything else just gets . . . blotted out.*

I want to disappear. I want to disappear.

And the door is the only way I can do that. I grab the doorknob, pull hard so the door slams into him. That, he didn't expect. For a second he looks at me very differently. Then he steps back, and finally, finally, I can get out.

I don't bother with the elevator. I don't want him catching me in the hall. Instead I run down the stairs. All fifteen flights.

MAX

Freshman and sophomore parties are lame. But the junior party is a whole different scene. Seniors deign to come, and all the lower classes want in so they can hang with the new seniors.

Which is why by the time I get there, it's a complete mob scene. We're having the party in a space made up of three big rooms: an entry hall, a dance floor, and a quiet room. We were supposed to be here at nine, but you can tell this party's been rocking for a while. As I make my way through the crowd it seems like a million people come up to me and say, "Loved your piece, man," "I was there when Haverford spewed, that was hilarious," "I forgot Mr. Weinblatt's tie!" Luisa gives me a big hug for mentioning her.

It's weird when people decide that you are good at something and all they want to do is tell you that.

Normally I'm not big on the whole party thing. But tonight, somehow, the noise and craziness of it matches my mood. Like, *We're free, man. We're seniors.*

Daisy

I have to laugh when I see Max surrounded. He never gets it, how great people think he is. Kind of hard to ignore now.

I look over at Jane. She should be pretty hard to ignore herself. From the neck down she looks incredible. But you look at her face, and it's the same old not-there, spacey Jane. And that's how she's been all night.

On the cab ride over I said, "What's up? You seem blue."

"I'm okay." She was sitting in the far corner, staring out the window.

I nudged her. "Hello, party time! The year from hell is over!" But she just retreated farther into the corner.

"Hey, Daisy . . ." Charles Tepper comes over, lifts me up in a big hug. "Next year we're going to do it, right, babe?"

"You mean the team, right, Charles? Hey, you know Jane?"

While Charles tries to talk to Jane, I make my way over to Max. As I go, there are a hundred people saying, "Hi," "Hey, can't believe we made it," "We're seniors, whoo!"

Not one of them is Leo.

But that's okay.

LEO

"Tobin, we should go, man."

"Yeah, soon." He takes another hit of vodka.

We're hanging in the park with a few other guys, drinking out of brown paper bags. The whole scene is a little skeevy bum for my taste, but how do you hide a bunch of drunken lacrosse players from your parents? So the park it has to be.

I check my watch. I want to be late, but not too late. Want to give Daisy a little room, let her see what it feels like. Then maybe she'll say, "You know, being without Leo isn't the greatest thing in the world."

Tobin nudges my arm with the bottle. "Time to drink. You got to catch up."

Jane

I don't have the first clue what to say to Charles. I think his name is Charles, it was hard to hear with all the noise. And of course, Daisy's long gone.

I ask, "So, how do you know Daisy?"

"Uh, go to the same school?" Which is code for "You're an idiot."

We stand there for a few moments. Then Charles says, "So, your mom's Julia Cotterell, right?"

I nod, look around the room.

MAX

A guy could do a lot worse than standing in between Daisy Stubbs and Luisa Martine. Even if they are both taller than me.

I'm actually high enough to tell them that, and they laugh. Luisa looks down at herself, then slaps my arm. "Yeah, you got the best view in the house."

"Perve," says Daisy.

"Totally," says Luisa. Then she asks Daisy, "Where's your guy?"

Which I've been wondering too but didn't have the guts to say.

"Guys' night," says Daisy. "He'll be here."

"Chugging in the park," says Luisa disdainfully. "How elegant."

Daisy gives her a look and Luisa changes the subject, saying to me, "Hey, I thought in the last issue of the paper you would reveal the name of the cheater."

I laugh. "Would have if I'd known it."

"See, I had this whole theory that they signed the letter, but Crowley said you couldn't say who it was because the school would be sued or some such thing—but that at the end of the year you'd print it in big letters on the front page."

"They didn't sign it, believe me."

Daisy

I'm sitting back in the conversation, trying to get over Luisa's little dig, when I see Kyra Fleming. She's near the door, hanging with some other Ivies.

And if she thinks I don't see her glancing at the door every ten seconds, and if she thinks I don't know who she's waiting for, no way is she smart enough to get into Yale.

LEO

I'm not gone. I know when I'm gone, and I'm not there yet. As opposed to Tobin, who is totally wasted. Like, the guy can barely walk up the stairs to the floor where the party's being held. His feet keep slipping. I don't know why they always have these things in old, rickety buildings where you have to walk up a million steps to get there. Doesn't it occur to them that some people might be trashed?

Not that I'm trashed. I purposely did not get trashed, because I knew if I did, it would piss Daisy off.

I think: *You know what? Screw Daisy. Who's she to judge?*

But I'll pretend I didn't hear that.

Jane

I'm just about to tell Charles I need to go to the bathroom, when I hear a huge roar coming from the other room, people shouting, "Yo, Tobin," and, "Le-o."

I say, "I think my friends are here, excuse me."

MAX

Most people just walk through doors. They don't parade through them like a pack of Roman generals who just kicked the crap out of Gaul.

But most people aren't on the lacrosse team.

Of course, neither is Leo, who's grinning and slapping hands with everyone like he personally scored every winning goal this year. *You don't even play,* I think at him. *You don't actually do anything, you just hang around people who do things and soak up their attention.*

I look over at Daisy, who's talking to Luisa. She has

to know Leo's here, but she doesn't seem to be in a big rush to get to him.

Which is good.

Daisy

Okay, Max, quit checking me out. I am not going to run over there and throw my arms around Leo, so chill.

Luisa glances at Leo, raises an eyebrow: *You want to say hi?*

I smile. "It's okay. He can find me."

Of course, to do that, he's going to have to get past Ms. Kyra Fleming, who actually has thrown her arms around him. Ms. Fleming has been downing cheap red wine all night.

I bet her breath stinks something fierce.

LEO

There are rules to everything. You can go this way, but not that. You only have a certain amount of time to make your decision. And once you've made your move, you can't take it back. No backsies.

I am very, very good at knowing what the rules are. Which is how I know I have a certain amount of time to get to Daisy before we get to the "I'm sorry" stage.

"You are so late, mister," Kyra is telling me.

"Yeah," I tell her, "look, I'll catch you later, okay?" I

step around her, head toward Daisy. Who, of course, is with my two favorite people in the whole world: Max and Luisa.

I give Daisy a kiss. She kisses me back, but the message is *Okay, that's a start. . . .*

And I'm like, look, I got here under the time limit, and we both know it. I blew off Kyra, and we both know it. I am not trashed, I have broken no rules here. So give me a break.

Jane

From the edge of the room I can see them: Daisy, Leo, Max, and Luisa. And all of a sudden I see what the group should be.

There is no hole in this group. Everyone fits perfectly. Luisa is friends with Daisy. She and Max like sports. And she is confident enough to stand up to Leo.

Luisa says something and they all laugh. Then Max says something else and they all laugh harder.

No one is saying, "Hey, where's Jane?"

MAX

"Where's Jane?"

Okay, I admit, I don't say that because I actually care where Jane is. I do, a little bit. But primarily I say it because it looks like Daisy's settling right back in with Leo—even though he made her come to this thing alone, even though he's drunk, and even though he let Kyra Fleming crawl all over him—and I want to distract her.

It works. Daisy immediately says, "Oh, my God, I left her with Charles."

Luisa laughs. "With Charles?"

"Well, he's sweet and cute. I don't know." She looks back at the other room. "I should go get her."

Leo says, "She's a big girl, leave her alone."

"I'm just going to tell her where we are," says Daisy.

"She'll figure it out if she wants to," says Leo. "Come on, don't . . ."

But he doesn't finish. Daisy says, "Don't what?"

Luisa tries to break in. "Guys, let's not—"

"No," says Daisy, "don't what?"

Leo's head sways over his beer. He looks like a stupid kid who's been caught shoplifting. He mumbles, "Rescue everybody."

And that's it for Daisy, who's gone.

Daisy

Screw him. Screw him. *Screw him!*

Do not tell me what not to do. Do. Not.

Did I tell you, "Don't get trashed with Tobin in the park"? No.

Did I tell you, "Keep away from that cheap-ass whore, Kyra Fleming"? No.

And now you're telling me . . . don't? I don't think so.

LEO

I'm not going after her. No way.

And I'm not hanging with Luisa and the shrimp, looking at me like, *You're a piece of dung.*

I spot Tobin and Kyra headed toward the dance room. Darkness and too loud music seems like a very good thing right now.

I say, "Excuse me," and split.

MAX

As we watch Leo head toward Tobin and Kyra, Luisa says, "Is this going to get nasty?"

I say, "Hope not."

But I wonder if that's true. If I really don't secretly want things to turn nasty. Because they are already. . . .

So why shouldn't it be obvious to everyone?

Jane

I should just go. Leave. Disappear. They'd never even notice I was gone.

I'm checking to see if I have enough money for a cab on my own—forget splitting one with Daisy—when Daisy comes in from the other room. From the way she's walking, I can tell she's really angry.

Gee, Daisy, have another fight with Leo? Bet you did. So of course now you want to hang out with me. Not when everyone's having fun. But when you're annoyed at each other, then it's, "Hey, where's good old Jane? Jane who always listens."

Or did Max decide he wanted to flirt with me again? Even though I'm not you? Well, even if I'm only second best, I'm at least okay to make you jealous.

I know it wasn't Leo who asked where I was. Leo's never really liked me. He just wanted to meet my mom—got stuck with me instead.

Did any of you think, just once, I might have something I want to talk about? Problems of my own? And that you don't have the first clue?

Daisy

Jane is in the quiet room. There's always one at every party, the place where kids who don't drink and are too scared to dance hang out and talk until they leave early. It's the place couples go to have arguments, where people pass out. At this party it's pretty empty; everyone wants to go crazy tonight. In fact, Jane and I are the only ones in here. There are windows that go all around the room, and they've put benches against the wall so you can sit and look out.

Jane's sitting on one of the benches. From the look of it, Charles is long gone. I wonder how long she's been on her own, and feel guilty.

I say, "Hey, everyone's waiting. Come and dance."

Jane shakes her head. "That's okay. I'm probably going soon."

I sit down on the bench next to her. "What's wrong?

You've been down all night." She doesn't say anything, so I guess. "I'm sorry I left you with Charles."

She looks at me. "No, you're not."

"I am."

She looks out the window. "You totally forgot about me."

If I'm honest, I have to admit this is a little true. I want to say, "You're right, I was obsessing about Leo. I'm really sorry, please come and dance. . . ."

When Jane says, "You're just users," I'm so shocked I don't know what to say.

Jane goes on. "You look at me, and you're like, *Ooh, movie star's kid. Julia Cotterell's daughter*—don't lie. *Yeah, she's kind of boring, but wow, you can get into some okay parties with her. And she has sort of a cool house.* But what you don't get? What none of you get? Is that all that means nothing to me. It has nothing to do with who I am. It's like you're talking about someone I don't even know."

She's standing up now, yelling. "Do you have any clue how much you don't know about me? Do you have any clue what goes on in my life? What it feels like to have someone after you and no one believes you? They just think you're crazy? And all the while you're like, *Wait, I know. I know this is happening.*"

"Jane . . ." I reach out, but she pulls away violently, sits far away from me on the bench.

Then she says, "I mean, you're all so stupid you didn't even have a clue it was me."

LEO

"How's it going with Miss B-ball?" Kyra smiles up at me on the dance floor.

"Can we not talk about Daisy?"

"Sure," she says. "No problem."

Then: "So, you never told me."

"What?"

"Your score."

I tell her. She smiles. Then tells me her score.

I say, "Congratulations. You win."

MAX

"Seriously," says Luisa, "you must have some clue about who it really was. You're a smart guy."

"Seriously, I don't. I had all kinds of theories, but none of them were right."

"Maybe they were and you just don't know it." She sips her beer. "You thought Leo."

"Sure. Everybody did."

"But you studied with him. You would know."

"I don't think we'll ever know."

Luisa looks like she's going to say something, when the music in the other room switches to something dumb, and a whole bunch of people come pouring into the room. Among them, Leo and Kyra. Who look like they crossed the No Touch Zone a long time ago.

Luisa takes one look at them and says, "Gettin' nasty."

Jane

What's funny is I meant to tell Daisy about James. Like, "Yeah, you think you're so sensitive, such a good friend. Well, here's what's really going on. . . ."

But at the last second I couldn't. It's just not something I can tell.

So instead I told her the other thing she didn't know: that I was the cheater.

The more I think about it, the funnier it gets. Particularly the expression on Daisy's face. Her mouth is literally hanging open.

Not to be mean, but she looks really stupid.

Daisy

The second Jane says it, I think: *I should've figured this one out a long time ago.*

"So, you wrote the letter."

Jane nods. "I felt bad when Crowley blamed you. I didn't expect that. So I wrote the letter and put it in your bag at lunch." She giggles. "I think it was when you got up to get a juice."

I'm thinking everything and nothing at once. All

the anger, all the suspicion and jealousy. All the "It was
you, it was you. . . ."

And all the time it was Jane.

"Why?"

"I didn't want everyone thinking you'd done it."

"No, not that. *Why?*"

LEO

The second I see Max and Luisa glaring at me, I think,
Reverse engines, and drag Kyra back into the dance room.
Where nobody really knows what you're doing and
nobody gives a crap. At the far end there are two bathrooms. Every once in a while the door opens and the room
gets a splash of ugly yellow light, then goes dark again.

Most times people go in there alone. But sometimes
they don't.

MAX

I say to Luisa, "You want to dance?"

She shakes her head. "This is not our problem."

"I'm asking if you want to dance."

She sighs, gives me her hand.

Jane

Actually, it's hard to remember now, how I first got the
idea. I remember Daisy telling me we were all taking the
test in separate places. It really bothered me because I'd
somehow thought it would be like the group: We'd go

through it together. I thought, *We won't even know if we all take the test. Someone could just walk out, the way Daisy did that first day of prep. But we'd never know. One of us could just make up some score; we wouldn't have the first clue.*

But I really started thinking about it after the Valentine's party. My birthday. Because, I don't know, I was just so tired after that stupid party. I didn't want to do anything. The practice tests were torture, and after a while I was like, *Forget this.* The thought of having to go to this strange place and sit with all these people for hours and hours . . . it felt like a nightmare. And for what? So they can judge you, give you some stupid number?

And then Leo just gave me the idea. When he said about Tory, "Yeah, maybe it would help if she took them for you." I thought, *God, that'd be great. Someone to deal with all this crap.* It was never about the score. Not at all. I only asked Tory because I knew she needed money.

It was like a little test of the system. I thought, *This will prove it doesn't matter. This test truly has nothing to do with who you are. What better way to prove that than by getting someone to take it for you?*

Would anyone say, "Hey, you're not Jane Cotterell"?

No, because nobody cares who Jane Cotterell is. She's just another kid among millions taking the SATs.

All Tory needed was my ID. She didn't want to take it at school because she was worried someone would see. So Saturday morning we met a few blocks away from the testing place, and I gave it to her. "Here you go," I said. "Now you're me."

We agreed: Any hassle and she would leave immediately. But there was no hassle. They took one look at her ID—my ID—and said, "Go ahead." Because she has dark hair and is about the same height, everyone just accepted she was me. Or they didn't care.

It was weird, waiting for the test to be over. I couldn't go home. Everyone I knew was taking the test. I had nowhere to go. So I just walked for a while. I don't even remember where. I purposely didn't pick any kind of direction. I guess you could say I got lost.

Then an hour after the test was over, and we could be sure everyone was long gone, Tory and I met up at the same spot. She gave me my ID back and I gave her the money. She shoved it in her pocket as fast as possible, like someone was going to say, "Hey, you, what is that girl paying you for?"

I said, "Well, okay. Bye."

She nodded. "Bye." She started walking, but then she turned around. "Don't you want to know how you did?"

"Not really," I said.

Then she just ran.

I should have known, now that I think about it. She was so freaked out by the whole thing, I should have known she wouldn't keep her mouth shut. I was really pissed at her for that. Because that was sort of my plan all along. I was always going to tell.

But then my mom was so happy about it. She was all excited that she had this brilliant daughter. And she actually defended me to James, like, "Nope, I believe her now." And I didn't want to ruin that.

It was so wild, when everyone was talking about it. "Did you hear?" "I heard . . ." Everyone guessing who it was, if they'd come forward, why they did it. I would walk through the halls, sit in class, thinking, *Me, they're talking about me.* Only, they didn't have a clue. I guess I didn't want to ruin that, either.

Writing the letter as the cheater? That was great. It was like giving the whole school the finger.

Daisy

I say, "Are you going to keep the score?"

Jane shrugs. "I don't know. I mean, who cares, right? It doesn't really matter."

"Jane, you cheated! This is not something to go, 'Yay, me!' about." I think of Lu, one room away. "People are seriously pissed about this."

"Why?"

"Because you don't deserve that score," I tell her. "That's not your score." Then I realize: If Jane and I wanted to go to the same school, she might get in because of that score. . . .

For a split second I see everything that's bad about Jane. Her money, her famous mom, the way she can't get over any of it and asks you to feel sorry for her for having all this stuff. I see all this and I hate her guts.

While I'm hating her, Jane leaps off the bench and screams, "Are you kidding? Not my score? Give me a break, who *cares*? You're the one who said it was all a lie, a big joke, that it didn't have anything to do with anything. Now you're like, 'Oh, it matters. It's the most important thing you can do.'"

I feel myself go red. "I did not say that. I never said that."

"But you do think it matters," Jane says scornfully. "Now that *you* did okay."

"No, I . . ." I don't think that, do I? No, I don't. But I don't know what I do think.

Except that cheating sucks. What matters is what you do. And cheating is claiming you did something when you didn't, that you are something you're not.

Slowly, I say, "You know what, Jane? You are what you do. If you really did it to prove the test was a joke, you would've signed that letter, said, 'Yeah, that was me. I did it.'" I stand up, because I have to be away from her. "But you didn't. You just let the lie go on."

Jane

I can't believe Daisy is being such a jerk. I mean, I thought she would totally get it. I thought she of all people would see how funny it was. Particularly after I got her off the hook when everyone thought she was the cheater.

She thinks it's all about the score—like I care where

I go to college. I want to tell her, "You don't get it. My mom believed me, that's what counts. People were talking about me. Maybe that happens to you every day, but it sure doesn't happen to me."

Only, I can't quite get the words to go from my head—where they're way, way in the back—to my mouth. I can see them, in the distance, but I can't pull them forward, make them real.

Actually, nothing seems real right now. Like it's a movie, but all out of focus.

Maybe this is what happens when you pretend to be someone else. You're not you, you're not them, you're this ghost.

Only, nobody sees you.

Especially not Daisy. Who turns around and walks away.

I guess I should tell her not to tell anyone. . . .

But then I think, *Who cares?*

Daisy

Leo. I have to find Leo.

Leo will be able to make sense out of this. He will say, "Wow, what a spoiled, miserable little . . . let's kill her."

Or, "Man, poor Jane, she is one screwed-up chick."

Because I feel both those things so intensely, I'm not sure which one is the truth.

But Leo's not in the next room. Not outside on the stairwell. And I know he wasn't in the quiet room.

So where the hell is he?

LEO

Kyra stands on tiptoe, says, "You know, we could just get out of here."

Supposedly, Kyra's just whispering into my ear. But she's not, and we both know it. For one thing, you don't use your tongue that way to whisper.

Tell her to stop it, Leo.

Why? There's nobody here who gives a crap.

"You know what, Leo? I promised myself if I scored higher than you did, I'd give you a consolation prize. Want to guess what it is?"

Kevin comes reeling out of the bathroom. He leaves the door open, like, *Next . . .*

For a second I think, *Not cool. Not with Daisy here.*

Then Kyra tugs me toward the bathroom. And I stop thinking.

Which is, I think, what I wanted all along.

MAX

Well, here's a choice.

Do I tell Daisy I just saw Leo go into the bathroom with Kyra Fleming?

Or not?

I could ask Luisa, but she bailed a while ago, saying she had seen enough and if Daisy wanted to know the truth, she could figure it out for herself.

Some choices get made for you. At least, that's

what I tell myself when Daisy comes up to me and says, "Have you seen Leo?"

Daisy

Max hesitates, does this looking-around-the-room gesture. I'm like, *Great, everything's falling apart tonight.*

I say, "Let me guess. He's bombed out of his gourd."

"Uh, no." Max says it so quickly—like, "No, *that's* not what I didn't want to tell you"—I know something's up.

Some of the lacrosse guys have drugs going, so I say, "He's not doing anything seriously stupid, is he?"

"It depends on what you call seriously stupid."

"Max, come on."

He opens his mouth, then shakes his head. . . .

MAX

I say, "I'm not going to do this."

I try to walk away. Really, I do try, but Daisy blocks me. "You've basically said there's something going on, now you won't tell me what."

"That's right."

"Max, you're doing . . ."

But I never get to find out what I'm doing, because at that moment Leo and Kyra come bursting out of the bathroom. And it doesn't take a genius to figure out what they've been doing.

Daisy

Some things hurt a lot less than you think they will. When I see Leo with Kyra Fleming, I'm like, *You want that instead of me? Fine. Your loss.*

Not my fault if you got a serious attack of bad taste. Not my problem at all.

But thanks for putting me in a position where I get to watch Kyra smirking at me like, Look what I got. *That, I really appreciate.*

LEO

"Fine."

That's all Daisy says. I guess I'm more bombed than I thought, because I'm like, "What do you mean?" You know, how is this fine?

I ask her that, and she says, "I mean it's fine. Have fun."

Big proud woman. I know this scene. This is where I'm supposed to say, "Oh, baby, I'm sorry, please forgive me."

Give me a break.

Although I wish Kyra would quit hanging off me and giggling. It doesn't exactly help.

MAX

I tell myself, *This is good. This is what should have happened.*

Leo screwed up. Leo got caught.

Except what I forgot is how much this would hurt Daisy. I didn't figure on her having to stand here staring at her jerk of a boyfriend with another girl in front of most of the junior class. Sure, most of them are going to think Leo's an ass. But they're also going to think, *Damn, doesn't Daisy ever learn?*

I tell myself I didn't tell Daisy anything. Or if I did, in any way, it was better she knew.

Also—and I really hate myself for this—even if I didn't stop her from knowing, there's no way she'll blame me.

Daisy

What I really want right now is to be in Guatemala.

Actually, no, I take that back. It doesn't have to be Guatemala. It doesn't even have to be another country. Frankly, anywhere but here would do. Anywhere where Leo is not right in front of me, sulking 'cause he's busted, and everyone watching, going, *Ooh, what's Daisy going to do?*

Leave. That's what Daisy's going to do.

As I turn around I hear Leo sigh, "Come on, Daisy . . . ," which just makes me walk faster.

LEO

I'm supposed to go after her, right? Supposed to say, "Okay, wait up, nothing happened."

Only, I can't say that because a lot happened.

"It didn't mean anything." *Yeah, then, why'd you do it?*

Because . . .

Because sometimes you just want to get bombed and say, "To hell with everything," and mess it up completely—and that's exactly what you do.

Of course, Max goes right after her. As he does he looks back, and I swear I know exactly what he's thinking.

You don't do *anything, do you?*

MAX

It's the weirdest thing. When I look at Leo, all I can think is, *How did this get so screwed up?* Then I run to catch up with Daisy.

I fall right in line with her, thinking we'll just walk out the door together, but she says, "Get away."

Which I get, but I say, "Okay, but . . ." Because I don't want her walking through a lousy neighborhood on her own.

"I'm serious, Max. Get away. Leave me alone." She wipes her arm across her eyes. "This is so screwed—"

"I know," I say. "I really know."

"You don't know. You don't . . ." She takes a big, shaky breath. "I mean, you don't even know about Jane."

"What about Jane?"

Daisy laughs a little. "Oh, nothing. Just that she's the cheater."

She starts charging down the rest of the stairs, and there's no way I can follow her.

Jane

There's always this big question with Hamlet: Does he actually do anything? Until the end, of course, when everyone dies. But what I thought was, *What about the ghost?*

Because none of it would ever have happened if it weren't for the ghost. Coming back from the dead and ruining everything by saying, "Hey! This is what's really going on." If it weren't for the ghost, Hamlet probably would have gone back to school, and Gertrude and Claudius would have lived happily ever after.

Ghosts have more power than you think, I guess. Of course, some people don't even think they exist. But I think that's just an excuse not to listen to them.

I can hear them all talking. Something's going on. Even from where I'm sitting, all the way in the back of the quiet room, I can tell: People are all excited. For a moment I wonder if Daisy told everyone: "Hey! Jane Cotterell is the cheater!" And what I'll do if she did. Any second now they could all come running in. . . .

But nobody comes running into the room. Only one person, and he walks in.

Max.

Who says, "Wow."

MAX

Jane says, "What's going on?" So casually that for a moment I think, *Wait, was Daisy kidding?*

"I think Daisy and Leo just broke up."

"Because of Kyra," says Jane.

"Yeah. How'd you know?"

"Pretty obvious."

"Really?" I sit down next to her. "Kyra and Leo. Guess I missed that one."

She says, "Guess so." And that's when I know Daisy wasn't kidding.

I wonder: How much wouldn't have happened if Jane had told us? Daisy and I wouldn't have had that fight. She and Leo wouldn't have suspected each other. You have to wonder, would Leo have gone in the bathroom with Kyra, would Daisy be storming home alone now, if Jane had admitted what she did?

Jane

Max doesn't have to say it. I know from his face exactly what he's thinking.

He's going to want to talk about it, do the whole "Why?" thing. I wish he wouldn't.

Because frankly, I just want to forget it ever happened.

MAX

I should be really mad at Jane, I know that. Because I was really mad at the cheater. I thought, *What kind of jerk would do this while the rest of us are working our butts off and freaking out like this?* I imagined them laughing at us: *You poor schmucks, suckered by the system.* But I don't think Jane's been laughing at anyone.

Then I remember something. "You didn't drop the dime on Daisy, did you?"

"No!" Jane shakes her head frantically. "That's why I wrote the letter. I hated that, that people thought she did it. They were so mean to her. . . ."

And you didn't want them being that mean to you, I think. *That's why you didn't sign the letter.*

Certain things you think you know. I knew the cheater was a bad person. I knew that people who cheat are evil—particularly rich people. That's an easy one. If you had told me the cheater was a rich girl who didn't really care about anything and could just get by the rest of her life, I would've said, "That person should be hurt. Bad."

But I can't say that about Jane. There's no *a, b, c, d,* or *e* answer here.

Here's what I can say: "You want to go home?"

LEO

When I see Max leave with Jane, I'm like, *What's that about?*

Kyra sees them too. "That's a weird pair."

"Yeah," I say without thinking, "wonder if Daisy knows . . ."

Kyra looks at me. "Uh, you'll never know, because I don't think she's going to be speaking to you."

And I'm like, *Why not?* Because yeah, I know this night was crazinesss, but it's not like that's it. I'll call Daisy, she'll yell, it'll be . . .

The booze isn't working so well now. The mellowness is fading, making way for other, darker things. It's like the earth starts breaking up all of a sudden, but you're telling yourself, *I got it, I'm fine, this is nothing I can't handle. . . .*

Your life can't change in three hours. You can't lose something like that in three hours. Three hours compared with an entire year? Come on.

No way do I mean this to be the end of things with Daisy. No way did I make a choice of Kyra over her.

Except . . .

Except that's kind of how it ended up.

No backsies.

MAX

In the cab Jane asks, "What did you think of me?"

"What do you mean? About the test?"

She shakes her head woozily. "No, forget that. Before. Like, before you even knew me, the group or anything. What'd you think of me?"

I have no idea what to say. Now that I know Jane's the cheater, it's hard to think of her any other way. But I try, "Uh, I thought you were pretty."

She turns her head. "Really?"

It hurts how happy that makes her. I wonder if anything would have been different if I had asked Jane out all those months ago, when Daisy told me to. Only, I didn't like Jane then. I only really liked Jane that one time at the diner. It wouldn't have been cool to ask her out.

Someone should have, though.

"What else?" she asks. "Come on, be honest. You thought, 'movie star's kid.'"

"Yeah, sure."

"And?"

I wrack my brain. I mean, what do you say? *I didn't think much about you, Jane. You didn't give us anything to think about. Except your mom's famous, and you are pretty, and . . . oh, yeah, your stepfather's a weird old horndog.*

God, yeah. That was the thing everybody knew about Jane.

Then I hear Jane say quietly, "What else?"

"Nothing." She looks at me. *Hey, Jane, you ever think maybe you are that smart?* I feel like she knows exactly what I'm thinking, that the worst thing I could do would be to pretend I'm not. Because it's three in the morning and there's been a whole lot of truth told already, and why stop now?

"People say stupid stuff," I tell her, and that's as far as I can go.

Jane turns, looks out the window again. She doesn't say anything else for the rest of the ride. I bring Jane upstairs because I don't actually trust her not to do something between the lobby and her apartment.

Getting her keys out and opening the door is a real adventure.

Which becomes even more so when Julia Cotterell opens the door.

She's wearing an old robe and no makeup. She doesn't look at all like an actress; she looks like a mom. A very tired and pissed-off mom.

Jane focuses a little. Then she tears away from me and stalks into the apartment. Ms. Cotterell says, "Jane," but Jane just yells, "No," and keeps right on going. A second later we hear a door slam. And there I am, just standing there.

Okay, so how do you tell a famous actress her daughter cheated on her SATs? That she thinks nothing matters—including herself—because she thinks all anyone cares about is the fact that she has a famous mom?

Somehow I get the feeling she knows all this already. But I say anyway, "You should probably check on her."

"Oh, I will. You're Max, right?"

"Yeah," I say. "I'm . . . Max."

"Well, thank you, Max."

You never want to go home from your junior party alone. As I walk home from the bus stop the streets are deserted, like I'm doomed to walk in no-man's-land forever. Or no-woman's-land.

It seems like all those compliments people gave me

at the party are from some dream I had: What would it be like if people liked me? "Oh, sorry, Max, that was just a dream. Time to wake up now. . . ."

I'm not even sure I'm friends with Daisy anymore. If someone else did to her what I did to her, I'd say to her, "What do you want with that loser? He's not a friend."

Also, if I'm honest, there's only so long you can like someone who doesn't like you without feeling seriously pathetic.

Maybe next year I should just start over completely.

But then I think of the group, that stupid SAT guy who couldn't find the books, Jane putting those notes on our lockers, and us recording our scores . . . like they mattered.

That goofy game we played that night before the SATs. Max, Daisy, Jane, Leo . . .

What happened to that? Is the only thing that's left out of the whole year, the one thing that'll last, our stupid score?

Daisy

I open the door super quietly, so as not to wake my folks. Not that they would freak or anything. But I can't talk about this to anyone right now.

I go into the kitchen and sit at the table. Dig my hands into my eyes. If you press hard enough, you can see flashes of light. And it hurts so much you get a headache, and you can think, *Well, dummy, if you'd stop pushing your eyeballs back in your head, it'd stop hurting.*

Only, then everything else would hurt worse.

I used to joke about it all the time. Yeah, I'm stupid. And what I meant was school. Tests. Things like that. Nobody's going to mistake me for Genius of the Year— ha, ha.

Life I thought I was pretty smart about. People— really thought I had that down. Well, think again, Daisy.

What's scary is, I think there's something seriously wrong with me. Like, why do I pick the worst guys— again and again and again?

That image of Kyra hanging off Leo is one I really wish I didn't have in my head. I hate that evil cow so hard it hurts.

Leo I can't even think about.

"Daisy?"

Oh, crap. My mom. I try to wipe the mess off my face. Probably just makes it worse.

She goes to turn on the light, I say, "Please don't."

"What happened?" She sits down opposite me. "What's wrong?"

I want to say, "Everything's fine, I'll be cool in the morning, don't worry." Instead I say, "I think . . . I actually am pretty stupid."

"Honey, that is crazy."

"No, it's not."

"Something happened at the party?" I nod. "Something with Leo?"

It's so humiliating that she figured it out that fast.

Daisy and her boyfriend problems. Then I remember, and say, "Oh, and Jane, too." My mom shakes her head. "Guess who the cheater was."

"*Jane?* Why on earth would she do a thing like that?"

"She said it was a joke. To see if anybody noticed. Nobody did. I sure didn't." I wipe my nose. "She claims she was going to tell everyone. . . ."

"But she kind of liked the score, huh?"

"I don't get it. How could I be that stupid? How could I not know someone that much? I even defended her to Luisa."

"Well, considering you had no reason to think it was her, that was the right thing to do." I shake my head, take a deep breath. "Want to tell me what happened with Leo?"

"Um . . ." At the thought of saying it out loud, my throat tightens. I barely get out the words, "Kyra Fleming."

"I'm assuming that's another girl?" my mom says gently. When I nod, she holds my hand tight. "I'm sorry."

"That one I really should've known, you know? I mean, I saw him do it to a million other girls. Oh, big surprise, he does it to me, too."

"I'm a little surprised. I thought he really liked you."

That reminds me of seeing Leo on the park bench, all the stupid things I felt, and I shake my head.

"Did you ask him why?"

"Uh, no. I felt stupid enough."

"You weren't stupid."

I sigh. "Yeah, I'm so brilliant. That's why I keep getting dumped on. It's my genius secret plan."

"Kyle you were . . . not as smart as you usually are," says my mom. "But everyone has a Kyle. That's how you learn never to have one again."

"Except I went on to Leo, when . . ." I'm about to say something about Max, but I stop. My parents adore Max. They would not think a lot of me for turning him down.

"Why don't you give it a few days and call him?"

"No way. That's it."

"Okay. But don't think you were stupid because . . ." My mom knows if she says anything about how I felt about Leo, I'll lose it completely. "'Tis better to have loved and lost . . .'"

"No, it's not. It sucks."

"Caring is not stupid." There's danger in my mom's voice; this is one thing she really believes. I used to believe it too. But I'm not so sure I'm there anymore.

"Then, why does it feel that way?" Because I think about all the times I asked people to sign petitions, went on marches, asked for donations. People always make fun of you. They always say how naive you are, how none of it does any good. And frankly, sometimes you feel like, *Maybe they're right. Who really got saved?*

Like, here's Jane so miserable she would cheat on

the SATs, and I never even noticed. Because, hello, I was all busy with Leo. . . .

Like someone pinched me hard: *God, I was stupid.*

I pull at my fingers. My mom may as well know what an idiot she has for a daughter. "Max told me he liked me this year, and I told him to get lost. Not . . . get lost, but that I didn't like him like that."

I'm waiting for my mom to say, "Are you crazy? How could you turn Max down?" She's a big one on physical appearance is meaningless. And I totally believe that it should be true . . . only, it's not. At least for me. God, I really am a shallow and awful person.

But all she says is, "That must have been hard."

"For me or Max?"

"Both of you."

"Really? Luisa thought I was evil."

"Well, honey, I didn't want to say it, but there were times you were working those flirt muscles of yours, and I thought Max was a pretty unfair target."

"I didn't realize it, I swear to God." She gives me a look that makes me squirm. "I thought he got it."

"That he was short and not so great looking, so he should understand that you would flirt with him but never actually go out with him."

I knew my mom would get me on this one; I just didn't know how much it would hurt.

She's not letting up, either. "You always say how unfair it is that some people have money and get things other people don't—and it is. But when did you decide that because Max is homely, he shouldn't have the same feelings about you that a good-looking guy like Leo does?"

"Okay, I get it. I suck." I put my head in my hands, wait for my mom to say, "No, you don't, honey." She doesn't.

I say, "I can't help who I think is attractive. I told you—I am seriously stupid."

"Of course you can't. And we can't help that some people have money and others don't—although we can make the system a whole lot more equal. I'm not saying you were stupid for not rushing into Max's arms, I'm saying—"

"That I was stupid because I didn't care about how he felt. That . . . not caring is what's stupid."

My mom takes my hands off the table, holds them in hers, and kisses them. "Told you you were smart."

Jane

In my room I think of what I should do next. Then what I could do next. Then all the things in between.

What it comes down to is this: Leave. Escape. Because that's the simplest thing. But what's not simple is where to go.

There's my dad, but I have a feeling Connecticut won't be far enough. There's California, where we used to live, but my mom knows too many people there. I don't know anyone anywhere else.

Mariah Fredericks

Maybe that's it. Go someplace where I don't know anyone. My mom was in a movie like that once. They put her in this crazy wig and sunglasses. She was running away from the mafia or something. She fell in love with a gambler at the hotel, and he saved her.

I do have a pair of sunglasses. More to the point, I have money. I could do it, go somewhere and be someone entirely different.

I imagine it, going up to the desk clerk in some seedy motel: "Hi, my name is Janet . . ."

Ugh, no. I hate the name Janet. "My name is Leonora Dahlbeck. I'd like a room." "Do you have any ID, Ms. Dahlbeck?" "Uh, no. No, I don't. . . ."

It's always a problem, ID. They never put that in movies. But you can't go somewhere and say, "Hi, I'm no one at all. Can you let me stay here until I figure everything out?" You always have to pretend to be somebody.

Or else people make it up.

I wonder if they'll expel me. At the very least, they might suspend me. If they do, I might say, "You know what? Let's just do it. Get rid of me. I don't want to be here anymore."

Because if I go back to school in September, here's what everyone will say: "Oh, there's Jane. She cheated on the SATs. Yeah, we all hate her for that. And her stepdad's a serious perve, which is kind of funny 'cause her mom's really famous."

All these things swirl around in my head: Cheater . . .

stepdad . . . famous mom . . . I feel like I'm drowning. I pull my knees up to my forehead, press them against my eyes until it feels like I'm going blind. I want to get out of this, get away from these voices.

Then I remember what Daisy said, "You are what you do. . . . You just let the lie go on."

I still think I hate Daisy, but there's something in what she said, something that feels new. Powerful.

Like an escape. And I don't even have to leave the house.

The next morning when I get up, my mom and James are in the dining room with bagels and the newspaper. Mom glances at me as I come in. But no lecture. At least, not right away. Probably not ever. Last night was upsetting. My mom doesn't do upsetting.

Then she starts talking about college. How she's planning this whole trip through the northeast, and we'll hit a bunch of places on my list. "Then, in between, we can do some camping, some hiking. . . ."

I hate camping. I hate hiking. The thought of visiting colleges with my mother makes me sick.

"I'm really excited," she says. "I mean, I've never seen places like Yale; it's supposed to be beautiful. Jane, if you go there, you can expect to see me every month. Soaking up the intellectual vibe. No, I'm kidding, darling, really, I'll leave you alone. But I just can't wait to see all these places. The choices you have are so exciting. . . ."

Really, Mom? They're not exciting to me.

I think of it, talking to some college interviewer. "Oh, yes, I'm quite brilliant. Oh, yes, I'd love to go to your school. I have so much to offer. Describe myself in five words? Okay, sure. I am wonderful, intelligent, committed, mature, and have a great sense of humor."

James is putting low-fat cream cheese on his bagel. For a second I watch him, because low-fat cream cheese? What's the point? Have the real thing. He looks up and for a second our eyes meet. Normally, I do anything not to have that happen. But this time I stare back. Like, *You see me? Guess what. I see you, too.*

Then I pick up my juice and say, "Hey, Mom? You remember about someone in my class cheating on the SATs?"

"Yes, I do," says my mom.

"That was me."

LEO

When you go to bed at five thirty in the morning, there's not much point in getting up before three in the afternoon.

Unless your little brother pounds on your door, wanting to watch cartoons in your room. I'm not sure my head can handle that much light and noise, but I let Zo in anyway. He sits up on my bed, while I stay under the covers. "You're a mountain," he says, and sits on me.

"Take it easy," I tell him. "The mountain doesn't feel good."

At the commercial he says, "Let's call Daisy."

"Let's not."

"I want to." He picks up my cell, says into it, "Hello, Daisy?"

"She's not home," I tell him.

He shoves the phone into my hand.

I hit the number, tell Zo, "It's ringing."

She picks up with, "Hello?"

"This is Leo Thayer, calling on behalf of Alonzo Thayer."

She doesn't say anything. But I know if I hadn't mentioned Zo, she'd be gone.

I put the covers over my head. "Seriously, please don't hang up."

She says, "You've got the wrong number."

"No, I don't."

"Yeah, you do," she says, and hangs up.

Daisy

If it weren't for what my mom said about Leo, I would never have agreed to see him. No matter how many times he called—or made Zo call, which is what he started doing.

But then I realized you can't end something like this by not talking. So a few days after school is over, I tell him we can meet in the park by the river. As I walk over there I pray that I won't be a total wimp, that this isn't just all some weird scheme on the part of my subconscious to take him back.

The first few days of summer vacation, before you start your summer job and are completely free, are always strange. It's like, *Wait, I can do anything I want?* You feel a little lost. For a while I watch the people biking and blading up the path, thinking, *That could be me, that could be me.* How come I have to be the dumb chick sitting here waiting for her cheating boyfriend?

Then I hear, "Hey," turn around, and see Leo. He's wearing a green T-shirt. He knows it looks good on him because I once told him it did.

I test myself: Do I care he wore the shirt?

No. And I know I don't, because it makes me sad that I don't.

"So," he says, "how do we do this?"

I nod toward the path. "Let's walk."

We don't talk at first. I guess because once you start a conversation like this, you're that much closer to finishing it, and we both know how this one ends.

Leo says, "What happens if I say that I was really wrong?"

"You weren't wrong." He looks at me. "You weren't. It makes total sense. You and Kyra want the same things: Yale, big job, money . . . that's who you are. You just decided to admit it, that's all." Leo winces. "What?"

"Kind of harsh?"

"What's the big hurt? It's true."

"Come on, don't do this."

For the first time I feel angry. "I didn't do anything, Leo."

"No, I know. But just 'cause I screwed up, don't make it like you're one kind of person and I'm another. We're way past that, you know?"

I want to scream, "Don't do this. Don't pretend like this is all going to work out if I let it, because *you* screwed up, you chose, and don't pretend you didn't. You did what you did—live with it."

I say, "We are different, Leo."

"Well, I didn't feel that way."

Well, neither did I until the party. But I don't want to remember anything I thought or felt before the party. All that feeling is like an avalanche, ready to crash down on my head with one wrong thought or word. *Keep it cold, Daisy.*

I say, "Yeah, you did. Or you wouldn't have hooked up with Kyra."

"And that was a total mistake," says Leo, like he has me dead to rights.

"This isn't a test you get to take again, Leo. Sorry." I walk a little ahead of him. So far he's playing by my rules. If I can keep this up, we'll be over in a few minutes. But he's going to try something, I can feel it. Any second he's going to say, "Let's stop this," or I don't know, "I love you" even, because he knows he's losing and Leo hates to lose.

Fake left. "By the way, I found out who the cheater was."

He sighs. "I so could not care less."

"Yeah? You should care. You know her." I feel the most wicked impulse to say, "It was Kyra—yeah, you doinked the cheater."

But I can't. Not even to Kyra. "It was Jane."

"Get out."

"Told me herself."

"Man . . ." He shakes his head. "Man, that's sad."

"It's not sad. It's disgusting." Leo shrugs. "Chick has everything and she pulls something like that? Give me a break. I'm not feeling sorry for her. She's a spoiled, whiny, self-involved cow—all the worst things I kept telling myself she wasn't."

Then Leo laughs, and I say, "It's not funny."

"Okay, it's not funny. But I have to remind you, there was a time when you thought I'd done it."

"No . . ."

"Or Max. And I thought you did it, so you know."

"No. What do I know?"

Leo shrugs. "Maybe I should be all outraged, but when people thought I did it, everyone kept saying, 'Oh, that Leo, man, he'll do anything, he's a jerk, you know it has to be him.' Oops, except it wasn't."

"So?"

"I'm just saying, we all had something people could point to and say, '*That's* what made them cheat. Leo's competitive, Max is under his dad's thumb, Daisy wants to give the system the finger.' And if we had cheated, everyone would have said about us: 'The worst thing we thought about them turned out to be true.' And . . ."

But then he stops. I guess because we both just realized there are two ways to hear the word *cheat*.

Leo shrugs. "And I guess that's all people would see."

We walk to the river, hang out and look at it over the chain-link fence. You're actually still far away from it. But it feels like you could jump right in.

I want to tell Leo that the worst is not the only thing I see in him—but I can't stop seeing it—when he says, "Look, when you get back from Guatemala . . ."

I shake my head.

Leo grips the edge of the fence. "I really don't want to end this here."

"It ended at the party." Leo looks at me. "Or it ended when I didn't want to go to New Haven, or whatever. It doesn't matter."

"Uh, yeah, it does."

These things are very easy when the other person doesn't give a crap about you anymore. But that's not what's going on here.

I cannot like Leo after what he did to me.

But I do, that's just the way it is.

Still, I say, "You know, we never would have even liked each other, except for that stupid test."

Leo looks down at the ground. "Yeah, yeah. Doesn't mean anything, doesn't have anything to do with who we really are—"

"It doesn't."

"Except it does." He sighs. "Man, I can't believe this. I mean, if I . . ."

He hesitates, waiting for me to say what it is he has to do to make this okay. He wants me to say something so bad that for a moment I'm tempted. But if I think about it, no one magical thing comes to mind.

It would be simple to say, "Hey, we'll see after the summer. We'll write, keep in touch." But we're coming to the end of the walk, and we know it's not true. We'll see each other next year, but it won't be any big thing.

I turn around, lean my back against the fence, and fold my arms. This is the crying point. Because it's the end of something and I hate good-byes.

Leo says, "I really hate the whole good-bye thing."

I laugh. "Yeah, me too." Tears again. I have got to stop with this; it's annoying already.

"So, next year . . ."

"Don't do that."

"Not even next year?"

I shake my head. He has to leave now, otherwise I'm going to lose it.

But he doesn't. I swallow, say, "Why don't you go on ahead?"

He looks down the road. "Don't want to."

"Have to sometime."

"True."

Words are out of the question now. Unfolding my arms, I hold out one hand. Leo takes it, gives me a fast kiss.

And then he's gone.

For a long time I just stand there watching the boats speeding up toward the George Washington Bridge. Some people try to swim in this river. Which is dumb, because it's so polluted.

It's still beautiful, though. And I guess when you get far enough away from here, away from the city and the garbage, where it's quiet, I guess then it turns clean and you can swim in it, drink it. Anything you want.

MAX

On Saturday, Daisy and I go to Luisa's graduation. When they call Luisa's name, we leap up and cheer—and we're not the only ones. Luisa shimmies back to her seat, waving her diploma, and the whole place goes crazy like they used to go when she scored a basket. I guess it's the last time everyone can let her know they love her all at once.

Luisa is one of those magical people, someone who manages to get through school totally being herself— and everybody likes her because of it. It was like a perfect match: Dewey and Luisa. You have to wonder, is she ever going to find another place that lets her be that great? I mean, how many times in your life do you get hundreds of people chanting your name, "Lu . . . Lu . . . Lu . . ."

I know Luisa will be fine. She's tough. She knows in the real world nobody gives a crap if you were the high school basketball star and everybody loved you. Or, for that matter, if you were the star writer on your newspaper. You've just got to go out and prove yourself all over again—no matter how many big moments you have in your past.

But a small part of me is glad that I haven't had my big moments yet. That means—I think, I hope—that they're still to come.

After the ceremony Daisy asks if I want to go to the diner for something to eat.

Right after we give our orders, I say, "I owe you a big-time apology."

She frowns over her straw. "For what?"

"The party. What happened. I shouldn't have told you about Leo."

She shakes her head. "You didn't. I mean, you did, but I knew it anyway."

"But I wanted you to know." I don't have to say, "I wanted you to be punished, wanted you to feel like crap, wanted to say, 'Ha, ha, shoulda picked me instead.'" Like I said, Daisy knows most things about me.

"For what it's worth," I tell her, "I hope things are okay with you guys."

Daisy sits back as the waitress puts our food on the table. Then she says, "Well, for what it's worth, they're not. It's over."

If you had asked me a month ago if anything could make me happier than to hear that Daisy and Leo broke up, I would have said, "Maybe the Mets, Knicks, and Giants all winning in the same year"—but frankly, it would have been a toss-up.

Now it just feels like another thing that's over.

Daisy must see what I'm thinking, because she says, "Hey, we got to catch a Yankees game before I leave."

I forgot Daisy roots for the Yankees. The one time she doesn't go with the underdog. I think it might have something to do with Derek Jeter, although she swears it doesn't.

That's one thing that's not over, I guess.

I say, "Or maybe a Mets game."

Nobody mentions Jane until we ask for the check. Then I ask Daisy if she's heard from her. She says, "Are you kidding?"

I dig in my pocket for some money. "I don't hate her."

"I don't . . . not hate her." Daisy throws some dollars on the table. "Why don't you hate her?"

"I guess 'cause when I thought about it, she didn't take anything from me."

"Yeah, what if she applies to Columbia?"

I don't tell Daisy *I* might not be applying to Columbia either. "If they want a Jane, they'll take a Jane. They want a Max, they'll take a Max. Why do you think she did it?"

"Oh, come on. She always felt so sorry for herself— you can see her going, *Oh, it's okay if I cheat, everyone's so mean to me, it's all so hard.* Give me a break."

I think of Jane in the cab: "What did you think of me?" Like I could introduce her to herself or something. I say, "I don't think that's why."

"Yeah, then why?"

"I keep thinking: She didn't need a high score. The whole time we were studying, she didn't care what she got. I think she just wanted to see, if she wasn't there, would anybody notice? Would anybody care? Like, who is she?"

"I don't think the SATs tell you that."

"Yeah, I can see how she got confused, though. I mean, the school wants it both ways. Be this unique, original individual—oh, and do incredibly well on this standardized test."

Daisy smiles. "Yeah, okay." Then she nods. "Okay."

I smile back. She's wearing an old Knicks T-shirt with Patrick Ewing's number on it. It makes her crazy he never won a championship. I want to say, "Hey, you love him. That's something."

Here's what didn't happen: Daisy did not say she was

crazy to ever like Leo and now she knows I am the man for her. And I didn't stop wanting her to say that.

But I also know she couldn't, and it wasn't because of Leo or Kyle or all those guys I thought were taking someone that belonged to me. People don't really take things like that from you—someone you think you could love, or your future. It either happens or it doesn't.

She's still the greatest-looking girl I've ever seen.

Part
I II III **IV**

End. Please Close Your Test Booklet.

Jane

In the end it didn't matter. Right before school started in September, my mom and me had a meeting with Crowley.

My mom started to tell him what had happened, but I said, "Mom?" and she stopped.

I looked at Crowley. "I was the one who cheated. I paid Tory."

I don't usually surprise people. I could tell. Crowley was surprised. For a while he just shifted files from one end of his desk to another. Finally my mom said, "She doesn't want to keep the score. She'll . . . give them back or whatever you do. Whatever's right."

That's when Crowley sighed. "Unfortunately it's not quite that simple, Ms. Cotterell."

I said, "It's totally that simple," as my mom said, "Why?"

Crowley stopped messing with the files and looked at my mom. "First of all it is no easy thing to erase a score. It can be done, but it can't be done quietly, not in the very small world of private schools and elite colleges. When a celebrity is involved, it becomes that much more difficult."

I remembered my fear from so long ago: *People* magazine and "Julia Cotterell's Daughter Flunks SATs!" Only now it would be "Julia Cotterell's Daughter Cheats on SATs."

I said, "I don't care."

Crowley looked at me. "You may not care for yourself, but you have to be aware of the impact it could have on your classmates. If one student from Dewey cheats, why not another? That shade of doubt could make a great deal of difference to top schools, when they consider our seniors."

For a second I thought of Leo and Yale. Then thought, *No, that doesn't matter.* I did what I did. I'm not going to let the lie keep going.

I could see from my mom's face, she was wavering. I actually felt bad for her. She likes lies, they feel right to her, even when she knows they're wrong.

I said, "It's not like everyone doesn't already know. The parents are all freaking out; they're not going to be happy with, 'Oh, we never found out who it was.'"

That made an impression. Crowley didn't want parents badmouthing the school or not giving money. But I couldn't figure it out; why won't he just let me say I did it?

Then I got it. It's the score. The number. He's thinking, *With that score and a famous mom, I could get this kid into a big-name school. Instead of three kids into Brown—or Yale, or Penn—I could have four.*

Probably when he threw his big hissy in the gym, he thought the cheater was some stoner. Or jock, like Daisy. He never figured it was a kid with a rich, famous parent.

Numbers and big names—it really is all about that.

Then my mom said, "I know this is an awful question . . ."

"Please," said Crowley.

"The girl who took the test, there isn't any chance she's going to go to the media, is there? I know that sounds paranoid, but you said she needed money. That's why she did this."

At first I had no idea what my mother was talking about. Then Crowley said, "You can rest assured, Ms. Cotterell. Tory understands the possible repercussions of going public. If anything, she stands to lose more than your daughter if this gets out. She has been admitted to a very good school and on scholarship. Obviously they would no longer admit her if they knew she had accepted payment to take someone's SATs."

Until then, it had never occurred to me that anything might happen to Tory. Of course, she'd be rejected from Stanford if they ever found out about this. Why didn't I ever think about that?

I told myself it wasn't my fault: Tory took the money. But how many bad things do people do because someone offers them money? That's why people sell drugs.

I looked at my mother, who was so worried about Tory going to the media, and something inside me switched. I'm not sure what it was. Just that *People* magazine covers are not going to be my first worry in life.

Then Crowley sat up like he'd just had a brilliant idea. "Let me propose an unorthodox solution. There's no question that this situation has created a certain amount of . . . emotion. So I will place a call to parents and inform them that the person who cheated has come forward, and she has agreed to erase her score. But for their children's sake, it's best that we now let the matter lie. We don't want it reaching the ears of certain college admissions people, who might be inclined to look more critically at all Dewey students."

My mom said anxiously, "Will you tell them it was Jane?"

Crowley said, "I really think given the fact that you are a well-known actress, that it's not advisable."

My mom nodded. Then said, "But she will give up her score?"

Crowley said blandly, "I don't think that'll be necessary."

And just like that, it was over. I wouldn't give up the score, but we would say that I had. Nobody would know it was me—but everybody would know. And I would never get the chance to say, "Yes, I did this."

The way my mom put it was this. I am under a lot of stress with the divorce and the new relationship in her life. Sometimes I have difficulty knowing what's real, what the consequences can be.

But that's not true. I know what's real.

And I know there are no consequences.

Mariah Fredericks

Daisy

Nobody believes Jane gave back her score. So Crowley says he did—who believes Crowley? Tory ended up going to Stanford, just like nothing happened. I wonder how many strings Crowley had to pull there.

At first I was furious, because I felt like they were just letting Jane get away with it. No suspension, no expulsion. I thought, Man, celebrity's daughter, you can't touch her.

Everyone at school knows she did it. It's the kind of thing when maybe if they liked you before, it could be okay. But if they didn't . . .

The things people say about her are really cruel. That she's stupid, an airhead, a slut. These two guys were trying to figure out what she'd do for them if they took her SATs for her. I told them they were sick, to shut up.

I saw her the other day. She was standing by the elevator, waiting to go up. The only place she would look was at the lights as they went on their way down.

She knew I was there. But all she looked at were those lights. And I thought, *No. She didn't get away with a thing.*

LEO

Kyra and I did go up to New Haven. And yeah, some of the things you'd expect would happen happened.

There are things I like about Kyra. There are certain

things I don't have to explain. Like she gets it about the drinking. She knows it's a stress thing, that I have to have a break sometimes. I have to have something that's for me.

Actually, Kyra's not averse to the Captain herself. As I found out. One night we were hanging in my room, and she said, "You know, it's so not fair."

I said, "Which thing out of a million?"

"Jane," she said, like it was obvious. "I mean, the fact that they're not doing anything to her when everyone knows she did it."

"She's giving back the score."

Kyra snorted. "Yeah, like you believe that? Just watch and see what college she gets into. If Crowley were really serious, he could, like, tell every college in the country that she's a cheater."

Which was true. But when I thought about it, whether I really wanted Jane strung up like that, I couldn't really get into it. I think about the past year, the one we're headed into, the way everyone thought I was the cheater. All the *She's this, he's that, they're blah, blah* . . . I don't know, maybe sometimes you don't judge.

Then Kyra said, "We should find out what colleges she applies to and write them letters."

And that's when I knew it was Kyra who dropped the dime on Daisy. She got it into her head that it was Daisy who cheated, that it was *unfair*, and it was her right to turn her in.

When we got back to the city, I said I'd call her. But I never did.

MAX

Today we all have to go to something called Senior Orientation, which is basically where they tell you, "Don't blow off your second semester, because colleges *are* watching." Like any college ever called anyone and said, "Hey, we hear you cut class today, forget it, we're taking back our acceptance." It's a bogus meeting, no question, but as we all head up the stairs to the auditorium you can tell people are excited because it's the first thing we're doing as actual seniors.

Even Daisy's a little excited, although she claims it's just because she has only one more year before she's out of here.

We finally get into the auditorium, and I say to her, "Where do you want to sit?"

She says, "Back."

So we do. I like the back. From here you can watch everyone else. I look out at the crowd, think, *This is my class.* People always talk about classes. Do you have a good one, a popular one, one with a lot of burnouts? I think we have a pretty good one, frankly.

Totally by accident I see Leo, sitting way up front with Tobin. He's stretched his legs out into the aisle, and he's laughing. It's strange to think I ever knew him. I heard he and Kyra got together for a little while, but I've never seen them, so I think it might be over.

Without thinking, I look for Jane. I'm not sure if I'd have the guts to come to something like this if I were her. But she's here, sitting by herself way off to the side. There are people around her, of course, but you can tell, she's by herself.

I glance at Daisy, see she's looking too. Somehow I know she's already seen Leo.

I say, "It's weird, isn't it?" She nods.

Then Crowley says, "Okay, people, let's get started. . . ."

Of course, when the meeting's over, there's the same crush at the doors, the crowds on the stairs. It's the end of the day, and everyone wants to go home. But it's all hurry up and wait while kids get off on various floors. You take one step, then wait, take another, then wait. Behind me Daisy says, "I'll meet you outside if we get separated."

Ahead of me, waiting and annoyed that he's waiting, is Leo. He looks at his watch, and for some reason that's funny to me and I laugh. He looks up. The crowd starts moving again, but he says something to Tobin and stays where he is until Daisy and I are near.

He says, "Hey."

I say, "Hey, Leo, how are you?" But he's watching Daisy.

Who, after a deep breath, says, "Hello, Leo."

People want to get past us, so we step back and huddle in the corner of the stairwell. Leo says, "Lame meeting, huh?"

"Yeah, I'm glad I know not to goof off second semester," I say.

For a second it seems like Daisy's not going to contribute anything. But then she says, "I don't know about you guys, but it was a real shock to hear that this is our last chance to beef up our transcripts."

The crowd has really thinned out now. Leo says, "So, what are you guys up to?"

I look at Daisy. "I don't know."

She looks at me and Leo. "Maybe pizza?"

We hear the door to the auditorium finally slam shut. The last kid has come out. At the sound we all glance up and see Jane at the top of the stairs.

And we wait for her.

As we head out of the lobby we pass by the bulletin board. It's covered with flyers for bake sales, basketball tryouts, Drama Club meetings. No scores, though.

They're not going to post the scores this year. After the whole thing with Jane everyone decided there was too much pressure put on kids over the SATs. The test had been "overemphasized," was how they put it.

I guess it's good. Now there's just everything else.

You know, like, the rest of your life.

About the Author

Mariah Fredericks does not have a clear memory of her SAT scores since that period of her life comes back to her only in snatches of nightmare. But she does remember the day her scores arrived. Her father met her at the door and said, "You did great on the verbal!" When she asked about her math score, he said, "We'll talk."

Nonetheless she did not take SAT prep. She would like to claim that this was based on principle, but in fact, she was just chicken. Attending Vassar college, she found several very good friends, including a husband. Not a single job interviewer has ever asked her where she attended college, what her GPA was, or, for that matter, how she did on the SATs.

Anna's To-Do List • Tuesday, September 22

1. Attend Act Now rally.
2. Try to sing off book in chorus. (Say something nice to Bridget?)
3. Ask Mr. Fegelson for an extension on biology project.
4. Water Mr. Kaiser's plants.
5. Walk the Dunphys' dog.
6. Get Mom to adopt Mrs. Rosemont's cats.

Does everyone think about bizarre things when they're brushing their teeth, or is it just me? The day after Mrs. Rosemont dies, I'm squooshing toothpaste in my mouth when I think, *What is dead, anyway?*

Yesterday Mrs. Rosemont was here—and now she's not. But what does that mean, except I won't ever see her again?

Is she just nothing? Or is she a spirit, floating around somewhere?

Part of me thinks she's a spirit. Because I can't believe she's gone. She doesn't *feel* gone. My mom told me last night that Mrs. Rosemont died in the hospital, but I don't feel the least bit sad. It's only when I think about her cats— Beesley, Tatiana, and Mouli, lost and missing their human—that I get upset.

Which is terrible. When someone dies, you should be sad about them.

I spit, then wonder, *So, if I died tomorrow, would anybody care?*

My mom and dad would definitely freak. Russell would demand he get my room. Eve would be psyched, because it'd be all macabre and she could wear black and flip out. But then she'd get tired of it and move on to something else. Syd would be sad, though. Genuinely sad. And they'd probably do something at school, have an assembly, tell people it was okay to cry if they wanted to.

But I'm not sure how many people would cry. More likely, they'd be like, *Anna? Anna who? Oh, her. Yeah, she was . . . okay.*

My little brother Russell is waiting for me at the door. He has two pencils stuck up his nostrils. Today, apparently, he is a walrus.

Russell is seven years old, but he's been strange since the day he was born. This doesn't seem to bother most people, for example, my parents, who you'd think would be a little worried that their only son lives on a diet of tuna fish and boogers. Just the fact that he's usually pretending to be some kind of animal should raise a red flag, right? I once looked up the traits of a psychotic personality. Russell had almost every single one. I told my mother, but she said, "He's just trying to be funny, Anna. Let him have his thing." Which made me wonder, *Do I have a thing? And if so, what is it?*

On the way to school I keep thinking about Mrs. Rosemont. This is the first day she isn't here, the first day she's missing. Everything that happens from now on she won't know about. And yet we're all just going along without her.

Once she gave me a piece of butterscotch candy, and I didn't eat it because it was old and kind of sticky. But she acted like it was this big deal, like she wouldn't give this candy to anyone but me. Now I wish I'd eaten it. Even though I hate butterscotch.

As we wait for the light, Russell sways and snorts and claps his hands like they're flippers. I tell him, "Walruses smell. Walruses get fat and roll over on baby walruses and crush them." He immediately starts shrieking like a baby walrus being squished.

I will have to talk to my mother. Russell is way too casual about death.

When we get to school, Eve is waiting for me on the steps. Today she's wearing her CUTE MAKES ME GAG T-shirt. It has a picture of a kitten and a red banned circle on it. Now, if Eve died, everybody at school would remember her. I don't know if they'd cry a lot, but they'd all have an Eve story. *Remember the time she farted at the mime show? Remember when she made Ms. DeLisi cry in English class? Or the summer she chopped off all her hair?* Sometimes I worry that I'm too tame to be Eve's friend.

As we go into school, I say, "Did you hear about Mrs. Rosemont?"

"Why would I hear about Mrs. Rosemont?"

"Because she died."

Eve shrugs. "Well, she *was* like a hundred and nine."

"God, Eve . . ."

"Uh, hello, old woman I met twice now dead, I'm supposed to be all boohoo?" Eve sees my face, says, "Okay, okay. Sorry. God, you like . . . care about everything."

Annoyed, I say, "I don't care about everything, but she's dead, you know? Have a little respect."

Eve puts her head on my shoulder, which is her real way of saying she's sorry. "It's Act Now. It's making me borderline postal."

"I get that," I say as we head up the stairs to assembly. Because I do. Eberly, our school, is heavily into "doing things." Penny drives, donating food, cleaning up the park. Our principal, Ms. Kenworthy, has a sign on her door: A GOOD CITIZEN IS AN ACTIVE CITIZEN. So every fall they kick off the year with a big Act Now rally to tell everyone what events are planned and how they can get involved.

Which sounds great, but sometimes I wonder if Ms. Kenworthy really knows what goes on at this school. She might tell us we're all the same and not to look down on anyone, but the fact is, there are a lot of kids at Eberly who *live* to look down on people. They wouldn't have it any other way. It's absolutely understood: There's a top ruling clique, made up of the über-cool. You have to *at least* be rich and *at least* be hot—so forget it for me and Eve right there (although I think Eve is very pretty, even if she isn't skinny-skinny and has her hair all cut up Goth style). These kids make fun of people for not wearing designer clothes, so it's a little hard to imagine them caring about the homeless.

Then, on the other end, there're the freaks, the lowest of the low. It's not as obvious how you get to be a freak. It's not about being ugly or strange or not having money—although those things help. What really does it is if you're targeted by the über-cool; if they decide to make you their little joke, you've had it. And that could happen to anybody; people try very hard at Eberly to stay out of the Freak Zone, which usually means joining in on the torture of existing freaks.

This is why I'm not sure if Ms. Kenworthy has the least clue. She should. All she has to do is look out and see how everyone's sitting. Über-cools like Chris Abernathy and his Cro-Magnonic bud Kyle are, of course, near the P&Ps (what Eve calls the "pretty and perfects") like Elissa Maxwell and Alexa Roth. Whereas Crazy Nelson Kobliner is sitting all the way off to the side, as is Planet Janet Epstein. (Janet's a little . . . heavy.) If Ms. Kenworthy did take the time to look, she'd see Chris pitching a balled-up Chinese menu at Janet right now. She'd see Elissa giggling and pointing at Sara Reynolds's hand-me-down sweater.

She'd also see Declan Kelso, as well as every girl in school staring at Declan Kelso. Declan is, without question, the hottest guy at Eberly. And not just in the eighth grade, either. I bet there are sophomores who would date Declan.

And what's really funny is that up until this year, Declan was a major freak. Not even a freak—a *geek*. You know Ark-Ark on *Ovidian Planet*? The dorky alien who's always screwing up? That's what Declan looked like. People actually *called* him "Ark-Ark." They knocked his books out of his arms, drew on his clothes with pen, and repeated whatever he said in a retarded voice until he almost cried. Some people found it quite hilarious.

But this year, when he came back to school, nobody recognized him. He was taller, wider—"babe shaped," as Lara Tierney put it. The glasses were gone, so everyone could see he had big blue eyes with the longest lashes. The brown hair was a little longer, so it didn't stick out anymore. The old Declan was always making weird jokes nobody laughed at. This Declan doesn't say much, just goes around with his head down and his hands jammed in the pockets of his army jacket.

Declan is the first major crossover from freak to über-cool, and every girl in school is crazy about him. The P&Ps think he's a babe, but geek girls think they have a chance because he used to be one of us. Naturally, everyone wants to see which girl he'll ask out, what group she'll belong to. It's a big topic of discussion on Zoe's World, a Web site run by official school gossip Zoe Friedlander. She even has a list of top candidates of future G.O.D.s (Girlfriends of Declan).

Needless to say, my name is not on the list. I'd like to say I don't care. That I find all this fuss over Declan Kelso pathetic and that, really, he's not *that* cute. . . .

But I'd be lying. I think he's amazing.

Frankly, I thought Declan was cute when he was Ark-Ark. Only I wasn't going to ask Ark-Ark out, right? Serves me right, because he's way beyond me now.

Ms. Kenworthy stands up and taps the microphone. "People, could we all calm down now and give our full attention to the matter at hand?"

Despite the fact that I think she's clueless about certain things, I sort of admire Ms. Kenworthy. All the things she wants us to think about are good things, and she is very . . . forceful. She's the kind of person you can imagine as a statue one day.

Now she says, "We have many exciting events planned for this semester. This year for Halloween, instead of the traditional dance, we will ask students to take to the streets in costume to ask for donations to Habitat for Humanity."

Eve frowns. "Whoa, no Halloween dance? That sucks."

Over the murmur of disappointment, Ms. Kenworthy says, "For those of you saddened by the loss of the Halloween dance, you will be happy to know that at the Thanksgiving Harvest Festival, in addition to our canned goods drive, we will have the first annual Eberly Turkey Trot and then our usual holiday party just before the start of winter break."

Oh. No. *The Turkey Trot?* Is she kidding? If it were anybody but Ms. Kenworthy, people would boo.

Raising her voice, Ms. Kenworthy says, "Finally, as we start this school year, I'd like each of us to think about how we could be kinder to one another. Humanity can be expressed in many ways. Even by reaching out to someone we don't know and asking them to lunch."

Hmm. Maybe Ms. Kenworthy isn't so out of it after all. Without thinking, I look over at Nelson Kobliner. Since Declan went "GreekGod"—Zoe's name for him—Nelson is now officially the weirdest guy in school. He's got a strange jar-shaped head, and he's always getting into fights. Kids might ask for donations to charity, but no way is anyone asking Nelson Kobliner to lunch.

Then Ms. Kenworthy says, "Thank you," and everyone is up and headed for the door. As Eve and I struggle to make our way through the crowd, I see Declan edging along his row to join the aisle. If I time it right, he will reach the aisle just as we pass.

I know it's dumb. I know I have no shot. And yet, I slow down. Because—I don't know. It can't be coincidence that we're about to collide like this. Eve pullson my arm, but I don't speed up. Just a few more seconds . . .

I feel someone pass behind me and look up. It's Crazy Nelson Kobliner, and instinctively, I back off. Maybe it's mean of me, but there is something scary about Nelson. He's so big, and it seems like he's always about to hit something. He carries this weird battered notebook everywhere. I can't imagine what's in it.

Then I feel bad. Two minutes after Ms. Kenworthy told us to be nicer to people, I'm already dissing Nelson. I try to smile at him, but he scowls and shoves past me. As he does, I move to make room and bump right up against Declan.

Which is totally perfect. But as I turn around, I hear, "Hey, Anna, ready to take over the altos this year?" The voice is Southern. And loud. And about three feet over my head.

It is Mr. Courtney, music teacher and chorus master.

It's useless to pretend I didn't hear Mr. Courtney; everyone hears Mr. Courtney. But I have to try—and I have to hope Declan didn't hear him. Because I do not want Declan finding out I am in chorus.

If being ugly or strange is a good way to join the Freak Zone, being in chorus is even better. It's a well-established fact that only losers, nerds, and geeks sing in chorus. But I've been in it since second grade because I like singing, even though I'm not so good.

Mr. Courtney has only been here a year. Old chorus teachers knew chorus was uncool and put up with what they got. Courtney is always trying to recruit people. Now, totally blocking the aisle so Eve, Declan, and I are trapped in front of him, he says to Eve, "You gonna sing in my chorus?"

Eve narrows her eyes. "Uh, how about I would not be caught dead?"

"Wouldn't be caught dead? Gal, you don't join my chorus, I'll catch you and kill you. Declan, when you coming to chorus?" Declan does a little half smile, shrugs. "You *want* to be in chorus, believe me. You want to meet girls, right? Well, the best girls are in my chorus. Girls like Anna Morris here. . . ."

I cannot even look Declan in the face. Someone please tell me: What did I do to deserve humiliation at the hands of Mr. Courtney? Meanwhile, Mr. Courtney's still yelling: "Still time to change your schedule, you know. I expect to see a whole bunch of you young men in my chorus next week."

Then he strides back down the aisle. For a long, awful, weird moment, Declan and I just stand there. Then I smile. Because maybe he's standing there for a reason, maybe he wanted to talk to me. . . .

Only Declan doesn't smile back. He says, "Sorry—can I get by?"

I leap aside. "Uh, sure. Sorry."

"Thanks." As he steps past me, I pray that no one saw me make a total fool of myself.

But my prayer is not answered as Eve says, "Okay, how long were we going to keep *that* little secret?"

Clutching my book bag, I mutter, "I don't . . . like him or anything."

"Oh, please. You went bovine."

"I did not," I say, even as I think, *Oh, God, did I?*

"You did," she says menacingly. "This *will* be discussed."

And from her tone, I know I *will not* enjoy the discussion.

Printed in the United States
By Bookmasters